WOLVES'
KNIGHT

P.J. MacLayne

Wolves' Knight

Copyright © 2015 by P.J. MacLayne

Wolves' Knight is a work of fiction. All names, characters, events and places found in this book are either from the author's imagination or used fictitiously. Any similarity to persons live or dead, actual events, locations, or organizations is entirely coincidental and not intended by the author.

ISBN: 1519717083
ISBN-13: 978-1519717085

Published in the United States of America.

ACKNOWLEDGMENTS

To K.M. Guth, for her wonderful cover design and positive attitude

To Cornelia Amiri, for her continuing moral support and editorial assistance

To Mary Beth Lee, for jumping in to help me whip my manuscript into shape, especially those darn commas!

WOLVES'
KNIGHT

ONE

Her tactical knife slid easily from its ankle sheath. With a curse, Tasha leaped out of the leather chair and slid across the wooden conference table, praying she'd make it in time. No matter how she played it, she couldn't stop the masked, gun-wielding intruder from shooting. Shifting to wolf form would allow her to spring on her prey, but the time it took to make the change gave him the opportunity to fire. No, her human body would have to stop the bullet before it struck Dot.

A fraction of a heartbeat later, feet firmly planted on the floor, she sensed another body skid in next to her, creating a larger barrier. Some of the board members stood, one appeared frozen in place, and one started to shift to what appeared to be a badger. Tasha sniffed, trying to figure out who had joined her without taking her eyes off the intruder. A female. Hopefully, a fellow warrior.

She bent her knees, shifted her weight to the balls of her feet, and adjusted her grip. A flick of her wrist and the knife would sail down the length of the table. As she tightened her muscles to make the throw, the interloper laughed and tossed his revolver onto the table. The gun was followed by the mask.

"I wouldn't have believed it if I hadn't seen it," said the young man who was revealed. With a broad smile, he added "You called that one correctly, Miss Lapahie."

As soon as Tasha realized he was no longer a threat, she relaxed and dismissed him from her mind. Granted, he was good-looking in a boyish sort of way, but shifter men tended to be attractive, and he didn't rank as anything special. She liked her men battle-tested and experience told her he didn't qualify.

Amid the babble of voices as everyone spoke at once, one rang out. "Thank you, Dustin. I see why the community theater uses you as their leading man." Tasha turned to see Dot Lapahie, her friend and now CEO of Lapahie Enterprises, standing at the end of the table. "This meeting is adjourned. Tasha, Samantha, will you please join me in my office?"

After indicating the chairs Tasha and Samantha could sit in, Dot calmly settled in behind her desk and brushed a lock of hair away from her face. Her ever-changing hair color was a light brown, and Tasha wondered if it was her natural color. Perhaps she'd given up dying it now that she was no longer on the run. Tasha had always admired her complexion, which reflected her Native American heritage.

"I like what you've done with your office," Tasha said, taking a seat across from Dot and looking around. The walls were a comforting light blue and the curtains the color of the early morning sun. The window overlooked a grove of trees. With a potted plant at each side of the windowpane, it almost made the frame disappear, creating the illusion that the room led directly into the tree tops. The sense of serenity the room inspired was in direct conflict with the adrenalin surging through Tasha's body.

"Not me," Dot laughed. Her desk was placed so she and anyone sitting across from her could see out the window. "Gavin insisted on hiring an interior designer after I complained how dreary the room was. It was my birthday present. Now even when I spend too much time doing paperwork I can still enjoy the scenery."

"He's a smart man."

"That's good since he's your pack leader."

And your mate, Tasha thought. I'm glad he's keeping you happy. Compared to Dot's tailored appearance, Tasha felt out of place in her wrinkled T-shirt and old jeans. She hadn't had time to primp before the meeting. They'd whisked her away from the airport and brought her straight to the former Choate village.

Samantha shuffled uneasily in the chair next to Tasha. Her slender frame and short blonde hair made her look boyish, but she moved with a grace that spoke of ballet lessons in her past. From her scent, Tasha determined Samantha was a wolf in shifted form. Probably one of the Free Wolves. There were many who had joined the ranks after Tasha went to Maine.

"Sorry," Dot said. "I haven't made official introductions. Tasha, meet Samantha Terral. And no, she doesn't go by Sam. Samantha is a martial arts expert. I use her as my personal guard when formal occasions demand it."

That explained her physique. Tasha wondered about the issue with Samantha's name, but now was not the proper time to ask about it.

Dot continued. "Samantha, this is Tasha Roeper of the Fairwood pack. She is an old friend and experienced in security."

Tasha kept the handshake cordial but swift. Until she'd figured out what Dot's agenda was, she was operating in business mode.

"I heard about you," Samantha said. "When I was with Miss Lapahie at the Fairwoods."

Tasha nodded. The quicker the meeting got past social niceties, the sooner she could get back to her family and the pack. She'd been gone too long. But Dot was as much of an alpha as any pack leader she'd ever met, and deserved respect. So Tasha waited for her to continue.

"I suppose," Dot said, "That the two of you are wondering about the demonstration in the board room."

That got her attention, but Tasha knew better than to think Dot really expected an answer. She leaned forward and fastened her eyes on Dot's.

"I have a problem," Dot continued. "And you two are the answer to it. I just needed to prove it to the board members."

Tasha frowned and looked away from Dot long enough to glance at Samantha. She also looked puzzled. "I haven't heard of any problems," Samantha said.

"Good. We've been working hard to keep the rumors under control." Dot got out of her chair and walked over to close the office door. "What I'm about to tell you doesn't leave this office. Agreed?"

"Naturally," Tasha said, a tug of excitement forming in her chest. She resented being shipped off to Maine during the middle of the pack wars, even though she knew it had been for her own good. She was overdue for a challenge.

"I'm worried about security."

Tasha barked out a harsh laugh. "You? Little-Miss-I-Don't-Need-a-Bodyguard? You want us to be your security?" She surreptitiously slid her hand down to her knife and caressed the handle. "Tell me who is threatening you, and I'll handle it."

"I'm not the one being threatened." Dot sighed. "Although Gavin's theory is that I'm a secondary target."

Samantha was clenching her fists as if she wanted to punch something. "So who is the primary mark?"

The CEO of Lapahie Enterprises stood up and faced out the window. Tasha hadn't seen her this nervous since the day she'd led a raid on the Choate village. In a voice filled with regret she said, "The Free Wolves are under attack."

Dot's hypothesis made sense, as much as Tasha didn't want to believe it. That the vehicles owned by various members of the Free Wolves movement began experiencing minor mechanical difficulties was mere coincidence. A loose battery cable here, a flat tire there and once a broken windshield. Yet the cars owned by the remnants of the Choate Pack somehow remained untouched. It stopped when people started locking their vehicles at night and installed alarms.

Then the vandalism in the classrooms started—but again, only the rooms used by the Free Wolves. Equipment stolen or destroyed, desks overturned and papers scattered about, small fires started in the bathrooms.

Increased patrols at night put an end to most of the incidents, but then the phone calls started. More than heavy breathing, the disguised voices threatened rape—and death—if the free wolves didn't return to their pack and abandon the training that Lapahie Enterprises provided.

"No one has left us early yet," Dot reiterated. "And a few of our graduates have stuck around to help out on patrols while classes are going on. But as the threats escalate, it's just a matter of time." Although Lapahie Enterprises was a software company, all of its profits were dedicated to the computer sciences training organization for displaced shifters, wolf or not.

"Free Wolves do not give up," Samantha said.

"And what happens when someone gets hurt?" Tasha asked. "Because once the verbal threats get nowhere, that'll be the next step. What are you going to do, put the whole organization on lockdown? It won't work."

"Exactly," Dot said. "And that's why you two are here."

Tasha leaned back in her chair and crossed her arms over her chest. It was time they got to the point. "What do you have planned?"

"That's up to the two of you. As Samantha will tell you, when we started this adventure, we didn't establish any official process for security. We didn't need it. The patrols were started more as a way of finding and welcoming the shifters arriving here rather than trying to keep people out." Dot picked up a pen and nibbled the end of it. "I've resisted doing this because it's like admitting defeat." She scrawled something on the paper in front of her. "You two are now Lapahie Enterprises' Security Chiefs."

Two

Samantha was shivering, but after Tasha's stay in Maine the chill in the air didn't faze her. Still, winter wasn't too far off. They rustled through the leaves that littered the sidewalk as Dot led the way to the house where she had a room. Not only was the porch light lit, it appeared every light in the place burned brightly. Beyond the lights, a shadow slipped in and out of the trees, tracing their path. They were being guarded.

"Someone having a party?" Tasha asked.

Dot shook her head. "No. More likely, nobody's home. I stay here only on rare occasions. The database administrators who live here full time seem to instinctively know when I need to use it for business. They're probably staying with friends tonight."

"So what's with all the lights?"

"They think it's more secure this way," Samantha said. "I've tried to tell them that lighting the house up like a Christmas display makes it evident to everyone that Miss Lapahie is there. It's a security risk, but they won't listen to me. Especially since the board agrees with them."

"First non-negotiable item," Tasha said as they climbed the steps, "If Samantha and I jointly make a decision in regards to security, the board doesn't get to override it. We work independently, or we can stop talking right now. We answer to you and you alone." The shadow that followed them drifted away into the darkness.

Tasha switched to mental speech for a private conversation. *"Does Dot know she's being followed?"* she sent to Samantha.

"It's an unspoken agreement. We pretend it isn't happening and she pretends that she doesn't see the guards."

"You don't trust my advisers?" Dot asked as she unlocked the door of the craft-style home. Samantha rushed in front, entered first, and disappeared around the corner. Dot sighed, but waited for Samantha to come back before going in.

"I didn't say that. But after their display in the conference room this afternoon, I doubt any of them are up to my standards in the art of war."

Dot stopped suddenly in the doorway to the kitchen, where several covered serving bowls waited for them on the table. "I've been avoiding the use of that word," she said. "I've had my fill of fighting."

"Unfortunately, you don't get to pick. Well, you do. You can either fight or give up. I don't see you giving up."

Dot swirled around and a flash of silver rotated in the air. Tasha shook her head in admiration as Dot caught the throwing knife and smoothly returned it to its original hiding place in her blazer. "I won't abandon everything—and everyone—I worked for. I've done that too many times."

"Good. Next item. You don't get to keep secrets from us."

"That works two ways. Besides, I can 'hear' a lot better than I used to. Does Dot know she's being guarded?' I caught every word of your 'private' conversation outside."

"I thought only alphas could do that."

"She is our alpha," Samantha said.

Dot sighed. "I keep trying to steer away from the traditional terminology, but there doesn't seem to be a replacement for it. I'm not your alpha, Samantha. You're a Free Wolf. And the Free Wolves are not a pack."

"I know, I know. We're a loosely-bound group working together to achieve a common goal for the good of all of us." Samantha raised her hands and made quotation marks in the air.

Tasha grimaced. "Either that or you're a bunch of pack rejects who think you're better than anyone else." She barely dodged Samantha's fist and prepared to avoid a second attempt.

"Enough!" Dot ordered. "We've heard it before." She glared at Samantha and Samantha dropped her fighting stance. "If you two can't get along this project is doomed before it starts."

"You sure act like an alpha. One of the good ones." Samantha said grumpily.

"Part of an ongoing discussion?" Tasha sent to Dot. "Sorry, Samantha," she said aloud.

"Too many times with too many people. If you can help me resolve it, I'd be grateful."

Dot may not call herself an alpha, Tasha thought as she took another forkful of the beef stroganoff, but she lived like one. Food this good didn't magically appear on her table. The old ladies of the village took pride in making sure Dot was well fed, according to Samantha.

In fact, during the survival part of her training, if Tasha didn't catch it or kill it, there was no food on her table at all. She'd gotten much better at tracking game during that month, in both her human and wolf forms.

Tasha had done much more with her time than survival training. The pack's security chief had taken her under his wing, and as good a marksman as she thought she was while with the Fairwood pack, she was many times better now. She'd also received training in military-style strategy and planning. Not the typical courses for a female in a pack, but the group in Maine prided itself in being unique.

"Any theories on who is behind the problems?" Tasha sent. That was one advantage to talking mind-to-mind; it could be done while continuing to eat.

"I have a couple of theories but no evidence." Dot replied.

Samantha joined the conversation. *"Where have the members of the Choate pack gone?"*

"Gavin has his connections tracing as many as he can but he can't locate all of them."

"Are you sure the women that remained aren't involved?"

"Did any of the men remain?" Tasha asked. Normally when a pack broke up, the men were forced to leave, but the stories she'd heard about the takeover made it sound anything but normal. The idea of a pack leader being overthrown by a female was unthinkable, but that's what Dot had done.

"A few. The ones at the bottom of the pack structure. They're being watched," Dot sent.

"I'd like to start with a list of the ones that are still here," Tasha said out loud, abandoning the mental conversation now that her plate was empty. "As far as the rest, will Gavin share his information with us?"

Dot winked. "If I ask him nicely."

Tasha suppressed the sudden unwelcome flair of jealousy the simple statement caused. She'd devoted herself to being just as good as any male in the pack when it came to weapons skills, but that had put her solidly in the "friend" category with her teammates. Marching for miles during a torrential rainstorm or listening as a teammate got sick after eating spoiled meat didn't lead to longings for romance or sex. Tanya, her twin sister, had snagged a series of boyfriends along the way. It had been several years since Tasha's last date.

She shoved the unwelcome thoughts into a dark corner of her brain. There'd be no possibility for romance. Now she needed to concentrate on the opportunity Dot had offered her.

"I'm surprised he lets you stay here. Or that he doesn't come and spend the night."

Samantha giggled and Dot grimaced. "I don't spend many nights here as I have my own office at Fairwood Industries headquarters and most of the time I work from there. I conference into meetings here if needed. But I make a point of being here at least once a week, even if Gavin doesn't like it."

"As stubborn as ever, I see. It would be safer if you stayed there until we can figure out the source of the threat." Tasha raised one hand, palm outward, before Dot responded. "We can discuss that later. Right now I'd like to get back to our list of suspects so I know what we're up against."

"I've been thinking about it," said Samantha. "How many packs are upset about what we're doing here? After all, by taking in strays and runaways, we're challenging their power."

Dot nodded. "I've talked to Counselor Carlson about it. He's heard rumblings, but nothing major. He promised to inform me if anything got serious."

Carlson was the head of the Council of Wolves, an organization formed to keep the peace between rival packs in the US. "Do you trust him?" Tasha asked.

"Yes. He says the Free Wolves provide a valuable service by giving disenfranchised shifters a safe haven and support system."

"But not everyone on the Council agrees," Samantha said. "The dissenters should be considered as suspects. The Free Wolves are monitoring the situation nationwide."

"Will they keep sharing the information?" Tasha asked "Now that we are partners?"

Samantha nodded vigorously. "As long as you commit to protect Miss Lapahie and Lapahie Enterprises, yes. A few hard-liners will push for you to renounce your affiliation with the Fairwood Pack, but they are a minority."

"That option is off the table," Tasha responded with a low growl.

"And I will make that clear to the Board. I don't expect or want it, and remember, you answer directly to me." Dot picked up her dirty plate and slammed it on the sideboard of the kitchen sink. Luckily, it didn't break. "No one will ever be forced to become a Free Wolf. That goes against everything the movement stands for."

Tasha followed her to the sink, carrying her plate as

well as the now-empty serving bowl. "And that's another group we need to consider. How many of the original members of the Free Wolves are upset about the visibility that Dot has brought to the crusade? Ones who were happier working in the shadows? Or may even be jealous of what you are accomplishing here?"

Samantha pushed her chair away from the table, its legs scraping against the tile floor. "The Free Wolves support what Miss Lapahie is doing,"

Dot sighed. "Tasha is right. As much as I would like to agree with you, Samantha, I know better."

"So who can we trust? We've eliminated the old pack, the Free Wolves and the Council."

"The three of us." Tasha held out one hand to each of her companions.

Dot took one of Tasha's hands, and held out her free one to Samantha. Samantha nodded and joined hands with Tasha and Dot. "The Three Musketeers," Samantha said.

"Not quite. Gavin is on the list as well," Dot said.

"More like the Three Amigos," Tasha said with a snort. Except she didn't fully trust Samantha. Not yet.

"Is there somewhere I can stay tonight?" As much as Tasha itched to go home, she was too tired after the long day. Dot was in her room talking to Gavin via the internet, and she and Samantha were sitting on the front porch stairs listening to the nighttime noises.

"You can bunk with me tonight, but we need to find you a permanent spot."

"From the look of things," Tasha indicated the small cluster of homes with a wave of her hand, "you're pretty well maxed out." Lights were on in almost every window, and each tree that lined the street cast more than one shadow. The shadows hid the worn-down look of most of the houses.

"Word spread quickly about what's going on here. We get lone shifters coming in on a regular basis. Not just teenagers and twenty-somethings either. We had a seventy-year old woman show up a while back."

"I don't see her as a student in the school."

"She's not. Dot dropped everything and went for a run with her. A couple of hours later, she was all settled in. She's now in charge of getting the paperwork our new arrivals need—birth certificates, social security cards, driver's licenses. She's a whiz at dealing with government agencies."

"No wonder people are so loyal to Dot."

"Yeah, and that's why the idea that someone is trying to sabotage her efforts pisses me off."

"Or it's not the Free Wolves someone is trying to destroy," Tasha said thoughtfully.

"What do you mean?"

"What if the real target is Gavin or the Fairwood pack? Think about all the resources Gavin will use to protect Dot. And how much that takes away from him watching out for the interest of the pack and the pack's business."

"Wow. This just keeps getting deeper and deeper. Should we mention it to Ms. Lapahie?"

"No, because she's as protective of Gavin as he is of her. I'll talk to Elder Fenner, the security chief of the Fairwoods, and get his input. I trust him. He's been my mentor for a long time."

"Yeah, I remember him from the time I spent with your pack. He seems like a good guy."

They fell into an awkward silence. Tasha watched as shadows circled among the trees that lined the yard. "Will they patrol all night long?" she asked after a fox came to the bottom of the stairs, sniffed, and slid back into the darkness.

"Yes, it's considered part of the training program. All students are required to take a turn several times a month. The instructors are given the schedule, so if a student is sleepy in class, they can give them a break if it's deserved." She switched to mental speech. *"We don't pay much attention to their backgrounds. It's a touchy subject for some of them if they come from a pack where they've been abused. Tomorrow, I'll start checking them out so we can weed out any that might be a risk. Switch them to a different duty."*

Good idea, Tasha sent. *I should head home tomorrow. Check in with the family, pay my respects to Gavin, pick up some belongings.*

I'll find someone who can give you a ride. Or do you want to hang out until Miss Lapahie heads home? She almost never stays more than one night at a time.

Sounds like a good idea. That will give you and me time to start on working on our plans.

Samantha yawned. "We should call it a night. No telling how long Miss Lapahie will be on her call. And we should get an early start in the morning."

"I need to find out where my luggage is first. I got hauled into the meeting this afternoon as soon as I arrived and I don't know what happened to it."

"Who picked you up?"

"A guy named Tony."

16

"Hold on." Samantha closed her eyes and puckered up her face. "Sorry," she said when her eyes re-opened. "My mental range is short and I have to concentrate to reach beyond a few feet. Anyway, Tony still has your suitcases and he'll take them to my room."

"I'm going to head inside and let Dot know what's up."

Samantha took a deep breath. "Someone will bring this up eventually, so I'll tell you first. We make a point of calling her Miss Lapahie as a title of respect because she won't let us call her Elder. I understand you're friends, but I wonder if you should too? At least when you're talking to folks around here?"

"Huh. I never thought of that. And I guess she is my boss now." Tasha brushed a mosquito off her arm. She'd also have to remember to call Gavin "Elder Fairwood" when she returned to her pack. "I'll give it a try when we're in public. But do you want to bet on how long it will take her to yell at me about it?"

THREE

The chill of the early morning air barely penetrated Tasha's fur, but it offset the warmth of her muscles as she loped through the woods. With Dot in a meeting this was as good a time as any to get familiar with the territory held by Lapahie Enterprises. The students were in classes and the employees were behind their desks, crunching code or numbers or whatever they did. Tasha didn't understand how they could forgo the joys of a run in favor of being stuck inside.

She ignored the rabbit that darted in front of her. Breakfast waited for her back at the house Samantha shared with five other single girls. Besides she needed to scent out each animal she encountered to verify it wasn't another shifter. No, this morning the joy was in the run, not in the chase.

She hesitated at a pine tree painted with a yellow swatch, marking the edge of the holding. A creek murmured a short distance across the line. The temptation to explore was great, but until she learned more about the neighbors, she would resist it. For all she knew the landowner was a trophy hunter who would love to boast about killing a wolf on his own property.

But the grove of pine trees a short distance south tempted her in its own way. The perfect place to bring a picnic lunch as a human, but the layer of pine needles on the ground appealed to a wolf. Tasha ran the short distance and dropped to her belly. It had been awhile since she'd had a good roll.

The odor of the decaying pine needles would only disguise her scent for a short time. And a truly skilled hunter could identify her even through the camouflage. But this was just for her personal satisfaction. The smell of pines was better than any perfume Tasha ever tried, and would linger after she returned to human form.

After thoroughly coating her fur and then shaking off the bits and pieces of needles and dirt, Tasha lay quietly, listening to the sounds of the woods. Different birds might flitter among the branches overhead than what she was used to, and it was good to be familiar with their calls. With her nose comfortably nestled on top of her front paws, she grew drowsy. A nap sounded inviting.

It didn't bother her that she was more comfortable in her wolf skin than in human form, although it had worried her trainers. There were precautionary tales of shifters gone rogue in their *other* forms who never returned to the human world. They were the stuff of nightmares for the non-shifter population. Tasha wasn't worried; her wolf was smart enough to know when it was time to return to her human nature. As *other*, she was free to be true to her warrior nature without the constraints of human rules.

Her ears picked up the distant sound of human voices and she went on alert. It could be students on patrol, but it could also be hikers straying past the "No

Trespassing" signs. She needed to figure out which before determining her response.

She slid from tree to tree, staying low to the ground, creeping ever closer to the intruders. There were advantages to not having the largest wolf form. Unseen reconnaissance was her specialty. The pack in Maine had trained her well. She needed to send the elders a thank you note.

Nestled behind a cluster of chokeberry bushes, she watched a young couple stroll into view. The breeze blew from their direction, sending their scents to her. She quickly identified them as shifters, and tension drained from her muscles. One scented as a wolf and the other she wasn't sure about. But the Free Wolves weren't exclusive, despite their name. Any shifter was welcome, and Tasha wondered what form this female took.

There were several ways to find out, but Tasha didn't know yet how far her authority went. Normally she'd act first and ask for forgiveness later, but she didn't want to step on anyone's toes this early in the assignment. She reached out with her mind, searching for one familiar signature. The cluster of buildings that once were the Choate holdings was a long reach, near the end of her reach. She wasn't sure of the strength of Dot's range.

So it surprised her when she made an immediate connection. Another reminder that Dot was indeed an alpha.

"*Please excuse the interruption,*" Tasha sent. "*But I have two young ones out here I suspect are shirking on guard duty.*" She'd heard enough of their conversation to realize that the couple was supposed to be patrolling the perimeter of the territory. Instead, the boy seemed more interested in playing with the buttons on the girl's shirt than paying attention to what went on around them.

"Your call. I trust you," came the terse response.

The corners of Tasha's lips curled in a wolfish grin. This could be fun.

"I ran circles around them for a few minutes," Tasha recounted to Dot on the trip home while Dot drove Gavin's old Jeep. "Getting closer each loop. They never even noticed. So then I started growling. At least that got Ruth's attention. She was raised in the city and is still freaked out by being in the middle of nowhere." Tasha snorted. "I wonder how she'd react to being dropped into the upper reaches of Maine."

"Ruth. Tall, skinny girl with bleached blond hair?" Dot asked.

"Yeah. Do you know all the students?"

"I try to meet with each of them." Dot glanced in the Jeep's mirrors before passing the slow-moving old pickup in front of them. "If memory serves me correctly, she's a mountain lion. Her parents were driven from their pack and she bore the brunt of their anger."

"I wish I'd known that before I scared them."

"What did you do?"

Tasha smiled broadly. "After my attention-getting tactics failed, I just leaped in between them. Knocked them both on their asses at the same time. When Roy, the boy, tried to shift, I kept hitting him, interrupting the process. He'll have a few bruises tonight. A bruised ego as well. He figured because his shifted form was bigger than mine, I'd be a pushover. He has a lot to learn."

"Roy." Dot sighed. "He's been in trouble too often. He's irresponsible and thinks that because he's a genius level, self-taught programmer he's better than everyone else. The trainers are having a hard time correcting his assumption."

"Hopefully, I brought him down a peg or two today."

"Or he'll file a complaint about being attacked."

Tasha thought back to her training. Being pushed mentally and physically had been a major part of it, and the physical punishments were designed to help her recognize her weaknesses and overcome them. Or figure out ways to work around them.

"Is there any reason to allow him to stay if that's the attitude he has?"

"I haven't given up on any of the students yet."

There's a first time for everything, Tasha thought. "How have the instructors been handling him?"

"I leave the details up to them and don't interfere." Dot glanced at Tasha. "I've learned I can't control everything."

"You tried, I bet," Tasha said with a smirk.

Dot chuckled. "Let's not go there."

They sped east and home. Tasha wasn't sure if the feeling in the pit of her stomach was excitement or anxiety or a mixture of both. She'd been gone from the pack for so long, and a lot had changed in that time. Hell, she'd been in some of the same training classes as Gavin and now he was the pack leader and the CEO of

Fairwood Enterprises. She reminded herself to call him Elder. It would be harder than to remember to call Dot Miss Lapahie. She'd known Gavin all of her life.

She'd even had a crush on him as a teenager before focusing her attentions elsewhere. Unless responsibility had aged him, he'd still be crush-worthy. Tasha quickly pushed away the image. He was now her pack leader and mated to her friend. She shouldn't be thinking of him that way.

A few deep breaths helped Tasha restore her equilibrium. She was just going home after all.

The reception waiting when they pulled into the parking lot rattled her. Not only were her parents and siblings there, but half the pack had gathered to welcome her back. Her parents waited at the front of the crowd with Tanya right behind.

Tasha turned to Dot. "You knew about this," she said.

Dot smiled. "Of course I did. Everyone has missed you, and we figured you'd sneak off to be with your family and not come out until it was time to leave again. We couldn't let that happen."

As Dot turned off the engine, a path cleared through the middle of the crowd. Tasha groaned, recognizing the figures striding through the gap. Under other circumstances, she'd worry she'd done something wrong. But maybe Gavin—Elder Fairwood, she reminded herself—was here to greet Dot.

No such luck. As Tasha swung her legs onto the curb, he extended his hand to help her out of the Jeep. She had no choice but to accept the proffered assistance even if she didn't need it.

"Welcome home, Tasha," Gavin said.

"Glad to be back, Elder." Before she could say more, he'd pulled her into a hug.

Then her parents were hugging her too, and Tanya, and Elder Fenner, and then she lost track of the number of hugs and pats on the back or shoulder rubs she received.

When things settled down and Tasha had caught her breath, the party moved to the village commons. Almost everyone in attendance was a shifter, so the outdoor heaters placed around the edge of the area weren't popular gathering spots. Only a few mothers with babies and the couple of elderly women huddled in their warmth.

Soon, Tasha abandoned her seat of honor, preferring to mingle with her pack mates. The cheerfulness surrounding her made her uneasy. Not too many months ago they'd been at war and she wondered if the lessons learned had been forgotten so soon.

Her mother and aunt chatted with one of their friends, and Tasha stood by them, pretending to pay attention to the conversation. Something about plans for the holidays. She focused on scanning the crowd, looking for any sign of potential trouble.

So when she spotted Elder Fenner occupied in much the same way on the other side of the clearing, she murmured a quick apology to her mother. It took her longer than she liked to get to his location, having to stop and make polite conversation with acquaintances along the way. But he must have seen her coming because he was still in the same spot when she finally got there.

He hadn't aged during her absence and remained as good-looking as he'd been when she trained under him. He'd kept his brown hair cut short, and the few wrinkles around his eyes had been there as long as she could remember. His main attraction was the air of confidence he radiated. She guessed he was at least twenty years older than her but it was hard to tell because he never seemed to change. "Welcome back," he said. "We missed you."

"Thanks. It's good to be back. But I'm not sure how long I'll get to stay."

One corner of his mouth rose. "So I've heard. It was strongly suggested I shouldn't schedule you for any duties."

"I'd rather be running patrol than doing this." Tasha indicated the party with a wave of her hand. "It makes me uneasy. Too many new faces. Where did they come from?"

"Not all the Free Wolves followed Elder Lapahie. A few realized they enjoyed the structure of the pack and stayed. Others formed bonds with pack members and gave up their free wolf status to mate."

"Fresh genes will keep the pack strong."

"But they come with their own challenges. We asked one young man to leave because he didn't honor his commitments."

Sounds like Roy, Tasha thought, but then she grinned. "You know Dot hates being called 'Elder' don't you?"

"As does Elder Fairwood. But it's a sign of respect."

"I've been asked to call her Miss Lapahie in public, not by her but by one of the Free Wolves. It'll be easier not to call her anything."

"Such is the way of pack politics."

"Which I'll be heavily involved in, I have the feeling," Tasha said. "I'd like to talk to you about it, get your advice."

"Gladly. But not tonight. Tonight you should relax and enjoy yourself."

At least she didn't have to worry about keeping her eye on Dot. Every time she spotted her friend in the crowd, Gavin had his arm around her waist. And they were never alone. The guards might shift with the wind, but there were always several pack members protecting the couple. She wondered if she could get Elder Fenner to share the technique with her.

FOUR

Tasha eyed the placement of the target. It was further away than the standard twenty-five yards, and the Sig Sauer nestled in her palm was an unfamiliar weapon. But she didn't have the luxury of taking practice shots. With only two rounds loaded, each had to count. She wanted to impress her former mentor.

She adjusted her stance and drew in a steadying breath. With a smooth movement of pure instinct, she raised the gun and squeezed the trigger. Without waiting to see where the first bullet landed, she fired off the second.

"Not bad," Elder Fenner muttered from behind her. He raised his binoculars. "Pretty impressive, actually."

Tasha feigned indifference, but his praise warmed her. Funny, although his given name was Mark, she could no more call him that than she could call Dot anything else. "Has a nice feel to it," she said, setting down the gun. "Is it a new addition to the pack's holdings or a part of your personal collection?"

He didn't answer, instead handing Tasha the binoculars. "Take a look."

Their hands brushed during the exchange, but

Tasha ignored the distraction of the tingling his touch always evoked. She raised the binoculars to her eyes and didn't hide her grin of satisfaction. Both bullets had landed at the edge of the bull's-eye. Pretty good, in her opinion.

"It's yours now."

"What? I can't take this." Tasha knew the reputation of this model, and that it was worth considerably more than her current weapon.

"Then consider it on loan. You need a better gun than what you've been using." Elder Fenner took a seat on a nearby stump. "You wanted to talk, let's talk."

It seemed as good a place as any for it. The shooting range was at the edge of the pack's territory and no one else was around. Tasha used her *other* hearing to verify they were alone.

"How familiar are you with the problem at Dot's organization?"

"Only the little Elder Fairwood has shared."

"The trouble," Tasha said, plopping on the ground, "Is there are too many potential suspects. I can't even verify who the real target is."

"Everyone assumes it's Lapahie Enterprises."

"I'm not convinced. It could be Dot, or Gavin, or it could be the Fairwood pack."

"That's quite a stretch."

"Think about it. What better way to ruin the pack than to destroy Dot and her company. Gavin would sink all of his time and money into saving her, and that would destroy our company. And voila, the pack would need to disband."

"Do you have any proof to justify that theory?"

"No. It's one of about five theories I've developed.

There's no evidence to back up any of them." Tasha plucked a piece of wild wheat from the ground and released the seeds, watching them float away on the breeze. "But I figure identifying where the threat is coming from is one of our first tasks."

"And how do you plan to do that?"

"For starters, I'm hoping Gavin's contacts have heard something and that he'll share."

"If not?"

"Surveillance cameras in the spots that get hit most often. Try to catch one of the culprits and make them spill the beans on who's behind them. Trace the numbers making the calls."

"Good steps. Anything else?"

"Question everybody." Tasha frowned. "That will take more manpower than we have available. Trying to figure out where to start is the tough part. We'll hurt some feelings and make people resent us, but I don't see any way around it. Samantha will need to do a big part of that.

"Speaking of Samantha, you wouldn't know who came up with the scheme to pair a free wolf with a pack member for this project, would you? And who suggested me? Somehow I doubt Dot came up with it on her own."

"Perhaps Elder Fairwood had something to do with it."

"Right. And you didn't put a bug in his ear. Not that I'm complaining. I'm glad to be back."

"We weren't sure you'd want to come back. The reports we got were that you fit in well with the pack in Maine. I half-expected you to find your mate."

Tasha knew the pack leader had sent reports back. At first she felt like a kid in school again, but soon decided that it didn't matter. It wasn't like she was a prisoner. She had been free to leave anytime she wanted.

"Have you been talking to my mother? Because she mentioned the same thing." She grinned. "I bonded deeply with many members of the pack, both male and female, and I can count on them for help if I ever need it. But none of the males appealed to me as anything but friends. My mother is worried because I'm well past the typical mating age for females, and I've never been in a serious relationship." Although Tanya hadn't mated yet, she'd had several long-term boyfriends. The older she and her twin got, the more they developed their own personalities.

"Your mother has mentioned her concerns to several of the elders. That's why I brought it up. As much as people push the whole concept of mates, there always have been exceptions to the rule. For a while, we thought Elder Fairwood might be one of them, that he might never choose a mate. That would've been a disaster for the pack."

"And then he found Dot."

"Yes."

Tasha smiled. "So the Elders gossip about the pack members' love lives."

"It's not gossiping," Elder Fenner said sternly. "We're showing our concern for the future of the pack." He grinned. "Don't tell anyone. It's a badly kept secret."

"Got it." She watched an ant crawling up a stem of grass, wondering if she should breech protocol and ask a personal question. "You never mated."

"No." He closed his eyes. "I came close once, but

she was killed in a pack war. Since then, I've devoted myself to making the pack as secure as possible so the same fate doesn't happen to anyone else."

"You've done a good job."

A V of geese flew overhead. "Am I good enough?" she asked quietly.

"Can you beat our strongest males in one-on-one combat in either human or wolf form? No. But what I've been trying to push into the pack's collective thick skull, including Elder Fairwood, is that it takes more than strength to be a leader. It takes intelligence and training and luck. You've got the first two. I can't do anything about the luck part."

"Dot seems to have more than enough luck to make up for any I'm missing," Tasha said with a wry grin. "Hopefully some will rub off on me."

A noise on the other edge of the clearing caused them both to stiffen. Tasha swiveled and reached out with her *other* senses. She spotted the vaguest outline in the bushes, mingling with the shadows cast by nearby trees. It was possible it was a pack member, but not likely. They were either at work or in school this time of day.

"Can you identify it?" she sent, dropping flat on the ground.

Elder Fenner sniffed. *"No, the wind is blowing the wrong direction."*

"Then the question is, does it see us?"

"Hard to tell. What's the plan?"

Tasha pushed away the thought that this was a pre-arranged test. *"Are the patrols out this morning?"*

"Of course. So chances of it being an intruder are low."

"But not non-existent. I say we observe it and see

if it reveals itself. I'll shift and try to get closer. You have more ammo for the Sig?"

His silent chuckle was the answer she needed, and she slipped the gun out of her waistband and laid it by his feet. He would pick it up when he was comfortable moving. She debated before beginning her shift; the jeans she wore were almost new and she hated to destroy them. But removing them and her shirt would create more movement and noise. She resigned herself to replacing them and prepared for the change.

"Wait. Look."

Tasha cautiously lifted her head the same time the wind changed direction. *"That's a beauty, and not another shifter,"* she sent as a large white-tailed buck stepped into a patch of sunshine. She counted the points on his rack. Ten. *"What's he doing here?"* They hadn't been quiet before the deer showed up.

Although the pack didn't depend on the local wildlife for food, hunting was a natural part of their lives, and few large animals were found on pack land anymore. Even rabbits and squirrels were not as plentiful as they were years ago.

"It's almost hunting season. He probably got chased out of his territory by someone scouting for a good spot for a blind. Are you going to take him down?"

"Does the pack need the food?" Tasha's *other*-self licked its lips in anticipation of fresh meat, but the deer was larger than she and Elder Fenner could eat in one sitting.

"No."

"Well, crap."

Elder Fenner chuckled. *"I agree. And I doubt he'll*

stick around until the next scheduled pack hunt. But wouldn't he be a prize?"

"I bet he'd give us a great chase." There were times when the hunt was more fun than the kill, but the combination of a good chase and large kill was a rare treat.

"Does the Lapahie holding offer good hunting?"

Fenner's return to spoken speech signaled the end of the need for secrecy and Tasha followed suit. "I didn't see anything but birds and a rabbit in my one run. I suspect the Choate pack killed everything off during the lean times. It'll take time for the wildlife population to make a comeback."

"Perhaps we can help. Occasionally the local game and fish department asks us to make a spot for an animal that needs to be relocated. It'll be tougher because they'd be moving them across state boundaries, but we could recommend they be transferred to the Lapahie holding."

"I'll suggest to Dot that she contact the local wildlife division. Somehow I can't believe the Choates were on good terms with the authorities and Dot might try to repair the situation."

"Good thinking." They watched the buck in silence for a few minutes as he grazed. "I'll add him to the banned list. He might attract some does if he sticks around and that'll build up the herd."

The pack maintained a list of animals they were not allowed to hunt. All pregnant females were protected, as well as those with babies too young to survive without their mother. And since shifters tended to attract other shifters, they made sure that everyone was schooled in identifying shifters versus wildlife. It was mostly a matter of a difference in scent.

A nearby gunshot sounded and the buck jerked his neck up, twirled, and dashed into the woods. Tasha breathed a sigh of relief that he appeared uninjured but another worry immediately took its place. *"Poachers?"* The pack didn't hunt animals with the weapons they owned.

"Let's find out."

FIVE

With the reloaded Sig tucked into its shoulder holster, Tasha crept through the brush. Her *other* sense of smell pointed the way towards her target. It would have been fun to track the intruders in wolf form, but this was business. Poachers were a major threat to the pack. But she knew the land well, having traveled it many times in both wolf and human form, and that gave her an advantage. Just as being able to call on her wolf senses while in human form put her in a better position.

Elder Fenner was circling in from the other direction. They could have communicated mind-to-mind, but Tasha preferred to keep her focus on her surroundings. It was too easy to make a mistake when listening to someone else's chatter. Since Elder Fenner had trained her, she knew he felt the same way.

The odor of burning weeds drifted her way, and Tasha's nose wrinkled in disgust. Bad enough smoke in the woods this time of year, with the potential for setting off a forest fire, but these fools were smoking a mix of tobacco and marijuana. If they'd laced the mixture with anything stronger, it would affect the way they reacted.

She leaned against the trunk of an old maple and listened to the poachers' conversation. Although they were still out of sight through the thick brush, her *other* sense of hearing picked up what they were saying. It didn't make her happy.

"The timber alone would be worth the price."

"Let alone the number of lots you could get out of the acreage. People will pay big bucks for a new development."

Tasha couldn't imagine the pack selling any of its property. It was more likely that they would want to add to their holdings as their numbers grew. She risked a quick thought to Elder Fenner to report the information.

After a short delay, he replied. *"Perhaps they are lost."*

She and Elder Fenner would find out soon enough. Tasha darted from tree to tree, working her way closer to the poachers. They were near the border of the pack's land, so maybe they had just strayed too far. Still, they were carrying rifles and using them, and hunting season was several weeks away.

From behind a stand of bushes, Tasha studied the two men. They were dressed like typical local residents in jeans, light jackets, baseball hats, and tennis shoes. Except for the rifles they carried at their sides, they didn't look like much of a threat. From their odors, she could tell they hadn't used bug spray, which was a mistake for normal humans. Unless they were lucky, they'd end up with deer ticks.

First, they'd have to deal with her. She unsnapped the cover of the shoulder holster and stepped out in front of them. "You boys headed somewhere in particular?"

If this hadn't been such serious business, Tasha would have laughed at their astonished looks. It was as if she'd dropped out of the sky. As it was, the shorter of the two men almost dropped his rifle.

They recovered quickly. "What's it to you?" the taller one asked with a sneer.

"You're trespassing on private land. And likely poaching." Tasha nodded her head towards their weapons. "Both are against the law. And you're smoking in the woods which isn't illegal but is damned foolish."

"We're just out for a hike," the first man said. "The guns are for protection. There are bears around here."

Not on pack land. "And you saw one. That's the shot I heard. Right."

"Wasn't us. Must have been someone else."

"You mean if I sniff the barrels of your guns right now all I'd smell is gun oil? Give me a break."

"It's not against the law to shoot at a stump."

"It is when you're trespassing in a posted no hunting area. Now why don't you empty the chambers of your guns, turn around and go back where you came from?"

"Who's going to make us? You and what army?" The second man tightened his grip on his rifle, but Tasha could draw her handgun and fire before he was able to get it to his shoulder.

In her peripheral vision, she caught movement off to her left and sensed it was Elder Fenner moving closer. She faked a yawn. "This is getting boring. I don't know what game you two are playing, but in my field I make the rules. This is your last warning."

"Or what? You'll take the ball and run home to your mommy?"

They weren't going to back down, at least, the taller guy wasn't. Tasha sent a quick thought to Elder Fenner with her plan. "That's a nice Winchester you have there." Tasha gestured towards the taller man.

Three quick steps, a dive and a roll, and she stood with the rifle in her hand. "Classic deer rifle. Model 70," she said, as she ejected the chambered bullet. "Not sure it has the power to kill a big bear, but it might slow one down enough to let you get away. Either that or just make it mad."

Fenner appeared from behind the two men and snatched the rifle from the second man's hands. "I've alerted Jaime," he said. "He wants us to meet him at the east gate."

"Jaime?"

"You haven't met him. He's the new Game and Fish Warden for the district. He was assigned here while you were gone."

"You got nothing on us," the shorter man blustered.

"We have two witnesses to loaded guns, trespassing on posted land, and," Tasha sniffed the barrel of the gun she held, "a fired gun. I don't think he'll need much more than that."

"You'd better give us our guns back and let us go or we'll sue you for false imprisonment. Take everything you own. You have no authority to hold us," the other one said.

"I'm a deputy game warden. I do have the authority." Elder Fenner slung the rifle across his back. "The more you argue the worse things get for you. Tasha, will you take the lead?"

She hesitated. "Shouldn't we search them for other weapons first?" She knew better than to turn her back on a potential attacker.

"Good call. I'll do the search. You gentlemen want to own up to anything?"

The prospect of being arrested appeared to have deflated the egos of the intruders. As the pair grudgingly handed over their hunting knives, Tasha spotted movement in the brush. She raised a questioning eyebrow, and Elder Fenner responded with the barest of nods. Reinforcements had arrived, but would stay hidden unless needed.

Tasha headed towards the east gate, deliberately taking the roughest path possible. Her jeans might suffer, but the men would fare even worse because they had no skills in maneuvering through the brambles. Petty, but it gave her great satisfaction.

Tasha had envisioned an older, balding man with a paunch, not this over-sized, red-haired bulk of a man whose shoulders strained to fit in the crisp uniform shirt he wore. From the easy way he moved, the bulk was all muscle covering his six-foot-something frame. The scruff on his chin added a hint of maturity to an otherwise youthful face. But when he turned his gaze onto the two offenders, there was nothing boyish about his expression.

"You two again?" he said. "I thought I told you to stay out of my district."

"You've run into them before?" Elder Fenner asked.

"Yep. Twice. First time I let them off with a

warning, second time I let them off with a sterner warning. Since it's clear they weren't listening, this time I'm going to charge them. We've got trespassing, unlawful firing of a weapon, anything else?"

"I didn't locate any sign of blood, so either they missed or they really did shoot at a tree stump."

The warden's mouth wiggled. Tasha wondered what he would look like if he smiled. "Right. Well, let's get the paperwork started. I'll need your ID's," he said, addressing the two offenders.

The shorter man reached for his wallet, mumbling something about "bad luck," and "we didn't do anything." Tasha kept her eye on the other one, her instincts screaming. Was he plotting something?

As the warden leaned into his truck for the needed papers, the second man bolted for the woods. Tasha didn't even take a complete breath before sprinting after him. He didn't make it very far. In less than ten feet, she tackled him and threw him to the ground. The wild punches he threw didn't stand a chance of landing when she sat on his back to hold him down.

"So we get to add resisting arrest to the charges, do we?" The warden was beside her in a moment. He pulled a set of handcuffs from his belt and with Tasha's assistance, fastened them securely on the struggling man's wrists.

"Police brutality!" the man screamed. "I'll sue!"

The warden rolled his eyes. "Anyone get this on video? No? It's a good thing my dashcam is rolling." He hauled the man to his feet. "It'll capture the audio even if we were out of frame."

The more Tasha heard his voice, the more she liked it. It was mellow, like a breeze on a warm summer's day. Too bad he wasn't a shifter. She didn't need to scent him to know that. He was close enough that she could see no hint of yellow in his deep green eyes.

She wondered if he was aware of the special skills of the Fairwood clan. The last warden had been part of the closely kept secret and made use of them in emergencies. They'd found more than one lost hiker and one time located a child who wandered off from his parents' home. Of course, they always arranged for the credit to go to a human volunteer so they could stay out of the limelight.

While she and the warden had corralled the attempted escapee, Elder Fenner had placed a call on his cell phone. "Backup is on the way," he said. "I wasn't sure if your truck was set up for hauling prisoners so I called the State Police. They'll have an officer here in ten minutes."

With more force than necessary, the warden shoved his prisoner into a sitting position beside his truck. "So you want to make a break for it too?" he asked the other culprit.

The smaller man held his hands up in the air. "No. I'm good. Just give me my summons and I'll hike back to my car."

With the warden doing paperwork and Elder Fenner guarding the prisoner, Tasha felt useless. Spotting a plastic bag lying on the ground, she grabbed it and wandered down the roadside, picking up litter.

It was mostly fast food wrappers and beer bottles. Since the pack worked hard to keep their territory clean, the amount of trash lying around bothered her. It didn't take long to fill the little bag and she realized she didn't know what do with it.

But evidently, the warden had seen what she was doing. "You can throw that in the back if the truck," he called. "And I've got garbage bags and work gloves behind the seat if you're interested in doing more. It drives me crazy seeing all the crap people throw out of their vehicles."

"Why don't we all hold hands and sing 'Kumbaya' while we're at it?" muttered the man on the ground.

"Ignore him," the warden said. Tasha planned to do just that. "With any luck he'll be assigned to a road clean-up crew as part of his punishment."

"Karma can be a wonderful thing," Tasha agreed. She peeled off the work glove and stuck out her hand. "I'm Tasha Roeper, by the way."

"I'm Jaime Zeiller. Thanks for your help catching him. You're fast." He took her proffered hand and shook it with just the right amount of squeeze and the perfect length of time to be polite. Why was she disappointed when he let go?

Six

By the time the state police arrived, Tasha had filled two trash bags with garbage. And by the time the prisoner was transferred to his car, one of the pack members arrived and gave her and Elder Fenner a lift back to the village, just in time for her meeting with Gavin and Dot.

They waited for her in his office. "I understand you had a little fun this morning," Gavin said, handing her a glass of ice tea. A beer would have gone down better, but business protocol demanded a non-alcoholic beverage.

"You could say that, Elder." She'd been here once before, when Gavin's father was pack leader. Little had changed, except for the computer setup and the pictures of Dot gracing the desk.

"In here, between us, I'd appreciate it if you call me Gavin. I'd get rid of the title if I could, but that's not going to happen."

"Pack tradition is hard to change." Tasha used her free hand in a futile effort to return her hair to a resemblance of neatness.

"I didn't realize how hard it would be." Gavin

frowned. "I thought that as our generation came into power, we'd be able to change all those things we talked about when we were younger. It never ceases to amaze me how many people our age are happier sticking with tradition because it's easier."

Tasha took a gulp of the ice tea, the cold liquid trickling down her suddenly parched throat. "They're unhappy with you and Dot being together? Instead of you choosing a mate from the pack?" She already knew the answer, but wanted to see Gavin's reaction.

Gavin got up and forcefully shut the door to the office. "What have you heard?"

"Rumors. Nothing solid. Overheard snatches of conversations. People suddenly switching the topic when I approach."

"Because they aren't sure where your allegiances are," Dot said.

Tasha nodded. "Or they're aware of the connection between you and me and assume I'm a spy."

"Where are your loyalties, Tasha?" Gavin asked.

"To the pack," she answered promptly. "As always. And as far as I can tell, you're the best person for the job of pack leader so that means I support you too. And since Dot makes you happy, I'm good with your choice of mate." She understood the disappointment of other women of the pack since Gavin hadn't chosen one of them, but a happy pack leader made for a happy pack. "Besides, you gave most of the eligible females a chance to win your heart before Dot come along."

One of Dot's eyebrows rose. "Including you, Tasha?"

"Including me." She grinned when she saw Gavin's cheeks redden. "As I remember, the date ended with the two of us trying to decide who could eat more nachos. I won."

"Your memory serves you incorrectly. I was still eating when you gave up. Then you had to be carried home."

"I ate five servings to your four. It wasn't the nachos that did me in, it was the beer I drank to wash them down. And it took two guys to drag you home."

"Sounds like you've had this argument before," Dot said with a laugh.

"We have," Tasha and Gavin said simultaneously.

"And I'm sure we'll have it again." Gavin grinned. "But not in public."

"The whole pack knows the story already. It's practically a legend," Tasha pointed out.

Gavin sighed. "At least no one dares to tease me about it anymore." He cleared his throat. "But we're here for serious business."

"Yes, we are." Tasha set her glass on the floor and leaned forward. She didn't want to risk a water stain on the wooden desk. "What did your contacts find out?"

"Not much." Gavin slid an almost-flat manila file folder across his desk. "If this is an organized effort, the conspirators are damned good at keeping secrets."

Tasha took a few minutes to flip through the contents of the folder. "Well, at least Elder Choate isn't involved." The former leader of the Choate pack was in a nursing home, apparently suffering from Alzheimer's. Lapahie Enterprises was footing the bill for his care. "Sorry, Dot, he's your grandfather and this is a terrible thing that has happened to him, but he was at the top of my lists of suspects."

Dot shrugged. "It's all right. He never pretended to care about me."

"And the Choate pack members responsible for your abduction are still in prison?"

Gavin and Dot exchanged glances. "All but one," Gavin answered. "He escaped from the jail before his sentencing. We suspect he had inside help, but can't prove it. And he's gone far enough underground that we can't locate him."

"I'll consider him a prime suspect then. Dot, do you still have the old files from the Choate Pack? I'd like to dig into them and see what I can find out about him. What's his name?"

"His name is Arnold, but he's probably using an assumed name. Unless he's had plastic surgery, he's got four scars in his left cheek—a gift from Dot." Gavin patted his mate's knee. "Although there are several other men with similar scars."

Tasha closed the folder. The information it contained didn't give her much to go on. "So tell me what you think is happening."

Gavin and Dot exchanged a glance. "Someone's trying to run Dot off," Gavin said.

"And you know what I think," Dot interjected. "Someone's trying to destroy the Free Wolves."

"The two aren't mutually exclusive. Destroying the Free Wolves would ruin everything Dot has worked for. And since Dot is now the 'face' of the Free Wolves, destroying her would cripple the movement." Tasha made the snap judgment not to voice her fear that the Fairwood Pack was the real target. She'd let Elder Fenner convey that information to his alpha.

"I'm not that important," Dot objected. "I'm just

the flavor of the week. Give it time, and the attention will fade away."

"We're friends, right? Because you might get mad at what I'm going to tell you." Tasha took a deep breath. "Let me explain how you look to everyone past that door.

"You guys are pack royalty. Not just to the Fairwoods, but to every pack in the country. Canadian packs too. Gavin, you're young and handsome, a war hero, and leader of one of the most influential packs around. What's not to crush on? But you're totally dedicated to your beautiful mate and that makes you even more of a fantasy.

"And Dot, you're better than Cinderella. You're the rags-to-riches success story. Not only did you capture the Prince's heart, you took over a business, pulled it out of the dirt and now it's thriving. But instead of keeping that money for yourself, you're giving it to orphans. At the same time, you're leading a movement to help all those poor little shifters without packs to depend upon."

Gavin's lip drew taut, and Dot opened her mouth to speak. Tasha held up one hand to stop her.

"I'm not done. Did you know bets are being placed on how soon you'll have children and what the kids will look like? But that's just the good stuff."

"What do you mean?" Gavin wrapped his large hand around Dot's smaller one.

"We're talking pack politics. There's always a down side. For example, you, Gavin, are a dirty no-good, backstabbing, ungrateful pup who threw your own father out into the cold. And Dot fucked her way into power. Why else would Counselor Carlson and the entire Council be at her beck and call?"

Gavin pushed his chair back and stood abruptly. If the desk hadn't been in the way, Tasha would have worried he'd attack her. As it was, she swore his fangs started to descend, the first sign of a shift. She was headed into dangerous territory, but she wasn't going to back down.

"Who said that? Nobody attacks Dot and gets away with it," he growled.

She got up, spilling the remnants of her tea, and poked her finger into his chest.

"You know how this game is played, Gavin. And if no one has told you this before, you need new advisers. You two are the ultimate power couple. Which makes you the ultimate target. So that's how I'm going to approach this mission. Yes, I'll work with Samantha and figure out who's behind the attacks at Lapahie Enterprises, but my goal is to protect the two of you."

Gavin gripped the edge of his desk with white-knuckled hands. Tasha let off the pressure from her finger and glared at him. Dot laid a hand on his shoulder, but the tension didn't leave his face.

"I suppose you're bucking for the position?" he snarled.

Tasha didn't blink. "Not a chance in the world, Tiny. I don't want anything to do with the power structure. I'm a behind-the-scenes kind of person."

"Tiny?" He closed his eyes for a second and his shoulders relaxed.

Dot grinned slightly. "Tiny?"

"That's what I said. Are you going to get all pissy on me now and demand I call you Elder Fairwood?"

Gavin's shoulders twitched. His fangs disappeared. The lines in his face smoothed out. "Tiny?" he chortled. He lowered himself into his chair, still laughing.

Tasha smiled broadly. "Lame, isn't it? Next time I'll come up with something better. How about Big Guy? Or Mr. Untouchable?"

"You think there will be a next time?"

"Absolutely. If you don't want the truth, don't ask me for my input."

"Don't you know about filters?"

She waved one hand in the air. "Buzzwords. I have no use for them. If you think I'm going to tell you only what you want to hear, or water down bad news with nice words, it's not going to happen. But I promise I'll give you the bad news in private."

"She's right," Dot said. "I've noticed it happening to me too. Most of the board members are afraid to challenge me and tell me when I mess up."

"The same rules apply to you, Dot. I don't want to attend board meetings, but if there's talk about decisions you're considering that will negatively impact the company, I'll tell you straight out."

"I may not like it, but as long as you're honest with me, I'll appreciate it."

"So what are your plans?" Gavin asked.

"I'm going to move in with Samantha and her roomies. I figure if I'm hanging out with the single women, I'll hear more gossip and be more approachable. I'll need to limit my time with you, Dot, pretend to ignore you. But with your skill in communicating mind-to-mind, we'll be able to keep in touch." Tasha grinned. "You've come a long way."

"Someone helped me." She rubbed Gavin's thigh. "It took lots of practice, but it's a useful skill." Her eyes went blank. So did Gavin's. Tasha realized they were communicating silently, leaving her out of the conversation.

She cleared her throat to bring their attention back to the discussion. "I'll want to take my bike. Spend more time over at Lapahie and not travel back and forth with Dot."

"Dmitri's been maintaining it and riding it once in a while, so it should be good to go." Lines creased Gavin's face. "But I hoped you'd be riding shotgun with Dot when she commutes."

"Did you base the need for that on any specific intel?"

"No, but I'd feel better."

"Me too. But I'm the wrong person for the job." Tasha chewed her bottom lip as she thought. "So we call it training. Dot, you go to Lapahie Enterprises once a week, right?"

"Yes," Dot said, but there was puzzlement in her voice.

"We call it an internship. One of the advanced students comes with you, works here for a week, then goes back with you. Next trip, different student. That gives you a chance to get to know the students better. The added body will make you less of a target.

"We can be selective in the students that get chosen. They'll need to be cleared through Samantha and me first. You can create an entire application process so we have the information we need to check their histories. Either of you see any flaws in the plan?"

"I hate bodyguards," Dot said. "And I use the drive to plan. I'm not happy losing that time for myself."

Tasha waited while Gavin and Dot engaged in another silent conversation. Finally, Dot broke eye contact with him and sighed. "Okay, you win. I don't like it, but I'll play along."

A knock on the door interrupted them and an older lady cracked open the door. "Sorry, Elder, but your two-thirty appointment is here."

"Thanks, Annie," Gavin said.

Tasha picked up the now-empty glass from the floor so she could remove it from the office. "Is there anything else we need to talk about?"

"I think we're good for now."

At the door, Tasha hesitated. "Have you met the new game warden yet? Is he aware of our specialized skills?"

Gavin smiled. "Jaime? Yes, he knows and will protect the secret. The old warden told him during the short transition period. He didn't believe it though, until I took him for a walk around our borders and demonstrated the transition. I've never seen a big man go pale so fast. Why?"

"I just wondered. He didn't hint at it this morning. Of course, the timing wasn't right. At least we won't have to worry about him spilling the beans." She opened the door the rest of the way. "Have a good afternoon, Elder, Miss Lapahie," she said, winking before she left.

Tasha felt like the proverbial third wheel. Tanya and her boyfriend, Rafael, snuggled in the booth across from her. The Pub, their favorite restaurant, was bustling, and their waitress warned them it might take longer than usual for their food to arrive. Under other circumstances, Tasha wouldn't have minded and would have sat back and enjoyed her beer, but she was too antsy to get into the party mood.

She'd already made the rounds to say hello to the other pack members who were there and dropped more than her share of quarters into the jukebox to play her favorite songs. Still, she was restless, anticipating trouble from an unknown source. So while she pretended to listen to what her sister was talking about, she studied the other guests.

Nothing had changed in The Pub while she was gone. The same menu, the same red and white checkered tablecloths, the same scent of yeast and tomatoes, the same pictures on the walls, and many of the same patrons. Nothing seemed out of place. So why was she so edgy?

The pizza arrived, and Tasha grabbed a piece, enjoying the familiar taste of her favorite variety, made with white sauce, spinach and feta cheese. Not a typical mix of ingredients for a wolf. Tanya and Rafael shared a pepperoni pizza, and Tanya shook her head after seeing what her sister had chosen.

"I thought that was just a phase," Tanya said. She smiled. "Real wolves eat meat."

"Real wolves eat whatever they want," Tasha replied, sticking with the old formula. But her attention was diverted when the front door opened. She sniffed, identifying the arrival before he got to their booth.

"Good evening, Miss Roeper."

"Evening, Warden," she said. "Please, call me Tasha."

"Only if you call me Jaime." He looked around. "Doesn't look like I'll be able to snag an empty table any time soon. But I wanted to say thank you for your assistance this morning. Those two med have been an annoyance since I moved here, and hopefully they'll finally be out of my hair."

"I'm glad I could help."

"Slide over, Tasha," Tanya said. "Have a seat, Jaime. I'm Tanya, by the way, Tasha's twin sister. And this is my boyfriend Rafael." Tasha had considered asking him to join them, but Tanya beat her to it.

Jaime slid into the booth next to Tasha, and she was reminded again about how massive he was. She had no doubt that he could hold his own against most male members of the pack if they stayed in their human form although she suspected his size intimidated potential opponents before a fight ever began. Now that he was out of uniform, she could see the muscles in his arms flex as he handed the menu to the waitress after she'd taken his order. Being wedged between him and the wall was not a position she would have freely chosen.

She snapped back to reality when he asked, "Is the food here as good as they say? This is the first time I've been here."

Tanya pushed the pan of pizza towards him. "Better. Go ahead and have a piece while you're waiting for yours."

"If you don't mind," he said with a smile, "I will. It was a long day and I missed lunch." After taking several bites, he turned to Tasha. "Elder Fenner said you'd recently returned from Maine. How is it up there? I've always wanted to go."

"It's a beautiful state but I didn't get to do much sightseeing," she answered. "I was doing specialized survival training." That had been her cover story all along. Pack business never got discussed with outsiders.

"Nice. Did you go too, Tanya?"

"Naw, only Tasha went. It didn't sound like my idea of fun."

The group fell into an uncomfortable silence, having run out of topics to discuss. The waitress brought Jaime his beer and pizza, and they busied themselves with eating.

Tasha normally enjoyed silence, but found the situation awkward. She decided to do something about it. "So where are you from, Jaime?" she asked.

He swallowed the bite he'd been chewing. "Fermer. A little town nobody's ever heard of in the southwest corner of the state."

"You're right. Never heard of it." Tasha grinned.

"I have," said Rafael. "Doesn't it hold an annual fall leaves festival? My mom dragged me to it once."

The two men started discussing how small town events seemed to be aimed at women with all the arts and crafts, and men were nothing but accessories. Tanya rolled her eyes. *"Typical male bonding,"* she sent.

Tasha nodded as she sipped her beer, glad that the attention was no longer focused on her. Besides, she liked the sound of Jaime's full and rich voice. When he laughed at some inane remark Rafael made, it reminded her of an old-fashioned Santa.

"He's a looker. You going to keep him?" Tanya kicked her under the table.

"Too bad he's not a wolf." Tasha flipped a scrap of pizza crust at her sister. *"You know my rule."*

"Never date a non-shifter. Blah blah blah. I think he's worth breaking your rule for."

"Not going to happen. I'm going to be out of here tomorrow."

"True. How about I go with you? I'd like to see the place."

"I'm taking my bike. You can haul some of my things over for me in your car."

"We'd better take this conversation to the spoken level before Jaime notices."

Tasha nodded, just as Jaime said, "Sorry, didn't mean to ignore you."

"That's okay, I've been to a couple of those things and don't really enjoy them. Tanya, do you have plans for tomorrow? I was going through what I need to take with me and don't have room in my saddlebags. Do you have the time to make a trip and take some of my gear to the school?"

"You ride?" Jaime asked.

"Yes. I have an old 700 Honda Shadow. It's not the biggest bike on the road, but it gets me where I'm going."

"I'm familiar with the line. I'm riding a dual sport myself so I can take it off road when I need to. Had to upgrade the springs, but that's a given in my line of work."

"He's perfect for you!" Tanya sent.

Tasha ignored her. "What made you decide to be a game warden?"

"Fate." Jaime shrugged. "I always knew I wanted to be in law enforcement, even got trained and hired on as a deputy sheriff after college. But I wanted to get outdoors more, so when this opening came up, I applied and got it."

Rafael said, "I understand the competition for the job of game warden is rough."

"They tell you that straight up when you apply. I got lucky."

Tasha put down her beer mug. "I'm sure your experience in law enforcement helped."

"That and the fact that I minored in Environmental Studies. These days, we work closely with the Department of Conservation because there's so much illegal harvesting of old trees going on, and sometimes we're the first ones to know."

Tasha remembered the morning's overheard conversation. "The men you arrested today mentioned something about the timber being more valuable than the land itself."

"I thought the Fairwood lands were under a land trust agreement," Tanya said.

"A conservancy, not a trust. It can't be developed except for a defined area where the village is," Jaime said. "That also allows it to be posted for no trespassing."

"He's smart too. You better grab him before someone else does," Tanya sent.

Tasha kicked one of her sister's feet. *"We don't even know if he already has a girlfriend. So shut up."*

Jaime picked up the pitcher of beer from the table and refilled both his and Tasha's mugs. "You said you were leaving tomorrow. Where are you going?"

"There's a school in Ohio I'm doing contract work for," Tasha answered. "Helping with security and training. The length of the assignment depends upon how well things work out, so I'm taking more with me than normal."

"Sounds interesting. Good luck. If I need you as a witness, is there a way to reach you?"

"Thanks. If you need me, just contact Fairwood

Enterprises and someone there will get in touch with me."

"He wanted your phone number," Tanya sent, hiding her grin behind the beer mug she raised to her lips.

"Grow up. If he wanted it, he'd ask for it."

SEVEN

"We need an office," Samantha complained to Tasha as they trudged through the parking lot of Lapahie Enterprises on their way to yet another meeting. "Make all these people come to us."

While Samantha and Tasha made their rounds, Tanya was off exploring the Lapahie grounds. She'd decided it would be fun to hang out with her sister for a few days.

"You can have your office," Tasha said, "I'd rather find someplace outside to hold these meetings."

"You won't think that once the temperatures fall and it snows."

"I like snow. Nothing like rolling around in it to cool down after a long run."

Samantha crossed her arms over her chest. "Just the idea of it makes me shiver. I prefer sunny skies and sandy beaches year-round."

"You won't see sunny skies here in a month or so. Why do you stay?"

"The Free Wolves. I believe in the cause. Growing up, my pack didn't allow women to hold leadership positions. I didn't like that, so I left. And I'm not welcome back. But Miss Lapahie gave me the chance to show what I'm capable of. This is my chance to help girls like me." She stopped in her tracks. "Sorry, there I go getting on my soapbox again."

"Not a problem. It's the same concept as loyalty to a pack."

"Only in some ways we're closer. Sure, the teachers have more authority than the students, but that's natural. What we have to watch out for is that the students that have been here for a while don't boss around the new ones."

They resumed walking and Tasha said. "You realize you have more authority than almost anyone here, don't you? If you consider this a pack and Miss Lapahie is the alpha, you're her second."

Samantha missed a step, but caught back up to Tasha easily. "Don't you mean we are her seconds?"

"Nope. I'm on loan from the Fairwood pack. You are a Free Wolf. Here, you rank higher than me. But don't expect me to take orders. This isn't a pack, and we're a partnership."

"Just as I was starting to get a swelled head." Samantha grinned. "Boy, wouldn't it irritate my pack leader. He thought women were good for nothing but cooking, cleaning, and increasing the size of the pack."

"So tell me about this guy we're meeting with next. Is he a male chauvinist too?"

Samantha consulted the clipboard she carried. "Norm Dillman. He's a non-shifter, and worked as a programmer for the Choate pack before Dot took over. He's old enough to retire but Miss Lapahie lets him stay on because he knows the history of the program. I guess he was an ace employee in his time, but he hasn't kept up with all the new technology and that's caused friction. So he sits in his office and does whatever he's assigned to do but doesn't mingle with the new people. He seems to like Miss Lapahie, though, because she spends a few minutes talking to him every time she's here."

"So why are we interviewing him?" Tasha pulled open a side door to the office complex and held it for Samantha.

"Because he's complained about people playing pranks on him. Turning his monitor display upside down, taking the batteries out of his keyboard, that sort of thing. Probably just his coworkers giving him a hard time, but I figured we shouldn't ignore anyone right now."

Tasha wondered if the light hurt his eyes. Mr. Dillman had the shades over his window closed and the overhead lights off. The glow from his monitors and one small desk lamp provided the limited illumination in the office. It made it difficult for her to read his body language as he and Samantha talked about his problems.

She'd already decided that the issue he was having wasn't tied to the problems of the Free Wolves. From the glances exchanged by his co-workers when they walked it, she'd figured out who to blame. Guilt and worry were written all over their faces. But he seemed like a lonely old man, and she saw no harm in letting him vent. Allies sometimes came from unlikely places.

"I got that from Elder Choate for twenty years with only one sick day." he said, pointing to a plaque on the wall. "It's nice, but it's just a piece of fancy wood. It didn't even come with a bonus." When he raised his arm, she noticed he was sweating even though it was cool in the office, likely a result of all the extra weight he carried.

Tasha made a mental note that Mr. Dillman was motivated by money, and wondered how long it had been since he'd gotten a raise. She'd have to ask Gavin's contacts to check if he was having financial difficulties or spending more lately. Still, she couldn't imagine he was part of a conspiracy, not when he seemed to have an almost-creepy fixation on Dot.

"I've never understood the gold watch tradition," Samantha said. "The last thing I'd want to do after retiring is watch the clock. Do you mind me asking why you haven't retired?"

"No reason for me to. I've got no plans, nothing to do and no one to do it with. My wife died five years ago."

"I'm sorry." Samantha reached out and patted his knee.

He cleared his throat. "Yeah, it was rough. Thankfully I had work to keep my mind off it."

The conversation was getting them nowhere. Tasha stood. "Thank you for your time, Mr. Dillman. Let us know if you see anything that seems out of place. And we'll look into how we can help you out in the meantime."

"What did you have in mind?"

"Install a security camera aimed at your door." He frowned and she added, "We'll let you share control of it so you can turn it off when you get to work and turn it on when you leave. That way you won't worry about someone looking over your shoulder all the time."

"And no one else would have access to it?"

"Just the security guards. And we'll let them know

not to invade your privacy. Will that work?"

He sighed. "It's sad that it's come to this, isn't it? No one respects their elders anymore. Not you two. You seem like a couple of nice young girls. And Miss Lapahie, of course. If it'll help her out, I guess it will be all right."

"We'll be in touch, Mr. Dillman," Samantha said, "When we get the parts to set the system up."

He nodded and turned his gaze to the computer screens. Tasha waited until she and Samantha were outside again before she asked. "What do you think?"

"I'll bet he's a pain in the ass to work with." She giggled. "But he seems like a lonely old man and I don't mind helping him out."

"Did you notice the stack of papers he stuck in a drawer when we came in?" As nice as he seemed, Tasha couldn't bring herself to fully trust him.

"Yeah, I saw that. I wonder what they were."

"Maybe personal info?"

"Could be. Or a project he's working on and isn't ready to release. Hard to tell."

Samantha nodded. "Hey, how much will a security camera cost?"

"A small one that he controls? Not much. We need to talk to Miss Lapahie about our budget. I'd like to install them other places as well. Like the parking lot and the exterior doors to the school.

"Do you know if there's anyone on the staff who can handle the job? It will save money if we don't have to hire out. In a school full of geeks, someone should be able to do the job. If not, I can check with Elder Fairwood."

"I'll ask around." Samantha picked up a piece of trash from the ground, crumpled it up and stuck it in her pocket. "I hate litter," she said. "We should add outside garbage cans to our wish list."

"We need to start a list. How is the company set up for weapons?"

"Weapons?"

Tasha grinned. "Your flying fists of fury can only be in one place at a time. The rest of us need to resort to guns, knives and bullets. I brought my pistols and AR-15 with me, but are the patrols properly equipped?" Her small Smith & Wesson was strapped to her lower left leg, but she hadn't seen a weapon of any kind in her encounter with the young couple in the forest.

"We can ask Chief tomorrow. He's in charge of the patrols."

"Chief?"

"Ex-Army man, coyote shifter. His pack disbanded after the alpha died and no one wanted the responsibility. He and two of the women showed up here looking for a place to stay for a few nights. That was six months ago and they're still here."

Tasha made a mental note to find out the man's real name and pass it along to Gavin. At the rate things were going, she needed to buy a notebook to track everything.

Tasha didn't think much of Chief's security measures. She'd been slinking around the village for an hour in wolf form, and no one had challenged her. The clusters of people she'd seen were busy chatting among themselves and not paying attention to their surroundings. The one solo young man she'd come across was so engrossed in his cell phone that she'd been able to sneak within touching distance without him sensing her. Granted, her natural wolf coloring blended in with the falling night, but he should have been able to scent her.

Samantha was prowling the southern border of the company's lands, checking out how efficient the security patrols were there. They weren't scheduled to meet up for another hour and Tasha was getting nothing but frustrated. She decided to stake out the school building as it was the target of most of the incidents.

The hedges growing in front of an oak tree offered the perfect hiding spot. From there, she could see the entire back side of the building. It was the most likely target for intruders attempting a break in because it was poorly lit in comparison to the front which faced the street.

She lay on the ground, wiggled her belly a few times to work away the pebbles under it, and put her nose between her forepaws. Even close up, with her eyes open only a crack, an unwary observer might think she slept. From the distance, she might look like a large rock.

It was a technique she'd learned to snag game. Find a spot along a trail, settle in and slow her breathing, wait, pounce when an unsuspecting animal happened by. She could stay in the same position for hours if need be. But the game she hunted tonight wasn't meant to end up as her supper, and she didn't have hours to wait.

The wind picked up and a gust almost covered the sound. Tasha's ears pricked forward at the shuffle of footsteps. A figure inched along the side of the building, stopping at a window. Tasha tightened her muscles, but didn't move.

Then he went on. Tasha was positive it was a male although the wind blew the wrong direction for her to catch his scent. Not even her tail twitched as he stopped at another window. Her ears caught the sound of him tapping on the glass. He moved again.

The third window sat in a pool of darkness. But Tasha's eyes watched as he raised the window. He grasped the window frame and started to lift himself inside.

And Tasha exploded into a snarling mass of muscle and fangs.

EIGHT

"Everyone knows," whimpered the fifteen year-old. Tasha had missed finding out his name when she'd gone home to return to human form and get dressed. "We all do it. At least, the ones who don't own computers. That's how we stay caught up on assignments."

She paced on the opposite side of the teachers' break room as the school nurse patched up the minor cuts on the boy's leg. Tasha had pulled her attack at the last moment, but not soon enough to avoid giving him a few scratches. His jeans were a lost cause.

One small part of her conscience felt terrible about the damage, especially after she'd figured out he was a rabbit shifter. But a larger part declared that he was lucky and could have been hurt much worse by a less-experienced sentry. She was having a hard time letting go of her surge of anger with nowhere to release it. She needed to go for a long run but wanted to stick around while the boy was being questioned to find out what she could learn from him.

"So this isn't the first time you've broken in?" asked one of his teachers, a male. Two of them were there, summoned from their beds to deal with the situation. Samantha and Chief were there too, but they were sitting back, watching the proceedings.

"I only do it once in a while," the student said sullenly. "I don't see anything wrong with it."

"But if the students can get in, so can anyone else." Tasha stopped her pacing long enough to stand in front of the young man and stare at him. He shrunk away from her. "Did you think about that?"

"Why would anyone else want to get in?" he asked. "It's a school."

"True. Filled with expensive computers and other electronics. Items that can easily be stolen and sold. I'll bet half the items on that on-line garage sale site everyone talks about were ripped off."

The boy's face was ashen. "But no one here would do that."

Tasha shook her head. "Are you that naive? Do you trust everyone here?"

"We're all Free Wolves! We stick together!"

That level of fanatical idealism had been beaten out of Tasha long ago, when she'd taken part in a fight between different factions of the Fairwood pack, each sure their way was the only way. Elder Fairwood— Gavin's father—made sure all participants received equal punishments. It taught Tasha that anyone was capable of putting personal interests over pack interests by twisting things to hide their true motives. She wondered how long it would take the boy in front of her to learn that same lesson. Some people never learned it.

She turned to the teachers. "Were either of you aware of what the students were doing?"

"I'd heard rumors," said the second one, an older woman. "Wasn't worried about it."

Chief, a scrawny man, jumped into the conversation. Tasha wondered if he got enough to eat or if his coyote form was responsible for his physique. "You didn't think there was anything wrong with the students sneaking into the building after hours?"

"What I'm worried about," Samantha sent directly to Tasha, *"is that the students don't have a way to complete their assignments after school hours."*

That was a valid point. They'd need to discuss it with Dot later.

"What I suspect," Tasha shot back, *"is that if one teacher knew, they all did. And they never told Miss Lapahie."*

"No one keeps their house doors locked here," the first teacher said. "And we don't have any problems. Why should the school be any different?"

Chief huffed. "Would you leave your keys in your car and expect no one to 'borrow' it?"

"Of course not! I always take my keys with me!"

"Can I go now?" the student asked. "You don't need me for anything else, right?"

"I'll be keeping my eye on you," Chief said. "In fact, I'll expect you to be at my office at six. You'll be on early patrol."

"But it's almost two!"

"So you better go straight home and get some rest."

The second teacher jumped to her feet. "I'll walk you home. Make sure you get there safely. We wouldn't want you to be attacked on the way."

Tasha had to stop herself from grinning at the dirty look the both teachers shot her. She could easily take them out.

The second teacher and the young man exited the room, and the first teacher trailed behind them. Chief stopped him. "I didn't say we were done."

"Does he have the authority to do that?" Tasha sent directly to Samantha.

"No. His job is to work with the students. Teach them how to run patrol, that sort of thing."

"Actually, we are done for now," Tasha said. "However, we'll set up a meeting with Miss Lapahie to discuss the situation and will want you there. Someone will be in touch."

"What right do you have..." Chief started but Tasha interrupted.

"We'll discuss that in private." She held the door open for the teacher. "Lock the outer door behind you when you leave. We'll make sure the rest of the building is secure."

Chief waited until the teacher was out of sight. "I don't know what you girls think you're doing, but I'm in charge here," he said between clenched teeth.

"Us *women*," Tanya shot back with a snarl, "are in charge of overall security for the entire organization. That means you answer to us. And you would have found that out in our meeting in the morning when we planned to discuss the procedures you've set up. But what you're doing isn't working. Do you want to hold that meeting now?"

"The two of you combined don't know half as much about security as I do," he challenged. "I'm US Army trained. I won't let you boss me around."

Tasha assessed his body language as he spoke. The rapid movement of his eyes was a dead giveaway. He was as nervous as hell. She wondered which part of his speech was a lie. "You want my credentials? Do you know who Elder Fenner of the Fairwood pack is? Only one of the most respected pack security chiefs in the country. I trained with him. And are you familiar with the Radferd pack in Maine?" The flicker of fear in his eyes was all the answer Tasha needed. "I've just come back from training with them. So don't even begin to question my credentials."

She moved in so they stood toe-to-toe. "Samantha and I were chosen by Miss Lapahie and that's all the authority we need. If you can't handle it because we're *'girls'* pack up and leave. Got it?"

"What did they train you for? Secretarial work?"

He didn't even have time to take a breath before the point of a finely sharpened knife pressed against his throat. "Men have died for lesser insults to the Radferds," she hissed. "You'd better consider what you say before you open your mouth again."

"Ease up, Tasha," Samantha urged. "Take a deep breath."

Chief backed up, his hands raised. "I was just kidding. Testing you. You passed."

Tasha pretended to clean under a fingernail with the point of the knife before she slipped it back into its sheath. "So will we see you in the morning?" she asked, her voice holding no sign of the tension of a minute before.

"Yeah, sure."

"We'll want to see the schedule of patrols—what students are assigned, when and how. Please have it ready."

"I'll make sure one of the girls-—women—pulls that together for you."

An arched eyebrow had him explaining more. "One of my secretaries."

Tasha inclined her head the barest amount before swiveling on one foot and turning his back to him. "Please verify that every window and door is locked before leaving," she said. "Tomorrow we'll figure out who will be responsible for that duty from here on." Samantha fell in step beside her as she left.

"Was that a smart thing to do?" Samantha asked as they walked through the village while Tasha noted which houses still had lights on. They could be the sign of someone having trouble sleeping or something more sinister.

"Probably not smart but necessary. He needed to be set straight right away. Besides, he ticked me off. How does he rate having secretaries?"

Samantha shook her head. "No idea. We'll need to ask Miss Lapahie."

"I hate having to bug her about crap like that." Tasha stopped and put a hand on Samantha's shoulder. *"Did you hear that?"* It was a sound right out of one of her nightmares, a scream of pain and fear.

"What?"

A sniff didn't provide any clues. *"I'm not sure. It's gone now. Want to take a run around the village?"*

"Don't you ever sleep?"

"Sleep is overrated." Tasha grinned. *"Besides, I'm too keyed up to sleep."*

They headed towards the house to strip and shift. Tasha studied the slender silver wolf Samantha had transformed into. *"You know, your wolf is beautiful."*

"People tell me that all the time, but I have a hard time believing it. I'm too small to be a good fighter. Now you, look at you. You're bigger than a

few males. And your fur is the perfect shade of black for hiding in the shadows. I stick out like a sore thumb."

"Maybe. But I bet you can fit into spots I don't. And you're a smaller target if someone's shooting."

"I guess that is an advantage."

"Besides, it would be easy to camouflage your color. Rolling in mud would darken it enough to make a difference. I'll show you some tricks I've learned."

"From that pack you were talking about?"

Tasha didn't answer immediately. They ran two blocks in silence while she crafted her answer. The Maine pack had secrets she wouldn't share. *"The Radferd pack was started by a Green Beret back in the sixties. After serving in Cambodia, he had trouble living among humans so he headed for wilder territory than his hometown in Connecticut. Other retired military men and women joined him—all wolf shifters. Now most of the males in the pack serve as SEALS or Rangers. A lot of the women join the military too now that they can train in combat skills. After they leave the service they become mercenaries—that's how the pack supports itself. And yes, they have a well-deserved reputation for kicking ass at the slightest provocation."*

"Do they take other wolves regularly?"

"No. But Elder Fenner's cousin is one of them, and they did it as a favor to him. Plus, although I can't get Elder Fenner to admit to it, I suspect he worked with them in the past."

"Why did you get to go and not one of the males from the pack?"

Tasha didn't answer for a long moment.

"I'm sorry," Samantha sent. *"Am I poking my nose in where it doesn't belong?"*

"Yes and no. I guess I should tell you the story." Tasha stopped and sniffed the air. Nothing smelled out of place, but her wolf senses were on high alert. She resumed trotting down the sidewalk. *"During the war between the Choates and Fairwoods, I was captured. I was drugged, brought here, and kept prisoner. They tied me up with silver-laced rope and injected me with a silver solution."* Talking about it reminded her of the pain of the silver infiltrating her bloodstream and circulating throughout her entire body.

"That's torture!" Samantha exclaimed.

"It took a combined effort of the Free Wolves and the Fairwoods to free me. It took time for me to recover physically. Elder Fenner recognized that I wouldn't be able to recover mentally while the war between the two packs was still going on so he arranged for me to go to Maine. I didn't want to leave at first, I felt like I was abandoning my pack, but it turned out to be the best thing for me.

"Miss Lapahie knows, but please don't tell anyone else."

"I won't, I promise." It was Samantha's turn to stop suddenly. *"Hear that?"*

Tasha listened closely. *"Do we have any young ones close to first shift? Someone without a parent or elder to guide them?"* She was all too familiar with the real chances for physical and psychological damage being caused by a shift gone wrong.

Samantha only needed a few seconds before she answered. *"Lars. We aren't sure how old he is. He says he's fifteen, but he looks younger than that. He lives in the boys' dorm. I'll lead the way."* She pivoted on her hind feet and dashed away.

That's another advantage to being smaller, Tasha thought as she followed. You can turn and take off quicker.

NINE

"Good job last night," Dot said. "I'm proud of all of you. You've proven you can work as a team. Thank you."

Having Dot displayed on the big screen in the conference room wasn't as good as having her be there in person, but it was better than nothing. Tasha missed the ability to send her a silent commentary on what was happening in the meeting. Still, the young men sitting around the table were awestruck at Dot's presence even it was by way of a computer display.

Tasha focused on one young man in particular. Lars. By the time she and Samantha had reached the dorm, Lar's roommates and neighbors were working on strategies to help him. A few of them went through training programs with packs and were guiding him as much as possible, but the shifting process wasn't going smoothly. None of them had ever worked with a Siberian Lynx before.

Neither had Tasha. In fact, she knew nothing about the species. And when she'd shown up in her wolf form, she'd only scared Lars more than he already was. Once she'd figured that out, she'd swiftly shifted back to human form. Samantha, on the other hand, stayed in her wolf form, which the boy didn't see as a threat. Her smaller size and coloring was closer to what he'd be once he shifted.

However, Samantha's mental voice wasn't strong enough to break through the barrier that Lars' pain, panic, and confusion had built. The other boys weren't able to break through to him either. He was stuck, mid-shift, until Tasha had wrapped herself in a blanket and sat beside him on the floor, ignoring the hazard of his extended claws.

While the others encouraged him with spoken words, she'd crooned silent chants of comfort and encouragement to him. When he'd calmed a little, she'd wrapped her arms around him to give him what physical comfort she could. Then, she'd reached out and helped him talk to the inner self he'd blocked, not understanding that it was a valid part of his dual nature.

Finally, she'd convinced the boy the momentary pain he'd experience would be nothing in comparison to the joy of finding his *other*. With his friends cheering at each change in his appearance, Lars released his fears and completed his transformation.

The paws came first. The ears and nose transitioned at the same time. The rest of the change happened so quickly that Tasha couldn't tell what came next. She only knew that a growling, fully formed cat stood beside her.

But to call Lars a cat was an insult. He was no more related to a common house cat than a wolf was related to a Chihuahua. His coloring, although light, was mottled with darker spots, perfect for hiding in a meadow in the fall. Or slipping between tree trunks and bushes in a forest. Tasha already had plans for him.

Although he'd been eager to try it again after shifting back to human form, both she and Samantha discouraged it. He'd used up enough energy for the night. Instead, they'd scheduled a lesson with him later in the day after his body recovered. Tasha pulled herself out of her musings when Dot spoke, her voice clear even through the overhead speakers.

"Lars, I look forward to seeing you as a lynx," Dot said. "I'm sorry I missed your first shift. Elder Fairwood is researching information on your heritage. It's a hobby of his, and you're the first Siberian Lynx he's heard of. If things work out and with your permission, he'd like to meet you."

It was no wonder the students were totally devoted to Dot, if she treated them all as if they were the most important person in the world. Lars who was seated next to Samantha, blushed. "Of course, Miss Lapahie," he said, beaming.

"I understand Tasha and Samantha will be working with you again. You're lucky they agreed to be your guides in this process."

"I know." Lars blushed and peeked at Samantha from underneath his long lashes.

"You've got an admirer," Tasha sent.

"What am I going to do about it?" Samantha asked.

"You'll figure something out."

Dot used her controls to sweep the room with the camera. "And remember, if any of you need help, please talk to any of the staff, including me. We're here to help you."

Tasha ducked her head to cover her grin. She

imagined the line of young men sitting outside Dot's office, waiting for their turn to meet with their benefactor.

"Once again," Dot said, "thanks to all of you. Now you need to get back to class. Have a good day!"

The students filed out of the room in a much more orderly fashion than Tasha anticipated. As they left, Tasha moved to sit next to Samantha. The next order of business required a united front.

After the last of the boys left, Chief came in, trailed by a young woman. One of his secretaries, Tasha assumed. A quick sniff verified she was also a coyote shifter. Seeing Dot was still on camera, he gave a brief nod. "Hello, Miss Lapahie."

"Good morning, Chief," she answered, pleasantly enough, but Tasha caught an undertone of something else. Impatience, perhaps. "What can I do for you today?"

"I'd rather talk to you alone."

"I understand. However, since I'm assuming your problem has to do with Tasha and Samantha, I'd prefer they stay in the room. That way we can make sure everyone is on the same page."

Tasha had never seen this side of Dot. Pure business. And she'd made the transition from surrogate mother to shark in the blink of an eye.

"I don't like that idea," he said.

"I'm sorry to hear that. You've expressed your concerns in the email you sent. Anything else you want to say can be said here. I understand that things didn't get off to a smooth start, but we are all going to have to work together."

"Working together is one thing, but they seem to think they are in charge."

"Did I not make myself clear in the email I sent you several days ago? They *are* in charge. I put my full faith and confidence in the fact they will do what is right and necessary for the school and the business."

If Chief was smart, he'd shut up now, Tasha thought.

"You don't appreciate the work I've done for you," Chief shouted.

Samantha tensed. "You owe Miss Lapahie an apology," she snarled. "She's treated you with nothing but kindness since you dragged yourself onto these grounds, half-dead. And look at you now. You have a house to live in, plenty of food to eat, and a good job. What else do you want? Others here work just as hard or harder."

Tasha kept one eye on the woman Chief brought with him. It bothered her that Chief hadn't introduced his companion. The louder and angrier the conversation got, the more the woman shrank into herself, as if by making herself smaller she could hide. She was pretty, despite a heavy layer of makeup, but Tasha spotted a discoloring in her right cheek. Had she slipped and fallen or had it been caused by something else?

Chief didn't seem to be able come up with an answer for Samantha. "I don't want anything special," he growled. "I just want to be respected. The other adults around here don't respect me and neither do the kids."

"We've talked about this before. Respect can go two ways," Dot said. "And you need to work on giving others respect as well. If you pay attention to how Tasha and Samantha interact with other people, you may learn something."

"So that's it? You expect me to take orders from them?"

Tasha didn't know how Dot was keeping her temper under check. It was taking every ounce of her self-control to remain seated.

"That is correct. For the immediate future, they are your managers. I expect you to give them your full cooperation. Now, let's move to the business at hand. Did you bring along the information Tasha requested?"

Chief scowled and motioned to his secretary. "Hand me that file."

She uncurled herself enough to pass over the manila folder she'd been clutching.

"What's your name?" Tasha asked.

The woman looked at Chief as if asking permission. He nodded. "Ariana," she said shyly.

"Pretty name. Thanks for putting that information together for us." Tasha held out her hand. "May I see that file?"

Chief sputtered. "I was going to explain it to you."

"Good. Why don't you let us look through the paperwork while you tell us about it? Is there more than one copy?"

Chief glanced at Ariana who shook her head. "No?"

"You only asked for one," she whispered.

"She's not a very good secretary," Chief said without a trace of apology in his voice.

"Or he's not a good boss," Samantha sent.

Tasha agreed. She was already planning to correct the situation.

"I'm really hoping you can straighten him out," Dot said much later after Chief and Ariana had left. Tasha and Samantha had moved again, arranging their chairs so Dot could see them both at the same time through the web camera.

"It'll take a lot of work," Tasha said. "His belief in himself far outdoes his actual knowledge. Can Elder Fairwood dig up information on Chief's military background?"

"With his contacts, he should be able to. Things were so disorganized when he arrived I wasn't worried about it. Chief talks a good game."

Not so good that Tasha hadn't spotted the holes in his procedures within a couple of minutes. They'd already patched one of the biggest ones—the lack of sentries in the village—by deciding to increase the number of students running patrol at any one time. Chief was unable to argue with them about it when Dot gave her immediate approval.

"We've got some other things we'd like to talk to you about," Samantha said. The lists of items they wanted to buy had been sent to Dot via email. "Things that aren't directly related to security but that we've noticed."

"Like?"

"The reason the boy was breaking into the school last night. The students are being given homework assignments and don't have computers to do them on. Since most of these kids are studying computer-related subjects, it's a problem."

"What do you suggest?"

"At least one computer in every dorm room, making sure every family has one. I know it will cost a lot. In the meantime," Samantha added, "have the teachers open up the classrooms for several hours every night and on the weekend. Or the older kids could be put in charge. Might as well invite the parents in too."

"What's the matter?" Tasha asked, noting the deepening frown on Dot's face.

"I swear we put some money in the budget for that," she said. "I'll go back and see if it got cut at the last minute. In the meantime, I'll work on getting the after-hours access set up. Anything else?"

"Lars was upset that he shredded his pajamas last night," Tasha said. "Until one of the boys said he had a spare set to give him. I heard him thinking that he was glad it wasn't his jeans. Who's tracking to make sure the students have enough clothes?"

"Joshua is in charge of supplies." Dot's fingers flew over her keyboard as she took notes. "Is that all?"

"One more thing." Samantha looked to Tasha for encouragement and Tasha's nod provided it. "You grew up packless, Miss Lapahie, so you wouldn't be aware of this, but in most pack schools they have a trainer to work with kids before their first shifts. My trainer was good at sensing when someone was getting close to the big event, and spent a lot of time instructing us on the finer points of what was going to happen. We need one of those here. Most of the kids that come to us are older and have already had their shift, but we're starting to see younger kids here. We may also have kids who could use a little extra help to make sure their shifts are as painless as possible."

"That's a good idea. Do you have any suggestions?"

"Not off hand, but I haven't had time to think about it." Samantha grinned. "I haven't gotten much sleep either. If you want, I'll ask around and see if I can get a few recommendations."

"I'd appreciate it. Maybe one of the older students who are getting ready to graduate? It makes me unhappy that so many of them leave to get jobs. It feels like breaking up family."

There it is again, Tasha thought. That's why Dot is so special to everyone here.

TEN

If she didn't get a break soon, she'd be running on fumes. Tasha bounced one foot up and down to get the blood flowing. She'd been sitting still too long and her leg was falling asleep. The rest of her body threatened to follow suit. But there was something about the schedules for the patrols that bugged her and she couldn't put her finger on the cause.

"Are you ready to go see Lars?" Samantha asked, stretching as she came into the kitchen. She'd taken a nap while Tasha had gone through paperwork. The steady drizzle outside made for good sleeping weather, but Tasha wouldn't be able to rest until much later.

"Is it that time already?" she asked, gathering up the papers. She'd commandeered the kitchen table as a temporary desk. There was no spot for a desk in the small room she now shared with Samantha. The three bedroom house was home for six people and spare space non-existent.

"Just about." Samantha covered her mouth and yawned. "I don't know how you're staying awake."

"I'll collapse later, take a short nap sometime between supper and going on patrol tonight." Tasha grinned. "I'll surprise Chief and make him go with me. What's the worst place to assign someone for that duty?"

Samantha smiled. "North border. I suggest you send him there and you go somewhere else. It's half-swamp."

"I want to see him in action. I'll call it a team-building exercise. Isn't that one of those phrases Miss Lapahie likes to throw around when she'd talking corporate speech?" Besides, she'd run thru a few swamps in the middle of winter before. At least the day had been warm if wet, so things could be worse. "Will you stay here as my point of contact? You may not be able to reach me, but I want to test if you can at least receive my thoughts from a distance. Did you have any plans?"

"I wanted to take a run around the village and take Lars with me. Give him a chance to see what he's capable of in his *other* form."

"Sounds like fun. You might invite some of the other boys along to act as chaperones."

Samantha's cheeks reddened. "He's too young for me. I'm almost old enough to be his mother."

"The point is you need to be careful around him. Try to figure out how to encourage him but not make him think it's anything but a teaching moment. If you take other boys with you, you can treat them all the same and not play favorites. Of course, you run the risk that they'll all end up with crushes on you."

"What am I going to do about it?" Samantha asked glumly.

Tasha thought about it. "Let's do the good cop-bad cop routine this afternoon. I'll be the good guy and praise the boys when they do things correctly. You stand around and look unhappy when they mess up."

"Will that work?"

Tasha shrugged. "We can give it a shot."

The plan didn't work perfectly, Tasha thought as she prepared to go out on patrol, but it took some of the glow from Samantha. At least Lars no longer looked at her as anything more than a teacher. But as good looking as Samantha was, Tasha anticipated that it wouldn't be the last time the problem occurred. Samantha was going to figure in many a young man's dreams for years to come.

As Tasha strapped on the Winkler belt knife and slung her AR-15 across her back, she hoped her other plan for the night would go as well. If Chief was a fraud as she feared, things might go downhill rapidly. On the other hand, he might prove himself and they'd have a place to start a working relationship. She placed the odds at an even fifty-fifty.

With another knife hung on her neck and a little camo paint on her face, she was ready. On a whim, she added three pink stripes to her cheek. A throwback to the days when Dot actively led wolves into scrimmages. She'd heard the stories of how the symbol had been adopted by Free Wolves through the country. The mark had fallen out of fashion, but reminding people of what it stood for might not be a bad idea.

Fully geared up, she strode into the living room where the rest of the housemates watched a chick flick. *"Wish me luck,"* Tasha sent to Samantha as she tossed Samantha one of a pair of walkie-talkies. The other was clipped to her belt.

"Holy shit!" Samantha almost dropped a can of soda as she grabbed the walkie-talkie. One of the other women let out a small shriek. "Good gods, Tasha, is that necessary?"

"It should be standard procedure," Tasha answered. She'd wondered if the camouflage pants and shirt were called for, but based on the shocked reactions she'd gotten they might become a permanent part of her wardrobe. "If an enemy is infiltrating your borders, you want to be as invisible as possible so you can catch them. If you stand out like a sore thumb, they'll take cover and hide until you've passed by."

"But we're not under attack," blurted the lady who'd screamed.

"That's the point. If you have the procedures in place, then you don't need to scramble if something happens. Don't forget, wolves are territorial, and trying to take over nearby packs' lands is part of the game."

"Doesn't sound like much of a game to me," muttered another lady. "Besides, we're not a pack."

"And that's what paints us with a big ol' bulls-eye. If someone gets it into their head we're going to be an easy target because we're a non-traditional group, they'll be at the borders and we'll be sitting ducks."

"You really buy into this shit, don't you?"

The chill that settled in the room seemed to emanate from Tasha's eyes. "Not everyone is here because they chose to leave their packs," she said harshly. "Some are here because their pack lands were taken and they were driven from their homes. Maybe if more people took this *'shit'* seriously that wouldn't have happened. Now if you'll excuse me, *I* need to go make sure *you* can sleep safely in your own bed tonight."

She fumed all the way to Chief's house, ignoring the stares of the people on their porches or strolling on the sidewalks. Standing on his doorstep, Tasha took a moment to think calming thoughts before knocking. "See who's at the door," Chief commanded someone inside.

She broadcast her response so whoever he was talking to would hear it. *"I suggest you get up and answer it yourself. I don't want to make one of your 'secretaries' faint. And I hope you aren't too comfortable because you and I are going to go check on the patrols."*

She didn't even blink when he yanked the door open and it hit the wall on the interior of the house. "What is this, a surprise date for a masquerade party?" he sneered.

Tasha calmly looked him over. He was dressed in nothing but a wife-beater T-shirt and a pair of ratty boxers. "You have five minutes," she said. "Then we're going to go check out how the patrols on the north border are doing. Dress accordingly."

"I'm off the clock. I don't get paid enough for this." He started to close the door, but Tasha was too fast for him and rammed it open with her shoulder. Through the open door she saw Ariana sitting on the floor, watching the confrontation with a puzzled look on her face. A second plot started churning in her brain.

"Can you hear me?" she sent to Samantha.

A short squawk on the radio was the predetermined response for yes.

"Security is never off the clock. You know that." Tasha made a show of checking the watch on her wrist. "You now have four minutes. I suggest you hurry. Don't forget your weapon."

"Whatcha gonna do if I don't play along?"

"Do you really want to go down that road? Because I'll be more than glad to take you down a peg or two. I'm capable of doing it even if I am a female." She'd had plenty of time to assess his physical capabilities and determine the winner in a fight in either human or shifted form. She crossed her arms and leaned against the doorpost. "Three."

For a moment, Tasha thought he was going to refuse. But she'd hung out with enough alphas to understand the power of intimidation so she stared at him, putting all her mental energy into her gaze. The trick worked and he turned, grumbling to himself, and headed into the interior of the house.

"Here's the new plan," she sent to Samantha while she waited. *"About five minutes after we leave, come get Ariana and the other lady who are Chief's 'secretaries'. Tell them you have an assignment for them. Make them keep track of when I contact you, the strength of my mental voice and where I report in from. In the meantime, let them watch the movie with you. Try to get them to enjoy themselves. That might be a challenge, so make sure the roomies are in on it. Oh, and don't ask a lot of questions to try to get them to talk. Just let them relax."*

The walkie-talkie's beep was the affirmative answer Tasha hoped for.

At least he knew how to dress for the occasion. Tasha gave him points for that. His worn jeans and flannel shirt were good choices although the revolver he'd tucked into his waistband looked woefully inadequate next to her arsenal. She gave him a curt nod. "Who's the armorer here?" she asked as she turned and walked down the steps and onto the sidewalk.

He had to hustle to fall into step beside her. "His name is Griego. From the looks of it, you've found the storage area."

She snorted. "These are from my personal supplies. I guess I need to meet with Griego. You should have better weapons at your disposal. You never know when you might need to fill in on a patrol."

"Samantha, make a note. We need to meet with the armorer and find out how well the organization is supplied in terms of armament and ammo."

The walkie-talkie squealed its response. "By the way," Tasha said as if she hadn't broken her train of thought. "We're putting your secretaries to work tonight too. Samantha and I are running an experiment in communications. They will be making notes for her." Now that they'd left the village, she picked up her pace from a fast walk to a jog.

"They work for me!" he protested. "You should have asked my permission!"

Tasha had anticipated the response. "Who pays them?" she asked. "You or the corporation?"

"The company, of course."

She nodded. "So the company will pay them for their work tonight. And I'll ask that they be given time off during normal business hours to make up for messing up their leisure time. It's only fair."

Tasha's preference was to work with partners who knew silence was golden while running patrol. Chief didn't seem to be one of those. "Where are we going?" he asked

"Can't you tell?" she asked sharply. Most shifters had an innate sense of direction.

"We're headed north, but why?"

They passed an old maple tree marked with orange paint and Tasha shot Samantha a mental picture of the location. Once she'd receive a response, she answered the question. "My sources tell me that the northern border is considered the worst assignment for a patrol. It's obvious we start there. There's an old adage about never asking an employee to do a job you wouldn't do. Same principal applies here."

He didn't argue with her and she noted with satisfaction that it wasn't because he was out of breath. So far he'd matched her stride for stride. He might not be a strong as her in some ways, but at least he had staying power. He'd need it. They were in for a long night.

Somewhere around the halfway mark, Tasha finally took pity on Chief. By then, they were both soaked from a combination of the drizzle, the swampy ground they marched through, and sweat. She found a relatively dry spot underneath a pine tree and sat, leaning against its trunk. After taking a swig from her canteen, she passed it to him.

"You look like you're enjoying yourself," he sent. She'd convinced him to switch to mental speech as practice after he'd admitted it was a skill that most coyotes never learned. He'd have a headache in the morning, and she'd already advised him to take some aspirin before going to bed.

"In a way, I am. I enjoy challenging myself, and this is a challenge in human form. It would be easier

as a wolf or coyote." As long as he was playing nice, so would she. That didn't mean she trusted him. Or would allow the switch in his personality to manipulate her instinctive feelings about him.

"I tell the students to run this in shifted form."

"Good. But do you see the flaw in that process?"

He curled his lips into a tight line as he passed the canteen back to her. *"No, not really."*

She took another swallow of water and set the canteen on the ground between them. *"No matter how big and bad we are in shifted form, we're no match for big guns. Especially if silver bullets come into play. I don't carry my rifle for show."*

"But we don't want the students to attempt interception of an intruder without help."

"How are they supposed to communicate with headquarters to send an alert? This distance is a stretch for mental communication. And a radio is useless to our shifted forms. I'm not sure the range of our current model is long enough. Besides, how would they carry it?"

"What's the alternative?"

Was Chief asking for her advice? Or was this whole evening an attempt to manipulate her into dropping her guard? Either way, she'd play along. *"Teams,"* she answered. *"One shifted, one human. The human carries weapons for both. Also a pack with extra clothes for both team members. I don't know about you, but I wouldn't want to make this run naked."*

An exceptionally large mosquito chose that moment to land on his covered arm. With careful aim, he slapped it with his free hand, killing it before it could fly away. *"I can see why."* He picked up the canteen and took a drink, replacing the lid before handing it back to Tasha. *"If I sit here much longer, I'll stiffen up. Shall we go find the patrol? We should be getting close."*

ELEVEN

Tasha hugged the ground, melting into the earth. The butt of the revolver strapped to her calf dug into muscle, but she dared not adjust its placement. The slight movement might give her position away to a watchful observer.

She raised her head enough to track Chief as he worked his way through the brush to the other side of the clearing. There, four people huddled around the campfire, but one looked drunk and half-asleep. That narrowed the odds to three against two.

He was the one who developed the plan of attack, and he'd taken the lead in its execution. She'd beaten him down enough for one night and wanted him to have bragging rights to something when they returned to the village. *If* they both returned the village.

Besides, the old philosophy of keeping her enemy close was a good plan.

A momentary flash of light signaled that he'd moved into position. Chief had developed the anticipated screaming headache ahead of schedule, so they'd resorted to more traditional forms of surveillance communication. The first move, as planned, was his.

"Ho, the camp," he called, deepening and disguising his voice as he approached from the darkness.

The resulting scramble was a disaster in slow motion, at least to Tasha's heightened senses, as three party goers scrambled to retrieve their weapons. A teenage girl who Tasha judged to be sixteen or seventeen was the first to get to hers. "Who goes there?" she hollered, pointing her pistol in the general direction that Chief's voice had come from.

Tasha gave her one point for bravery, but immediately took it away because the girl remained standing, her silhouette clearly defined against the campfire. Two other teenagers joined her, the three facing the same direction, their backs to Tasha. It was her turn.

She rose stealthily, barely stirring the bushes that served as her hiding place. Despite the wet combat boots on her feet, her footsteps were noiseless. The scattered beer cans presented easily avoided obstacles as they glittered in the glow of the fire. Disregarding the now-awake drunk who stared at her with wide eyes, she crept into place behind the other three. Chief sent a one word thread of thought. *"Go!"*

A grim smile played on her lips as she reached out with both hands, placing one on a shoulder of the two outer students. "A fine night to run patrol, isn't it?" she asked quietly.

It was a damned good thing Tasha had taken that nap because it promised to be another night with no chance for sleep. Hell, she hadn't even bothered to clean up except for discarding her combat boots and slipping into the fresh socks and sneakers Samantha brought her. They'd sent the four students to their beds an hour ago after extracting as much information as possible from them. Now she and Chief were waiting for the last of the teachers to arrive. The teachers were the closest thing the organization had to elders and personally she thought they were a poor substitution.

And Dot was on her way. Over the protestations of Chief and others, Tasha had called her. In Tasha's mind, the anticipated discussion was too important to be handled by a web meeting. Dot would need to read the body language of the people in the room, and Tasha didn't know if that could be done over a computer display. Besides, as alpha, Dot might pick up stray thoughts of the people present. Not everyone realized that alphas had that ability.

Tasha knew the minute Dot pulled into the parking lot outside. *"How bad is it?"* Dot sent by way of a greeting.

"Bad. Like a lot of the residents here, most of the teachers don't believe that patrols are necessary." Tasha rested her crossed arms on the table and placed her head on top of them. It looked as if she was taking a moment to rest. *"In fact, they believe they take away from the students 'educational experience'. They aren't even giving Chief complete class rosters, they're using it as a form of punishment. So their 'favorites' rarely have to run patrol.*

"But Chief isn't blameless in this. He clings to the notion that women are incapable of handling anything beyond the traditional pack roles of having babies and raising children. So he won't give deserving female students the opportunity to take leadership positions and they're about ready to rebel.

"And he has his favorites that get the easy routes. Samantha got the information from Ariana and Rosa, the two women he brought with him, the ones he calls his secretaries. The students are aware of the unfairness."

"I kept hoping that my first impression of him was wrong," Dot sent. *"I'm glad I convinced Gavin to stay home. I may need to exert my authority and I don't want anyone thinking I can't handle this on my own."*

"You brought a guard with you, didn't you?" Tasha had a sudden vision of this being an elaborate trap. Probably the result of an over-tired and overactive imagination.

"Yes. Gavin insisted. So Tanya came along."

"It's been too long since you and I have fought together." A new voice intruded into Tasha's mind and she smiled at the familiar touch. *"I may just hang out and bunk with you for a while."*

It wouldn't be the first time they'd shared tight quarters. *"This could get ugly. I'm going to need all the help I can get. I'm glad you came."*

Tasha's *other* sense of hearing picked up the click of high heels striding down the hallway, and she raised her head. *"Front and center,"* she sent to Samantha. *"The boss is here."*

"Words can't express," Dot said, looking around the crowded room, "how disappointed I am. Not only in tonight's events, but in everything that had led up to them." Tasha had abandoned her seat to make room for one of the teachers, and she, Samantha and Tanya each stood guard in the corners of the room. Dot, despite the early morning hour, looked as fresh and sharp as if she'd had hours to get dressed, not minutes. "I've been briefed on the situation and am considering my options for addressing it. One of which is to abandon this experiment, sell the business to the Fairwoods, and wash my hands of the whole thing. As the majority stockholder of Lapahie Enterprises, I would be within my legal rights to do so, with or without action from the Board of Directors. That has been confirmed by my legal counsel."

Murmured protests came from various people, but most of the room's inhabitants looked too shocked to speak. Tasha carefully kept her face expressionless. She didn't believe for a second that Dot would take that extreme option, but it certainly was an attention grabber.

Dot held up on hand and the room quieted. "I will say that is not my first inclination. However, if you don't support my aims and goals I have no other choice."

The protests were louder this time. "We've been behind you since the beginning," said one woman.

"Yes, if it weren't for a few of you, I wouldn't be alive today, and I haven't forgotten that. But I have the distinct impression that others are only here for the paycheck." She stared intently around the room, her gaze resting on a few of the teachers longer than on everyone else. They shifted uncomfortably in their chairs. "When each of you was hired, I made abundantly clear what the goals of this organization are, and each of you agreed to support them. So what has changed? Or did you lie when you signed on the dotted line?"

The room came alive. Everyone was on their feet, declaring their innocence or shouting insults at perceived offenders. At Tasha's signal, Samantha and Tanya moved in closer to Dot. *"What the hell are you doing?"* Tasha sent.

"Watching their reactions. Figuring out who is on my side and who isn't."

Dot allowed the yelling to go on for what seemed like forever to Tasha before she raised her fingers to her mouth and emitted a piercing whistle. "That's enough! Now sit down and shut up!"

It took a long moment before everyone settled back into their seats. "I want an unofficial show of hands. Everyone who wants the school to continue and is willing to re-commit to the goals raise their hands."

About half of the people in the room raised the hands immediately. A quarter more raised their hands slower, but with enthusiasm. Of the remaining quarter, Tasha spotted about three who appeared to raise their hands due to peer pressure, and one who didn't raise his hand at all.

"Thank you," Dot said, her eyes circling the room. "You may put your hands down now." Tasha had no doubt that Dot had recorded each person's response. "Over the next few days I will meet with each of you individually to determine your future with the school."

"What, by computer because you're too good to stay here with us?" The remark came from the one man who hadn't raised his hand.

For a moment, Tasha wandered if he'd survive long enough to regret his outburst. She took two steps his direction, knowing that as much as she hated it, it was her job to protect him too.

The momentary look of hurt that flashed across Dot's face was quickly replaced by a bland, expressionless visage. "Thank you for your input,

John," she said. "All of you are aware that this method of work was developed by not me, but the original founders of this organization so that I could split my time between it and my commitment to my mate. Since you were not part of that original group, perhaps you should seek out one of them to voice your complaint."

"Or maybe you should resign if you don't like it." Tasha recognized the speaker as the lady who'd been one of Dot's original supporters. "Some of us appreciate the sacrifices Dot has made and continues to make for us. She doesn't have to donate the entire profits of Lapahie Enterprises to the school."

"Like she needs the money. She's got a rich sugar-daddy taking care of her."

That crossed the invisible line so far that Tasha couldn't stand for it. She swirled the man's chair around. "That's enough," she roared. "It's one thing to question the goals of the school, but you will *not* insult my pack leader or his mate and get away with it. I am within my rights to call you out right here and now to settle this like wolves." She allowed her fangs to descend and she bared her teeth. "We can take this outside. Just say the word."

"Tasha! Stand down!" Dot ordered.

Tasha held her position.

"She's right, Miss Lapahie," Tanya said. "By Council rules Tasha and I have the right to call out anyone who insults our pack leader."

"Then I guess John is lucky we operate as Free Wolves here and not under pack rules." Dot's voice was quiet but filled with authority. "Tasha, stand down. That's an order."

Tasha backed off a few steps, but didn't allow her

stare to drop. She sensed other people moving in behind her, giving her moral and physical support. To her surprise, Chief was one of them.

"You have placed yourself in an unsupportable position, John. Please draw up your letter of resignation, effective immediately," Dot said calmly. "Perhaps there is a pack somewhere willing to take you in or you can seek a position among the human population. If there is a particular city you have considered relocating to, I'll put out feelers to help find you a new job."

"You can't do that!" he sputtered.

"No, but the Board of Directors can. I'm confident they will back me on this decision. Now, I suggest you go home and start packing."

The tension in the room lifted slightly when he was gone, escorted out by two of his co-workers. Eventually, the rest of the teachers were sent to their homes and classes canceled for the day. Chief had the task of using the next shift of students scheduled for patrol to spread the news. Only Dot, Tasha, Tanya and Samantha remained in the room. The first hint of sunrise crept in through the windows and Tasha stifled a yawn. She dared not think about sleep yet.

"I hate to tell you this, Tasha," Dot said. "But you stink."

"I hate to tell you but sometimes I smelled worse than this while I was in training. Figure a night like last night every night for a week."

Dot pretended to shiver. "Then my first request is that you go home, get cleaned up and catch a nap. You need to be thinking clearly."

"What's the plan for the rest of the day?" Samantha asked.

"I have no idea." Dot tried to smile but there was no trace of cheerfulness in her expression. In fact, Tasha thought she saw the glimmer of tears in her eyes. "I have to figure out how to stop this wave of disaster from engulfing us."

TWELVE

The four of them huddled in her office. Tasha, despite a long hot shower and a short nap, still felt dirty. Not physically, but emotionally, as if the happenings of the morning had soiled her soul. She needed a long run in wolf form to sweat out the experience and cleanse her spirit.

Dot looked as fresh as ever, even though worry etched her face. Samantha had also had a nap while Tanya had stayed awake to guard Dot. From the look of the papers scattered across her desk, Dot had been hard at work while they slept.

"I've got some additional information from Gavin's contacts," she told them. "Before I share them, tell me what your impression is of Chief."

"He's in over his head," Tasha answered promptly. "His Army training is limited to the basics, the things every recruit is taught. Plus, he has a chip on his shoulder. I think I know why, but it's based on a pretty broad assumption."

"I'd like to hear your theory."

Tasha blew out a deep breath. "There are long-standing prejudices against coyotes in the shifter community. They are seen as sneaky and trouble-makers. That attitude still exists in many wolf packs, and quite a few won't assist a coyote in trouble like we'll help other types of kin. If Chief has run into that belief, he may be fearful that it will happen here. On the other hand, I don't sense anything malicious about him so I don't think he's the source of the problems."

"That doesn't excuse how he treats women," Samantha burst out. "I went through those schedules for patrols, and not only are female students denied leadership roles, they're given the worst runs."

"That is a problem," Dot agreed. "It bothered me when I saw how he interacted with his secretary yesterday. I need to figure out how to get the two who came with him assigned elsewhere. I can't justify him having two secretaries when they could be more useful doing other things. And Tasha, your instincts are correct. Chief never saw combat. He was assigned to a mechanics division."

"Are you going to throw him out?" Tasha asked.

Dot grimaced. "I've thought about it. But I'd rather have him where I can keep an eye on him than somewhere plotting against us. You seemed to have impressed him last night, so I'm going to ask you to keep working with him. Teach him how to do all those things he claims he knows already."

"Keep your friends close and your enemies closer?" Tasha asked.

"Something like that." Dot nodded. "On the other hand, maybe if we give him a chance he'll turn into a useful part of the community."

Ever the optimist, Tasha thought.

But Dot had every right to be an optimist. Tasha watched as she moved around the gymnasium, stopping to greet people, chat with them, and exchange hugs. Everyone wanted a moment with her, and she was doing her best to accommodate each of them. So many photos were snapped Tasha wondered if Dot had a headache from the brightness of the flashes.

Dot had come up with the idea of a community supper. They originally planned to hold it outside on the common area, but a light drizzle that started late afternoon forced the move indoors. The gym was the only place big enough to host it. Someone had gone to the last-minute effort to bring the outside in by scattering colorful leaves on the tables. They didn't do much to brighten the otherwise drab space, though the sound of laughter echoing all around was the best embellishment possible.

Dot had miraculously obtained enough fresh steaks for everyone while not forgetting the few people who were vegetarians. There was a large selection of vegetables too. Everything else was provided by the residents—a variety of casseroles, breads, and specialty dishes, as well as the myriad of desserts. It reminded Tasha of an old-fashioned Thanksgiving feast, minus the turkey.

Having the dinner inside provided an extra advantage. It was easier to control who attended. Guards were posted unobtrusively at each entrance, and although they may have looked as if they were greeters, their job went deeper than that. Each wore a hidden weapon and had permission to use it if needed. The giant dogs that lay at their feet were not dogs at all, but experienced security personnel borrowed from the Fairwood pack for the evening.

Still, she, Samantha and Tanya were taking turns watching over Dot, hanging in the background, keeping their eyes on the people closest to her. Tasha didn't anticipate any problems, but she wasn't taking any chances. The setting was too open for her comfort.

"You can at least pretend you're having fun," Tanya sent from across the gym.

"What? And betray my street creds as an enforcer?"

"I keep hearing what a good mother you'd make after the way you dealt with the boy who was making his first shift."

"Obviously not from the same people who nearly had to restrain me from tearing out that fool's throat this morning."

"Don't be so sure of that. They think that goes to prove how far you'd go to protect your own children."

"So that's why so many of the mated women are inviting me for dinner. They're trying to line me up with a cousin or friend or something."

"You'd make a good catch."

Tasha located her twin across the gym, and even from the distance saw her broad smile. Her laughter sparkled in Tasha's mind. She couldn't help smiling either. *"Imagine this,"* she sent, *"Me with my AR-15 cradled in one arm, a baby cradled in the other, slogging through the brambles of the territorial border."*

"And your mate beside you, carrying a second child on his back. Maybe a certain big brawny redhead?"

A momentary vision of Jamie and her strolling side by side along a gentle path deep in the woods flashed through Tasha's brain. It would never happen. It was against her rules. *"That joke's going to get old real fast," she* warned.

"Who says I'm joking? Didn't you see the way he looked at you?"

Tasha was saved from needing to answer by a sudden commotion near the double doors, which opened to the main floor of the school. A group of giggling children ran into the gym, carrying brightly-colored daisies. "Miss Lapahie, Miss Lapahie," they called and a pathway cleared between them and Dot.

One by one they went up to her and either curtsied or bowed. "For you," each one said as they handed her their flower. "Thank you." Tasha noted that every child's cheek bore pink stripes.

Tasha sensed Dot's warring reactions as she gave each child a hug, holding back tears of happiness. After the last child, no more than three years old, reached her, Dot knelt to receive the flower and a kiss on the cheek, and to hug the little one. The toddler giggled and ran off to find his mother, and when Dot stood Tasha saw traces of tears on her cheeks.

She had no time to recover before the chanting started. First two voices from somewhere in the far corner of the gym. Then four, then the entire room joined in. "Lapahie," the chant rose, "Lapahie, Lapahie."

Jars of face paint were passed hand-to-hand and pink stripes appeared on the cheeks of the villagers.

And still the chant went on. "Lapahie, Lapahie."

An elderly woman carrying a solitary wild daisy pushed her way through the crowd and stopped in front of Dot. The crowd fell silent. "I am Lorena," she said. "Originally of the Choate pack."

"I remember you, Lorena," Dot said. "You were present at the fight between my grandfather and myself. If I remember correctly, you cheered for me then."

The old woman smiled. "I did. And I was among the first to paint my cheek when you took over."

Dot reached out and gently touched the woman's cheek, which once again bore three pink stripes. "And you stayed here when others left."

"This is my home. You've given it back to me and my children and grandchildren and the rest of the Choate women when others wanted to take it away from us. We didn't have the honor of helping you to grow up, but you've proven that you are part of our family."

"It's been my honor to help you."

Pretending to push away a stray lock of hair, Tasha surreptitiously wiped a tear from her own eye.

"We've heard the rumors," Lorena said solemnly, "that not everyone feels the same way and that saddens us. So we," and she waved her arm to include the entire assembly, "want you to know we stand behind you. No matter what you call yourself, you are Choate and one of us. We are pack, and you are our leader." She raised a fist in the air. "Lapahie!"

"Lapahie!" roared the crowd. "Lapahie! Lapahie!'

Tasha moved in, fighting her way through the throng that surrounded Dot. Everyone wanted to hug her, touch her, be part of the moment. *"They're going to crush her!"* she screamed to Samantha and Tanya.

"I'm with her," Samantha sent. *"So far they're being orderly, but I could use backup in case things get out of hand."*

Then Tanya was there with a chair so Dot could sit. With a little urging, the crowd became a line. To the unaware, Tasha and Samantha were only keeping the line straight, making sure everyone had a turn, while Tanya made sure that no one person took up too much of Dot's time. Because after all, why would Dot need to be guarded?

With the long evening over, Dot escorted to the house where she stayed, and patrols evident in the village, Tanya, Tasha and Samantha were relieved of duty. Tasha volunteered to take the couch and let Tanya have her bed. However, she only pretended to settle in for the night, waiting until the others had time to go to sleep before she slipped out the back door, removed her pajamas, and shifted.

She made her presence known to the first security patrol she sensed so they wouldn't challenge her as she roamed among the shadows, verifying everything was secure. She worked her way to the outskirts where there were no houses, and then further. If anyone had been tracking her, they would have seen a standard patrol routine.

But Tasha had a goal in mind, a small hill south of the village. Once she was sure no one was following her, she made a beeline to it. There, a lone wolf stood guard.

Tasha approached the wolf in submissive fashion, crawling the last few feet. When she was close enough, she touched her muzzle to his and licked him.

"You don't have to do that," Gavin sighed.

"I know. But tonight reminded me of the value of packs and tradition and it seemed appropriate." She stood, shook off the stray weeds that clung to her belly and sat beside him where she could keep an eye on the village. *"Does Dot know you're here? One of the pack told me you were coming."*

"She sensed my presence the minute I crossed the border."

"She is of Choate blood, and I believe that ties her to this place. Just as your skills increase when you are on Fairwood territory. It's too bad you couldn't have been at the celebration with her."

"I would have liked to see it. But it's important that she is the one in charge, standing on her own."

Tasha sent him a wordless nod of agreement and they were silent for a minute. They watched as a few lights flickered off in the village and night-owls sought their beds. *"What are you doing here anyway?"* she asked.

"I wanted to be close if I was needed. It's my duty to protect my mate."

And it was her duty to protect him. She sat, listening to the night noises and enjoying the cool air. A howl drifted to them through the night and Gavin rose and answered. His lips curled in a wolfish approximation of a smile.

"She comes," he sent.

"Is she guarded?"

"Yes. By one of the pack. You can go home and to bed now."

"Is that an order?" she teased.

He growled, but it was a playful noise.

She rose and stretched. *"May your path be clear*

and your puppies numerous and healthy." It was an old pack saying to a mated couple, and it seemed fitting to use it. She hoped their mating would be fruitful.

As she trotted down the hill, she heard his response, the traditional one to an uncoupled wolf. *"And may you find your mate and happiness."*

THIRTEEN

The words taunted Tasha as she surveyed the fresh damage in one of the second-floor classrooms. Whoever had smashed the monitors and torn apart the computers was clearly an unhappy person. They'd pulled the posters off the walls and ripped the textbooks apart. The bleach they'd dumped over the desks and floor covered any scent left behind.

"I checked every one of these rooms myself before supper," Chief said, not for the first time. "Everything was locked. And we had patrols running all night long."

"But the building itself was open during the event. Who's not to say that while we were celebrating, someone didn't sneak away and do this? We couldn't track everyone every minute. And it's not that hard to jimmy the locks on these doors. They're old enough that it can be done with a credit card and a little persistence."

"Did everyone come last night?" Samantha asked.

"Where was that teacher Miss Lapahie fired?" Tasha added.

"He stayed in his house the whole time. We had

someone posted nearby the entire night. As far as everyone else, we didn't track attendance or anything," Chief answered. "Why would we? How often do people turn down a party? We even split the shifts for the patrols so that everyone had the opportunity to be there at least part of the time."

"That was good planning." It didn't hurt to stroke Chief's ego when he did something right. "So let's assume that someone slipped away during the party and did this. Or a couple of people. Who was at the party last night that didn't want to be there? Who was reluctant to add the pink markings?" Tasha closed the door to keep the bleach smell from infiltrating the hallway more than it already had. Even with the windows open in the room the odor was overpowering.

"I spent most of the evening outside," Chief said. "I didn't have the chance to observe what was going on inside."

"And we were busy with crowd control," Samantha said.

"Who's the biggest gossip?" Tasha asked. "Who loves to talk shit about anyone they don't like?"

"Gerta," Samantha said promptly. "But she's gone, visiting a friend in Cleveland."

"Any security cameras in the gym?"

"No," Chief answered. "There's been talk about installing recording equipment for school plays and conferences, but it hasn't happened."

"Cell phones," said Samantha. "Someone had to record the party on their cell phone. But how do we find out without raising a big stink?"

"Easy. We put out the word that Miss Lapahie wants the video to show to Elder Fairwood. People will fall all over themselves to help her out." Tasha grinned. "Better yet, we say we're putting together clips of the event to present to her as a surprise. That way she won't be bothered by folks stopping her to show her their pictures. It would be nice to give her a video of the evening. If we screen the excerpts first, that's even better."

Chief nodded. "I'll put my secretaries to work on it. They can talk to the students on patrol for starters."

Tasha avoided looking at Samantha so she wouldn't reveal her thoughts. *"I take it Miss Lapahie hasn't talked to him yet,"* she sent in a tightly controlled thread to Samantha.

"She slept in this morning," Samantha answered. *"At least that's what I was told. Maybe she was up late doing paperwork or something."*

Tasha nodded. It was all she could do and keep a straight face at the same time.

She wasn't laughing later when Dot reviewed the pictures of the damage. "Damn it, Tasha, they can't let me have one good night, can they?" Dot pounded her fist on top of the stack.

"You think this was personal and not an attack on the school?"

"That's how it feels." The tears that stained Dot's face were not tears of happiness. "I try so hard, and this happens."

"You can't please everybody."

"But they aren't hurting me alone—they're hurting the kids who coming here. How can I make sure they get the experience they need to make it on their own if I can't provide them with the right equipment?"

"They haven't stopped you—just delayed the process. And won't insurance help cover the cost of replacements?"

"I haven't filed a claim yet." Dot pulled a tissue from a desk drawer and blotted her cheeks. "If I do, I'll need to file a police report, and I can't risk having the state police here. Besides, I'm afraid that will make our rates go up and cut into the budget for other things."

"I've let you down." Tasha was no longer certain of her ability to protect her friend and the other Free Wolves, and it stung. She'd been so sure of herself.

"You've accomplished miracles in what, two days? Nobody will blame you for this."

"But I haven't done enough yet. I haven't got a clue who's to blame."

"Be realistic. It'll take time."

Although Tasha agreed, she still worried that she'd failed her assignment. While Dot took a phone call, Tasha wandered around the room, looking at the various knick-knacks decorating the office. Many of them were influenced by Native-American art, which wasn't surprising because of Dot's heritage.

But a few were dreadfully out of place. The sculpture that looked like a banana, for one. Tasha picked up the vase, decorated with a painted-on screaming face, to examine it more closely as Dot finished her call.

"Ugly, isn't it?" Dot asked. "But it was a gift, and it's rude not to display it. I need to arrange for it to get 'accidentally' broken."

"Did you try turning the face to the wall and putting flowers in it? Tasha set it back in the original spot.

"I tried putting a bouquet in it—once. I've never seen flowers die so fast. There must be something in the coating that killed them."

Tasha wiped her hands on her jeans. She'd need to wash them carefully before she ate.

"It's supposedly by a famous artist," Dot continued. "But I don't think I could even give it away."

"Donate it to a charity." Tasha picked up the monstrosity again and turned it upside down, looking for the artist's signature. And promptly returned it to the shelf.

"Nothing to show the creator," she said as she strolled over to Dot's desk. She picked up a pen and scribbled something on the current page of the calendar pad, ripped it off and handed it to Dot. "Want to go get coffee?"

"What do you mean the vase is bugged?" Dot asked as they carried their coffees outside so they could talk without being overheard.

"I don't know a whole lot about electronics, but I recognize a listening device when I see one. And that's a bug, clear as day. Do you remember who gave the vase to you? And how long ago?"

Dot took a sip of her coffee, blowing across the surface first. "It's been a few months. And I don't remember where it came from. Why?"

"No wires. It has to be battery powered. How long

the battery would last is not part of my expertise.

"So what do we do?"

Tasha scowled. "With all the computer geeks here, you'd think someone would know about these things. Question is, who can we trust?"

"I can ask Gavin for a recommendation."

"Are you heading back tonight?"

"I'm going to spend the night here. I want to show that I won't run away from the problem, that I'm committed to the school and the community."

"And last night proved how the residents feel about you." A thought struck Tasha. "You haven't told them about the problems, right?"

"No, I don't want to worry them unnecessarily."

"I'm willing to bet they've heard about at least one of the incidents, especially after today's. There's no way the students didn't talk about this, tell their friends and parents, who then shared it with the neighbors."

"And?"

Tasha smiled. "It's the power of the pack. Call a community meeting tonight and tell everyone exactly what is going on. You'll have so many volunteers willing to run patrol your head will spin. Can you imagine the reaction when you are the first to volunteer?"

"I'm not sure it's a good idea." Dot perched on the edge of a picnic table. "It's my job to protect them."

"And their job to protect you. So let them."

"There's a problem." Dot set her coffee cup down. "Well, two really. The first is that I don't know how to run patrol. I wasn't allowed to when I was with the Fairwoods."

"Easy enough to fix. You'll be paired with the most

experienced partner we can find. What's the second problem?"

"Gavin will hate the idea."

Talking Dot into the plan was the easy part. Convincing Gavin was the hard part. At least she didn't have to do it face-to-face. A phone call was easier.

"We'll assign her to the easiest run," Tasha told him, "with the most experienced partner."

"We can't risk her," Gavin insisted.

"And this is too important not to try. You should have seen her reaction when she saw the pictures of the damage."

"Then I need to be with her."

"You can't be and you know that."

"She's my mate and I need to protect her."

Tasha had anticipated his reaction. "She'll be on the Eastern run. You can provide extra coverage by setting up security on the road leading to the gate. As long as you stay far enough away from the border she won't know you're there. If my theory is correct she won't be able to sense you unless you cross onto Choate pack lands."

"If she gets hurt I can't guarantee you'll ever be able to return to the pack."

"I'll be dead before I let anyone hurt her."

The impromptu meeting went even better that Tasha anticipated. The group was large enough to ensure that Dot's message would be distributed widely. They met the bland recitation of the incidents with quiet murmurs, confirming Tasha's instincts they'd already heard about them. But when Dot announced she was going to be on patrol starting that night, the crowd exploded.

With her as an example, almost everyone signed up to be part of the patrols. Ariana volunteered to gather the names and organize the effort, but she ended up needing help to get the job done. She soon had a committee of older women who were no longer physically up to the demands of patrolling to assist her.

Then someone suggested that the students too young to patrol be trained as messengers. If other forms of communication broke down, they'd carry messages back and forth between patrols and central headquarters. The only people left out of the effort were the children who hadn't made their first shift. Watching Dot's face, Tasha suspected that she was plotting how to change that.

"This isn't much different than getting ready to go on a raid," Dot said as she strapped on the belt that held her throwing knives.

"In a way; it is," Tasha told her. "Only instead of going to your target, you're searching for someone coming to you. Which can be even more nerve-racking."

"I wish you two could come along."

I will be, Tasha thought, but not officially.

"Chief agrees with you, but it wouldn't look right," Samantha said. She was double-checking Dot's preparations. "You have to do this on your own."

"Do you know how many times I bugged Gavin to

let me run patrols with the Fairwoods?" Dot adjusted the shoulder harness for the revolver that the arms master had supplied. "And he'd never let me. I can't believe he caved and agreed to this scheme."

"I guess he realized how important this is," Tasha suggested.

"Either that or someone blackmailed him. What do you have on him, Tasha?"

"Me?" Tasha fluttered her eyelashes and attempted to look innocent. "All I had to do was explain how important this is."

"I'll force you to tell me later." Dot turned around slowly. "What am I missing?"

She didn't look like the CEO of a growing organization any more. Instead, she'd gone back to her roots and looked every inch the warrior. From the combat boots on her feet to the cropped hair tinged with streaks of red, she was prepared for battle. Tasha decided it was a good thing that Gavin wasn't there to see her. They'd never make it out the door. Nothing was sexier to a male wolf that a female prepared to do battle for her cubs.

"One minor detail." Samantha reached into her pocket and pulled out a small, round container. "Pink stripes on your cheeks. Then you'll be ready."

A small cluster of people waited for Dot when she reported to the staging area for her patrol assignment. As she shook hands with her well-wishers, Tasha used the diversion to slip away. She had her own preparations to make.

FOURTEEN

It was easier tracking in wolf form, but Tasha wanted her weapons available. She'd run the border in daylight hours and picked out hiding spots. The last thing she wanted was for Dot to know she was being guarded. Which meant she had to swear Samantha to secrecy after she walked in on Tasha making her preparations.

The team—Dot and two men—stopped to examine a break in the fence line. The top rail of the crude wooden barrier had fallen—or been knocked—to the ground. They milled around, arguing about the potential cause, and mixing their footprints with any that might have already been there. It didn't take Tasha's *other* senses to detect the fragrance of manure, and her theory was that a cow tried to get to the greener grass on the other side of the fence. Either that or used the fence as a scratching post.

The patrol leader came to the same conclusion after stepping in a pile of what the cow left behind on the other side. Tasha watched with amusement as the two men struggled to put the rail back in place. They must not have played with wooden building logs as children.

Dot stayed out of their way while they worked, her eyes constantly roaming the area for any signs of trouble. With the rail finally finagled into place, the group moved on. After waiting for a few minutes, Tasha took their place, using all of her senses to see if they'd missed something. Avoiding the cow-patties, she searched the pasture across the fence for signs of any intrusion by anything besides cows. Finding nothing, she hurried to catch up with the patrol.

It was clear that the two men were treating Dot as a less-than-equal partner, and even clearer that she knew. Tasha admired the level of patience Dot showed, pretending to pay attention to their over-simplified explanations of patrol duties. Half the time they spoke out loud instead of using mental communication. A major mistake, as they could be heard from a long distance away in the relative quiet of the night. An approaching enemy would have time to hide. Chief needed to make more changes.

The boundary didn't follow a straight path, instead meandering along an old stream bed. The trio followed the well-worn path along the edge. Tasha, on the other hand, moved in a straight line and soon worked her way ahead of them. On edge and alert for any sign of trouble, she jumped at the caw of a crow. It was unusual for one to be calling at night, especially when even the night birds were silent.

She dropped to the ground and reached out with her *other* senses. The yellow streaks in her eyes glowed as she surveyed the forest and her tongue darted in and out like a snake's, tasting the air. But it was her ability to overhear the thoughts of others that alerted her to the intent of the intruders.

There were four of them. Tasha crept closer to where they hid behind a cluster of blackberry bushes. Two of them she could handle on her own, but it would be suicide to tackle all four by herself. She needed to separate them.

"They should be here any time," one whispered.

"Are you sure this is a good idea?" another asked.

"We all go through it," the first one answered. Tasha figured he was the ringleader. "If she wants to show off and act like she's all that, we'll give her the real experience."

"It's all in good fun," said the third.

"Don't chicken out on us now," added the fourth.

Nothing like peer pressure, Tasha thought. She wormed her way closer. She couldn't figure out how to warn Dot without revealing her presence.

"Don't worry, I sensed them about five minutes ago," a voice intruded into her mind. *"Just like I knew you were along for the ride shortly after you joined us on the trail. As far as I can tell, neither of my guides know you've been trailing us."*

"Sorry, Dot," Tasha sent sheepishly. *"But you know I had to do it."*

"I'll deal with you later. In the meantime, let's give these cubs a taste of their own medicine."

With wild war cries, the boys rushed out from their hiding place waving flashlights that acted as strobe lights. One tripped and fell within a few feet, landing hard, losing his light and knocking the breath out of him. Before he could recover to join his friends or look around to figure what he'd stumbled on, a dark form was on top of him. A knife was pressed to his throat.

"Keep quiet and stay here," Tasha hissed. *"And I won't hurt you. Agreed?"*

Still trying to catch his breath, the boy nodded. Tasha kicked the flashlight out of his reach and slipped back into the night to where the real battle was taking place. A sudden silence made her fear the worst.

But Dot already controlled the situation. One boy slumped at the base of a tree, as pale as a moonflower. A throwing knife was stuck in the trunk only inches from his head.

As Tasha watched from the shadow of the trees, Dot caught the ringleader by one arm as he rushed her, twisting it behind his back. With a little pressure, she forced him to the ground on his knees. With another of her knives, she cut off a lock of his hair before turning to the remaining attacker. Her lips curled into a sneer. "What are you waiting for?" she asked.

The last boy backed away, hands up and palms outwards. When the lights flashed, illuminating his face, Tasha detected moisture forming in his eyes. "It was a joke, Miss Lapahie. We didn't mean anything by it."

Dot examined the edge of one of her knives before tossing it in the air. It glittered in the artificial light before she caught it on its downward spiral. "A joke, huh? And you play it on all the newbies?" A second knife, then a third, joined the first one creating a flashing whorl of metal.

They were gathered in Dot's office. They'd drug chairs in from the outer office to give everyone a place to sit. With the four practical jokers, the two men that had been on patrol with Dot, Chief, Samantha and Tasha all in the room, it was crowded and stuffy.

Tasha made it back to the village before Dot and the others. In fact, she'd had time to slip out of her combat gear and into jeans and a T-shirt. So the only witnesses to her participation in the events had no reason to reveal the truth.

"And what made you think Miss Lapahie was a newbie?" Tasha asked, her voice harsh. She had no sympathy for any of the males in the room. As far as she was concerned, they all were part of the conspiracy. "Haven't you paid attention to the stories about how she fought her grandfather to gain control of the business?"

The ringleader squirmed. "We figured they were exaggerations," he said. "Every time we see her, she's in a fancy suit and high heels. You can't fight dressed like that. We've never even seen her shift."

A slim blade flashed by his cheek and landed in a cork board on the wall. The blood drained from his face and he wilted in his seat.

"You're lucky she's an experienced warrior." Tasha poked him in the chest. "And that she was able to identify you rapidly. You might be dead otherwise." Her eyes scanned the room. "What did you know about this?" she asked the two men Dot had gone on patrol with.

The one who had given Dot the hardest time cleared his throat. "We'd heard rumors," he admitted. "Didn't think much about it." He glanced at his partner. "We didn't think anyone would actually do it."

"In fact, you thought it was funny," Dot interjected. "It's not like you take running patrol seriously. Hell, you rarely shut up the whole time. If there was an enemy at our gates, they'd hear you blabbing long before you got close enough to see them."

A second knife shot out of her hand and quivering, landed next to the first in the corkboard, almost touching. Dot contemplated the placement, and with a move so fast Tasha could barely track it, added a third. "I believe you and I need to have a discussion about your training methods, Chief," she said. "But later, not now."

Tasha had a few things she wanted to say to Chief herself. She hoped Dot would include her in the meeting.

"The question," Dot said, "is what's to be done with these four?"

"The traditional punishment for someone who disrespects their alpha," Samantha said, "is banishment from the pack. At least it was in my pack."

Is that what had happened to Samantha? She'd stood up for herself or disobeyed an order? Tasha had never asked her why she'd left. It didn't seem to be a topic that needed to be discussed.

"Coyotes have similar rules," Chief said.

"Then it's a good thing I'm not an alpha," Dot said. "Because these boys would have nowhere to go if we kicked them out. What do you think, Tasha?"

"Public shaming might be good. I'd say make them clean latrines if we had any. What if we assign them to clean up the houses of our more elderly residents? Not that there's anything shameful about that, but it might remind them they're part of a community and everyone plays a part in making the community work no matter their skill level or age."

Dot stood and stared out the window, her hands clasped behind her back. "I like it," she said eventually. "I suspect some of the grandmothers of the village are lonely. Having young men around might cheer them up. Samantha, can you find someone to organize the effort?"

"I'll be glad to, Miss Lapahie." Samantha grinned. "In fact, I have the perfect person in mind. Gerta should be back in a day or two."

"But she talks all the time," one boy muttered.

"Then you will listen to her," Dot said. "And you'll do it with a smile. Agreed?" They nodded and she continued, "Go get ready for school. And no sleeping in class either."

After they'd shuffled out, Dot retrieved her knives and slipped them back into her belt. "Now what am I going to do with these two?" she asked no one in particular, indicating the two men she'd run patrol with.

Chief, who'd stared at the floor much of the time, raised his head and asked, "What do you mean?"

Dot raised an eyebrow. "Really? They disrespected me more than the boys did. Talked down to me, treated me like I was too fragile to do the simplest tasks. And they should have known better." She turned to them. "What do you suggest?"

They exchanged a glance. "Maybe we could help the younger boys?"

"That's the best you can do? Add the lack of imagination to your list of failures. What do you suggest, Chief?"

"Perhaps they can be assigned to the northern border for a month or so."

"Better, but not good enough. That won't fix their sloppy habits. Tasha?"

"Neither of them has a mate or children," Tasha said slowly. "Send them to the Fairwoods to train with Elder Fenner. He can either train the bad habits out of them or advise you that they are worthless and let you decide whether to kick them out or not. And since they won't be able to do their duties here, they won't get paid."

"So kill them or cure them. And if they straighten out, when they come back they can help train the younger students, both female and male. That is, if Elder Fenner gives his blessing." Dot nodded thoughtfully. "I like it."

"You expect us to just give up our jobs for that? I'm up for a promotion!"

"You're lucky you won't be asked to pay for the training you'll receive," Dot snapped. "It's a generous offer. If you don't like it, you're welcome to leave for good."

Tasha was worried. What would Dot think the appropriate punishment for her transgression would be?

"At least give us a couple of days to get ready."

"Agreed. I have to make sure Elder Fenner has the time for you first. Now get out of my office before I change my mind."

With them gone, the office seemed bigger but still stuffy. Tasha wished she was outside running in the woods somewhere.

"Chief," Dot said. "You've disappointed me again. If you were working with your trainees correctly, none of this would've happened. What am I going to do with you?"

"You can't pin this on me." Chief straightened and crossed his arms defensively. "I didn't have anything to do with it."

"So you didn't know that's there's a tradition of trying to scare newcomers? And never once has a trainee told you in the briefings about it happening? What does that say about your ability as a leader?

"And I suppose you're going to tell me you didn't hand-pick who would be on patrol with me?"

Hadn't Ariana created the schedule? Tasha forced down the growl that rose in her throat. Her instinct was to grab Chief by the neck and slit his throat. Her hand moved towards her knife.

"Don't," Dot warned. *"I've got this covered."*

"Tell me, Chief," Dot said, "what is the traditional punishment in a coyote pack for a member who betrays his alpha?" The question was simple, but the threat it contained was clear.

Chief remained silent but his hands were white as he gripped the arms of his chair.

"No answer?" Dot asked oh-too-sweetly. "I've done a little research and the answer is death."

FIFTEEN

With a strangled noise that might have been a yelp, Chief made a dash for the office door. Samantha was too fast for him and with a flying kick, hit him in the back and sent him smashing into the wall. Tasha wrapped an arm around his neck before he had time to fall to the floor. "Can I kill him now?" she asked between clenched teeth.

"Not yet," Dot answered. "It's a good thing we aren't obligated to follow pack rules here. Besides, I want him alive. I think he's stupid, not malicious, and that doesn't deserve the death penalty."

"What's the alternative?" Samantha asked. The rage evident on her face matched how Tasha felt.

"Banishment. But I'm not sure that's a good idea either. I don't want him running around loose where he can make trouble for the school. We've already got our hands full."

Chief grabbed Tasha's arm with both of his hands and tried to pull. In response, she tightened her arm. "Is there anything handy we can tie him up with?" When he continued to struggle, she kneed him in the back.

Samantha had another idea. She pressed several fingers onto his neck until he slumped against Tasha's restraining arm. "You can let go of him. He should be out for a while," she said.

Unceremoniously, Tasha released her hold and let Chief fall to the floor. She didn't resist the urge to kick him when he was down. "Now what?" she snarled.

Dot rubbed her forehead. "I don't know," she admitted. "I didn't plan for things to go this far. Any suggestions?"

"I've got an idea." Tasha pulled off her shirt, then drew her knife from its sheath. She cut a strip from the bottom. It was an old one she didn't mind sacrificing for the cause. She used one strip to tie Chief's hands behind his back, a second secured his feet. "I'll need to request a favor to make it happen."

"What do you have in mind?" Dot asked.

Tasha put the remnant of her shirt back on. "The Radferd's cook is getting old. He's still makes a mean barbeque, but lifting heavy dishes and washing pots and pans is getting to be too much for him. He needs help, and it seems like a perfect job for Chief. The Radferds won't put up with his shit and there's little or no way for him to leave the compound."

"Banishment with a twist." Dot nodded thoughtfully. "It might work. Do you think your contacts at the Radferds will go along with the idea?"

Tasha shrugged her shoulders. "It's worth asking, but I can't predict their answer."

"What are we going to do with him in the meantime?" Chief groaned, and Samantha gave him a shove with her foot to gauge his reaction. Satisfied that he was still out, she resumed her wary pose. "There's no place here to secure him."

"And too many people I don't trust who might try to free him." Tasha frowned. "We can't keep him tied up long enough to make the arrangement."

"How about with your mate's pack?" Samantha suggested. "Can they help out?"

Dot sighed. "I'd prefer not to bother Gavin, but it might be an option. I'll call him. In the meantime, let's move him downstairs to his office. Gag him and post guards—ones you trust."

Gavin himself showed up to supervise the transfer. Chief had regained consciousness by then, and when he saw the size of the men that accompanied the Fairwoods' leader, he grudgingly went with them. Or pretended to. They untied his feet and allowed him to walk. When he made a dash for freedom, he was tackled and injected with a drug that knocked him out again.

"He's not very bright, is he?" Gavin asked Dot, watching as his men loaded Chief into the back of a van. Tasha stood nearby, ready to protect both of them if needed.

"I'm not sure how much is stupidity and how much is fear," Dot said. "And the lack of a good example when he was younger. But I've run out of chances to give him."

"You think he was behind the problems you've been having?"

Dot considered the question. "No. No, I don't believe he'd do anything that left a trail."

"You want me to send some of the pack here to help with security?"

"There is a sudden opening in my staff."

"Samantha and I will deal with it," Tasha said. "We were going to step in anyway. The community here needs to handle the crisis without too much help from outsiders."

Gavin nodded. "Can Samantha manage it by herself for a few days? I'd like you to return with us."

Tasha knew the request was an order from her pack leader. *"Is that my punishment?"* she sent to Dot.

"Not my idea. He didn't tell me this part of the plan. But you and I still need to talk."

"Can Tanya stick around and help out? She can work in the background. I'm not sure Samantha knows the in-and-outs of managing patrols well enough to tackle it by herself. And I haven't been here long enough to suggest someone with the skills to assist her." It might be a good idea to give Samantha a second person to work with. Tasha didn't know if Dot would ever trust her again.

Gavin nodded. "Works for me. I'll ask her." He got that semi-vacant stare in his eyes that indicated he was having a mental conversation with someone. His eyes returned to normal and he said, "That's set then. I'll clear the time off with her boss."

Tasha had left some of her clothes at her parent's house, so it didn't take long for her to retrieve her motorcycle and gas it up for the trip back to the Fairwood village. The majority of her weapons were stashed in the closet at the house, but the pistol Elder Fenner had loaned her was securely stowed in her saddlebag.

She pulled in behind Gavin's Jeep and shut off the bike's engine. As long as she was still given the honor of acting as a guard, she couldn't be in too much trouble. Besides, Gavin had approved the plan, so why was she stressing about it?

Or something else had her nerves on edge. She scanned the central commons area, looking for anything out of place. Spotting nothing, she decided it was her imagination, or a result of too many things happening and not enough sleep.

She wondered what was holding up Gavin and Dot. She thought they'd just gone to retrieve the bugged vase in Dot's office. There weren't any experts on the technology among the Fairwoods, but Gavin knew someone who might be able to help.

From the corner of her eye, she caught movement among the trees at the edge of the parking lot. She pretended to check her hair in the mirror of her bike while she tracked the motion. Two female figures emerged, lugging overstuffed suitcases. Something didn't smell right.

She didn't need to be a genius to recognize the one figure. When the two started walking down the road that left the village heading south, Tasha could no longer contain her curiosity.

Even her normal walking pace was faster than the limited progress the two women were making. It only took a few seconds to catch up with them. "Going somewhere, Ariana?"

It was clear from their puffy eyes that both women had been crying. "We figured we'd leave while we could take our things with us." Ariana sniffed. "The last time Chief got us thrown out of a pack, we had to leave everything behind."

"We don't have much, but we wanted to take the most important things," said the other lady. Tasha couldn't remember ever meeting her, but her guess was that it was Chief's other "secretary."

Tasha stuck out her hand. "I'm Tasha," she said, "I don't think we've been introduced."

The woman seemed startled by the gesture, but was unwilling to set down her suitcase. She ignored Tasha's outstretched hand but mumbled, "I'm Rosa."

"Well, Ariana, Rosa, why don't you tell me what's going on here? Because the truth is, I'm confused."

"You can't stop us from leaving." Ariana shifted her hold on her suitcase.

"If you really want to go, I won't get in your way. But why don't you explain why you want to leave?"

"Nobody will want us here after what Chief did."

"Who told you that?"

"Chief. He says that we're worthless and that the only reason people put up with us is because he covers for our mistakes." Rosa's bottom lip quivered and Tasha was afraid she was going to start crying again.

"And we don't have any money to pay to stay here," Ariana added.

It was a good thing that Chief was already on his way to the Fairwoods, because Tasha was ready to kill him.

"What happened to the money you were paid to help Chief?" she asked.

"He took it. Said it was to cover our share of the rent and food." Ariana hesitated. "I saved some money from the little bit he gave us to buy women's supplies. It's not much but it should get us to another pack."

"Dot! You need to find out if Chief had a bank account and freeze it! He's been stealing Ariana and

Rosa's paychecks!" Tasha hoped her message would reach Dot.

The wordless curse that came back to her reassured Tasha that Dot would handle it.

"Those suitcases look awfully heavy." She waved a hand at a nearby bench. "Can we go sit down? There's something I need to explain to you."

Her heart broke a little at the fear she caught in their unspoken communication. No words, just emotions, but that was enough. She had to find a way to get through to them. She was a warrior, not a diplomat, but she had to try.

"You understand that Free Wolves aren't just wolves, don't you? They're rabbits and dragons and foxes and even coyotes. And they won't judge you by what Chief did. This is a safe place for everyone and you're welcome to stay."

"She's right." Tasha had been so intent on Ariana and Rosa that she hadn't even heard Dot come running up behind her. "No one will chase you off. I'm sure we can find new jobs for you. Ariana, you're already helping by organizing the volunteers for patrols, and I really appreciate it. If I haven't said it before, thank you."

A blush rose in Ariana's cheeks. "It was the only way I could think of to help. We don't know how to fight, so we couldn't go on patrol."

"And it was a big relief. I don't have the time to do the job right."

Tasha and Dot caught the change in Ariana's expression at the same time. "What's wrong?" Tasha asked.

"It's my fault," Ariana said.

"What is?" Dot asked.

"That the patrols were messed up. I tried to tell Chief the schedules were bad, but he told me to do it his way. Maybe if I tried a little harder, he would've listened, and you wouldn't have been put in danger last night."

"Oh, Ariana," Dot poured so much love into her voice that Tasha caught her breath. Dot put her hands on Ariana's shoulders. "No matter what *he* told you, none of this is your fault. In fact, it's my fault. I should have seen how Chief treated you and put an end to it long ago. Do you understand? This is not your fault! None of it!"

Then she swept Ariana into a hug. A moment later, she pulled Rosa into her embrace as well. The three women wept, and Tasha fought to hold back her own tears.

Sixteen

Tasha strolled into Gavin's outer office five minutes before the meeting time. They'd arrived at pack headquarters near midnight, and she'd had time for nothing more than a quick bite and a short conversation with her parents before tumbling into bed. Between the lack of sleep the previous couple of nights and trusting the security patrols running outside, it didn't take long to fall asleep. As a result, she felt refreshed and ready to tackle whatever Gavin threw at her.

Annie, Gavin's secretary, smiled at her. "He'll be with you in a minute. He's meeting with someone else right now."

Tasha was glad she didn't have Gavin's job. Nothing worse than being stuck inside a building all day long. She idly picked up a magazine from the end table and took the nearest chair. She wasn't in a hurry.

After admiring the classical wedding dress that graced the cover, she flipped past the ads that filled the first few pages. And then leafed through the next few. After checking the title of the magazine, she asked "Anything I should know about, Annie?"

"What do you mean?"

With a grin, Tasha held up the bride's magazine. "Who's getting married?"

"That's where that got to," Annie said after a moment's hesitation. "A friend of my niece is getting married, and we were discussing the newest styles of dresses."

"Right. A friend of a friend." Tasha tossed the magazine on Annie's desk. "You better take that home before rumors start."

Gavin's secretary hastily stuck the magazine in a drawer at the same time. Gavin opened the door to his office and stuck his head out. "Tasha! You're here! Come in, please."

Tasha winked at Annie as she walked by her. She'd have to remember to check Dot's left hand for any sign of a ring.

Her mood changed abruptly when she realized who else was in Gavin's office. "You've met Jaime," Gavin said. "He's got a proposal for a joint project and I'd like you to be our representative."

"Yes, Tasha was most helpful in arresting those two poachers." Jaime smiled and held out his hand. "Good to see you again."

Tasha hoped her sudden nervousness wouldn't show. There was no polite way to avoid it, so she shook the offered hand. It seemed as if he held on to hers a shade too long. "I don't want to abandon what I'm working on right now," she said, her voice tightly controlled.

"I don't expect the project to kick off until next spring," Jaime said. "There'll be a few planning meetings between now and then, but they can be arranged around your schedule."

With Gavin standing there beaming at her, there wasn't a graceful way out of it. She was representing the pack and had to at least act interested. "Why don't you explain your idea?" she asked.

"You want coffee?" Gavin asked. "Have a seat, I'll ask Annie to make some. Here's a file with the basic information Jaime prepared for me."

He was acting like a matchmaker and there was nothing Tasha could do about it. She glanced through the papers while Annie brought in a tray with a coffee carafe and several mugs. Besides, if Tanya had put him up to it, it was her sister who'd get an earful later.

The proposal looked interesting, she had to admit. Jaime theorized that because of the long-term ownership of the Fairwood territory and because many parts had never been developed, rare species might be found there. He wanted to do a survey, and if possible, transplant small portions of the colonies to other protected areas.

As she filled a cup, she asked, "What does this have to do with being a game warden?"

"Nothing." Jaime smiled. "Just a personal interest. I spend enough time tromping around that I've seen what we're losing each time another housing development or shopping center goes up. I've also had the privilege of meeting people devoted to saving the gifts nature shares with us. I'm looking for a way to combine the two."

His enthusiasm was contagious and Tasha found herself nodding as he talked. Besides, she liked the sound of his voice.

"So what do you think, Tasha?" Gavin asked.

"It looks interesting so I'm in, as long as it's understood this isn't my main priority. A few of these plants are familiar looking." She tapped the folder. "Most I don't recognize, but I'm not an expert."

"I didn't expect you to be. I hear you're mostly a meat-eater." Jaime's smile spread across his face.

It took a moment to sink in. Had he actually cracked a joke about her *otherness*? The last bit of tension eased away and Tasha smiled in return. "Yeah, I'll take a good steak over a salad any day."

"I still remember the performance you gave on the debate team in high school." Gavin sat on the edge of his desk. "When you had to speak in favor of being a vegetarian. You convinced half the audience it would be a good idea."

"That was more acting than debating. It was hard for me to keep a straight face the whole time."

"It was hard enough for me to believe this guy is a wolf." Jaime jerked his thumb towards Gavin, "But you. I can't imagine you as a wolf at all."

If he saw her as a house cat or something similar, the friendship would be at an end before it ever started. "What do you see me as?" Tasha asked.

Jaime looked her up and down. "A mountain lion," he said, "A compact bundle of muscles that may not look dangerous at rest, but is a world of trouble if provoked."

She could live with that. "If you were a shifter, what would you be?" she asked.

"Me? Not a clue."

Gavin grinned. "With a bulk like yours, you could be a bear. Although you'd work as a wolf as well. What do you think, Tasha?"

"I've never met a bear shifter," she answered, eying Jaime critically, "so I can't say. But he'd make a great wolf." Too bad he wasn't a shifter. She'd jump at the chance to date him if he was. But she had her rule for a reason.

Tasha had dated a non-shifter for several months. Things had been progressing well, and she'd considered revealing her secret. She'd even gone as far as discussing it with her parents. But then they'd gone to a movie in which a werewolf was the hero. After listening to him rant for days about how a werewolf could never be the good guy, she'd put an end to the relationship, and decided to never date a non-shifter again.

Besides, there were too many horror stories about mixed relationships ending badly. She didn't want to take the chance on adding to the statistics.

"Thanks. I presume that's a compliment." Jaime chuckled, and Tasha decided she liked that sound too. "Can I get your phone number? I'd like to call you directly when I set a meeting instead of bothering Gavin."

Tasha ignored Gavin's quiet laugh in her mind. *"Let's see you get out of this one,"* he sent.

"Fair warning," she said. "Be prepared to leave a message. There are lots of times I don't have my cell phone on me or am out of tower range."

"You mean you don't carry it around when you're in wolf form? The wolf doesn't come with built in pockets?" Jaime asked, his eyes sparkling.

Another joke? Tasha considered revisiting her rule. But first he'd have to ask her out. She still didn't know if he was already taken.

She scribbled her number on a sheet of paper from Gavin's desk and gave it to Jaime. In return, he handed her a business card he'd pulled from his wallet. "The number on the front is the office," he said.

"The one on the back is my personal cell if you need to reach me after hours."

He tucked his wallet and looked at his watch. "I've got to run," he said. "I have another meeting in half an hour and it'll take me twenty minutes to get there."

Gavin held out his hand. "It was good seeing you again."

"Likewise," Jaime said as he accepted the proffered hand. "You too, Tasha," he said with a nod. "I'll be in touch."

"Do you remember the way out? Or do you want Annie to show you?"

Jaime got that grin on his face again. The one that created wrinkles at the corners of his eyes and lit his entire face. "I can find my way through the forest. An office building isn't too much of a challenge for me."

Tasha was confused, unable to read the signals Jaime was sending. Usually she could tell when a man was coming on to her, but he was different. His attention had been focused on Gavin, not her. Once he was gone, she filed the incident away to analyze later, and turned to Gavin. "Is there anything else?" Surely he hadn't pulled her from her post at Lapahie Enterprises just for that.

"Actually, yes." Gavin settled himself back behind his desk. "Give me an update on your progress at Lapahie. I know you've only been there for a few days, but what have you found out?"

"I've been too busy putting out fires to make any headway into determining who's setting them. The security flaws I've identified are a symptom, not the cause. The new patrols may slow down the attacker, but I don't think we've stopped him. Or her."

"Tell me about your impression of Chief."

"Where is he?" Tasha asked.

"Infirmary. Dr. Tracy is keeping him sedated for now but a guard is stationed there as well. I hope you hear from your friends soon."

Tasha had placed the call first thing in the morning but hadn't got an answer to her request yet. "He plays a good game," she said. "But it's all on the surface. He had me convinced he was willing to change his methods, but after he tried to sabotage Dot, I had no sympathy for him. And when I found out how he abused the two women from his pack..." she shook her head. "Let's just say it was a good thing he was where I couldn't get my hands on him."

"About them. Should I offer them a place here?"

Tasha considered the offer. "It would be a nice gesture, but they're better off staying with the Free Wolves. I'd like them to move into a house with other women. It might help them to see the way they were treated before wasn't right. Maybe they'll build some self-confidence working with Dot. You're a great leader, but I think they need a female role model right now."

"Makes sense. And what is your assessment of our new game warden?"

"How long has he known about or special abilities?"

Wrinkles appeared in Gavin's forehead. "A month or so. Why?"

"He was awfully comfortable with it. Most people don't adapt that easily. I don't fully trust him."

"Is that why you're being so standoffish towards him? He was pretty freaked out when I shifted for him."

Tasha grimaced. "Was it that obvious? I tried to hide it."

"I don't think he picked up on it. But then, he also didn't pick up on the signs that you're interested in him."

"Where did you get that idea? He's not a shifter. I have a rule about that."

"I've heard about your rule. But since you're not having any luck finding love among the pack, it might be time to expand your search criteria."

"Why is everyone so interested in my love life? Right now, I need to concentrate on figuring out what's going on with the attacks at Lapahie. I don't have the energy for anything else."

"Speaking of that," Gavin said, "My accountant has been analyzing the budget. Dot was concerned that items she thought were budgeted for aren't being bought. We're scheduled to meet this afternoon. Do you want to sit in on it?"

"I probably won't understand half of what she says, but yes. If there's anything shady going on, I want to know about it."

"Good. I'll see you then."

SEVENTEEN

She had time for a good run before the afternoon's meeting and the weather was perfect for it. Tasha sniffed the air and caught a trace of musk aftershave mixed with the smell of crumbling leaves. It was the same scent Jaime wore, and she was surprised that it lingered so long and the gentle breeze hadn't blown it away.

"Just the person I was hoping to see," said a familiar voice from behind her.

She turned around, feigning total calmness, hiding the sudden rush of excitement. "Hey, Jaime. What are you doing here? I thought you had a meeting."

"They canceled on me before I got out of the parking lot, so I decided I'd hang out and try to catch you. I was wondering about that buck you spotted."

"What about it?"

"Did you notice if it was wearing a transmitter? I got an email about a tagged buck the scientists lost track of, and they've been picking up random signals from the transmitter in this general area."

"Would it have been wearing a radio collar around its neck? Because I didn't see one."

"Oh well, it was worth a shot. Thanks anyway."

Tasha decided to go out on a limb. It had been so long since she'd dated a human she'd half-forgotten the rules of the game. Still, there was no harm in asking. "We can take a stroll out that way and try to spot it. I'd be interested in seeing if it stuck around."

She sent a separate thought to Gavin. *"Are there any restrictions on where I can take Jaime? I'll explain later."*

"Normal guest protocol."

That left out sensitive areas of the settlement—so Gavin didn't fully trust Jaime either.

"I'd like to, but I'm not dressed for it," Jaime said regretfully. He was right, his business clothes wouldn't survive a walk in the woods. Not considering the paths Tasha liked to follow. "Can we go tomorrow?"

"I'm not sure how long I'll be here. I'm consulting for another firm." That was the pack's code wording for working with another pack. Tasha thought she saw a flicker of disappointment on Jaime's face, but it disappeared so quickly she wasn't sure.

"Another time, then. Well, it was nice seeing you again."

She waited while he climbed into his truck. He rolled down his window and leaned out. "Any chance you'll be at The Pub tonight?"

Tasha planned to have supper with her parents. Her mother had mentioned home-made lasagna. "I might drop by for a beer."

"I'll look for you." With a smile and a wave, he pulled away, leaving Tasha more confused than before.

Normally a run in wolf form helped Tasha clear her mind, but by the time she returned home, she was as puzzled as ever. There was no sudden clarity about the problems facing Dot, and no understanding of Jaime's behavior. Maybe he was just being polite, and she was misinterpreting his intentions. Not that it mattered. She didn't have time to date anyway. And she had her rules.

Elder Alejos had been the pack's accountant for as long as Tasha could remember and now Tomas, her son, was stepping in to carry on the family tradition. Tomas looked like a clone of his mother, except for her silver-gray hair. But then, wolves were slow to age. Tasha grinned to herself. Unlike the myths, they weren't immortal.

The screen was lowered from the ceiling in Gavin's office and the first slide of their presentation was already projected on it. Elder Alejos sat behind Gavin's desk working the computer, while Gavin, Dot, Tomas and Tasha had arranged the chairs as if they were going to watch a movie. But the thick packets of paper that Tomas passed out ruined the illusion.

"Do you want the long explanation, or do you want to get to my findings?" Elder Alejos asked once they'd turned off the room lights.

Tasha had sat through one of her long presentations at a pack meeting once and hoped she'd never have to do that again. The detail had almost put her to sleep.

"In the interest of saving time, why don't you give

us the overview first? If we want more in-depth information, we can come back to it," Gavin suggested.

Tasha heard the old woman mumble something about no one appreciating her job. Gavin must have heard it as well because he added "You and I can go through the whole report later."

Elder Alejos skipped past the first few slides, still mumbling to herself. She stopped at one that had a bar chart with columns in red and blue. "What these charts show," she said, "is that on the surface the books are balancing correctly. Although there's some variation in expected income versus real-time income, it's within anticipated percentages."

She flipped to the next chart. "And these are expenditures." The graph looked similar to the last one, but the columns were green and red. "They seem to match the quotes again within expected parameters."

"So if everything matches up why are things not getting bought?" Dot asked.

"I'm getting there." Elder Alejos rushed past several more slides and stopped at one in red. Yellow and green. "Actually, Tomas spotted it first." She moved the mouse pointer over the shorter column in green. "We compared what Lapahie is paying for select items and what we are paying. The green is us. The red and yellow are Lapahie."

"So Lapahie is paying more for the same things?" Gavin asked.

"But we're using the companies you recommended," Dot said.

"Exactly." Another slide, this one appeared to be a list of items ordered. Red ovals highlighted a handful of the numbers. Tasha tried unsuccessfully to figure out their significance. "These items," the elder went on, "are what Lapahie Enterprises paid—at least on the surface. But I called my contact at the company and asked them to send me a copy of their version of this same order." The next slide appeared. "Here it is."

Gavin caught on first. "The numbers don't match."

"Precisely." Several more slides flipped by. "All of these show the same pattern. And I only checked with one company, but I anticipate seeing the same pattern with others."

"How is that possible?" Dot asked, exactly what Tasha wondered.

"If the proper safeguards are in place, it shouldn't be. Not unless more than one person is involved."

"What's your estimate on the total amount that has been misappropriated?" Gavin asked.

"It's too soon to give you a figure." Elder Alejos said. "We need access to more records to determine that. It could take days to get an accurate figure. Our best guess is that will total in the thousands of dollars."

"Humor me," Tasha said, "because this is not my area of expertise. What you're saying is someone is changing what the company is being billed, paying the suppliers the original amount and pocketing the difference. Right?"

"That's our theory." Tomas finally spoke up. "We haven't figured out how they're accomplishing it."

"You said something about the proper safeguards being in place. What do you mean?"

"If the bookkeeping in a company is structured correctly," Tomas explained, "no one has access to both the ordering and the payments sides. Sure, it happens in a small company, but Lapahie is big enough that there's no reason it should happen. That's why we think more than one person has to be involved."

"I don't know that we've ever looked at that," Dot said "I've trusted our more business savvy professionals to handle that."

"Perhaps it's time to do an audit," Elder Alejos said. "And I don't mean a monetary audit. We'll do that anyway. I mean a personnel audit."

"This is so out of my league," Tasha said later. "Plus, I don't see how it ties into the attacks."

Dot and Gavin looked up from where they were huddling over the stack of papers Elder Alejos had provided. "We didn't mean to ignore you," Dot said. "Why don't you take off? If we need you we'll be in touch."

"Is there any reason for me to stick around here? I hoped to head back to Lapahie tomorrow. They're predicting a storm moving through in a few days, and I'd like to get back before that."

"Can you stay one more day?" Gavin asked.

"Do you have an assignment for me?"

His answering grin was lopsided. "Your mother," he said "is upset that I brought you back from Maine and didn't even give you time to spend here before assigning you to work with Dot. She thinks she should have a few days to spend with you."

"That's why she was talking about cleaning house tomorrow." Tasha groaned. "She wants to talk my ear off and catch up on all the gossip I've missed. Can I please leave tomorrow?"

Gavin tried to look stern, but his eyes sparkled. "As

your pack leader, I'm giving you a direct order. You will stay one more day, you will spend time with your mother, and you will enjoy it. Do I make myself clear?"

Tasha sighed. "Whatever you say, oh Great and Glorious Leader."

Her mother's mood was upbeat during supper, and Tasha played along with making plans for cleaning. But after supper, when her parents settled into their favorite chairs to read, she excused herself. "Don't wait up for me," she said. She leaned over and kissed her mother on the cheek.

"Don't stay out too late. I want to get an early start."

Tasha forced a smile as she pulled on her leather jacket. As chilly as the nights were getting, even it might not be enough, but it would have to do. "It'll be fun," she said. She felt bad telling her mother a white lie, but it was easier that way.

She listened to the rumble of the bike's engine for a moment before slipping on her helmet. She wasn't sure where she was going. She just wanted to ride, to feel the power of the engine between her legs and the wind in her face. Riding her motorcycle was a close second on her list of favorite things to do, the first being running in wolf form. And doing both on the same day—just the thought made her smile.

She sniffed the wind, looking for a clue to help her decide which direction to go. What she got was the whiff of exhaust as Dimitri pulled alongside her in his 1960-s era Mustang. He had three pack members with him. "Going anywhere in particular?" he asked. "We're headed for The Pub if you want to tag along."

That must have been Fate's way of pushing her in the direction it wanted her to go. "Sure." She grinned and gunned her motor. "Whoever gets there last has to buy the first round."

If she'd been honest with herself, Tasha would have admitted a slight twinge of disappointment when a certain burly game warden didn't seem to be at The Pub when they got there. But that was easily covered up by the shared joy of her victory over Dmitri. And after the first beer, she was having so much fun catching up with old friends that she stopped looking every time the front door opened.

EIGHTEEN

Tasha made the switch to soda long before the night was over. Another of her personal rules—never ride drunk. She'd started watching the clock, trying to decide how soon she could leave without seeming impolite. If she didn't want to disappoint her mother, she needed to get home early.

As the evening progressed, the crowd got noisier. With the start of a headache coming on, Tasha stepped outside for a minute to clear her head. There was a cluster of smokers hanging around the door, so she walked down the front steps to get away from them.

A row of benches lined the sidewalk in front of the restaurant, and Tasha took a seat on the one farthest from the entrance. She closed her eyes and leaned back, breathing deeply. The sound of footsteps reached her a moment before the distinctive scent of his aftershave did.

"Hey," Jaime said, sitting next to her.

"Hey yourself." Tasha didn't open her eyes. She didn't need to. "I didn't know you were here."

"I didn't want to interrupt you and your friends. You looked like you were having a good time."

Tasha opened her eyes and sat up. "We had a lot of catching up to do. But no one would have minded if you'd said hello. It wouldn't hurt for you to meet other members of the..." she caught herself. "Community. You might need to work with a couple of them one day."

"Maybe another night. I'm ready to head home."

"Me too. I promised my mother I'd help her with some major housecleaning tomorrow. I was gone for over a year and she wants to spend time with me. This way we won't just sit and stare at each other. Then I'll have to head back to my assignment."

"What do you do?"

"Security. Both personal and institutional."

Jaime whistled. "You mean like a bodyguard? That's a tough business. I'm impressed.

"You sound like you know someone else who does this."

A shadow crossed his face. "Well, when you're in law enforcement you run into all types."

Tasha sensed there was more to the story but didn't want to push for details. She decided to change the subject. "So your hobby is endangered species of plants? How did you get interested in that?"

"It started out as a bet among me and a couple others taking the same college biology class."

"Hey guys, I found her!" Dmitri called from the doorway of the restaurant. "We wondered where you got to, Tasha. We're getting ready to take off and didn't think you'd leave without saying goodbye."

Regretfully, she stood. "I guess I should go with my friends. It was nice talking to you again. You can tell me the rest of the story next time."

Jaime rose, and she had to look up to see his face. "Tomorrow night? Supper?"

"Sorry, I'll be gone," Tasha said with real regret.

"That's too bad. Can we do it another time?"

"I'd like that." That was the story of her love life. Nothing ever worked out. But she wouldn't let it bother her. She had to focus on her job, and Jaime would have been a distraction.

She felt his eyes watching her back as she walked away. When she reached the other members of the pack, Dmitri asked "Who's the giant?"

Tasha had gotten used to the men of the Radferd pack who all seemed larger than life, so Jaime's height hadn't struck her as extraordinary. "That's the new game warden," she said. "He showed up when Elder Fenner and I ran into those poachers a few days ago."

"He seemed interested in you."

Tasha was not about to play that game. "Wouldn't matter," she said. "I'm not going to be around. I have a long-term commitment at Dot's company."

"You want me to ask Gavin to get you out of it?" Dmitri teased.

"No. I need to see it through. I've only scratched the surface, and my gut tells me it's only going to get worse. Dot's safety comes first."

"That bad, eh? Well, I'm sure Gavin picked you to handle it because he knows you're the best person for the job."

Tasha hoped he was right.

Housecleaning had never been Tasha's favorite activity, but she was glad to help her mother wash the walls of the front room and kitchen. Despite being in the best shape of her life, her arms and legs were tired by lunchtime. She'd taken the upper part of the walls while her mother had tackled the areas near the floor. When her mother suggested they take a break for lunch, Tasha was all for it.

She took the opportunity while her mother was in the kitchen to call Samantha to get an update. To her great relief, the answer was "nothing to report."

"But that's the pattern, isn't it?" Samantha asked. "I've been studying the records. There's an incident, then things quiet down for a week or so."

Tasha thought back to Elder Alejos' graphs. "I'd like to see that charted out. You know, what days of the week each incident occurred and the date. See if there's a pattern."

"Let me talk to Tanya. She's the computer whiz. I bet she can figure out a way to do that. When are you going to be back?"

"Late tonight." Tasha's mother came back to the dining area with a plate of sandwiches. "Gotta go, I'll call if anything changes."

"Everything all right?" her mother asked as Tasha tucked her phone back in her pocket.

"Yes. Just checking in with a friend."

After lunch Tasha got a call from the pack leader of the Radferds. He'd already spoken to Gavin and conveyed his willingness to deal with Chief. In fact, he was sending two of his personal guards to pick the miscreant up and take him back to Maine. The fact that both were women with the ability to kill a man with their bare hands seemed appropriate.

With her mother satisfied with the work they'd done, Tasha had time for another run—this one in human form. There was a distinct difference in the experiences, and sometimes Tasha craved the adrenalin rush that came with running on two feet instead of four.

She set a hard pace as soon as she hit the street and kept it up as she ran through the open field just past the last of the Victorian-style houses. She kept the punishing stride as she followed the well-worn path to the shooting range. By the time she reached the fence marking the boundary of the Fairwood holdings, she had to slow down, not only to dodge the trees and brambles, but to ease her labored breathing.

But still she kept running. Endurance was as important in human form as it was to her wolf form. She might not be able to outrun a wolf, but there weren't many humans who could match her for the combination of speed and distance.

Even when she reached the point where forward movement was more instinct that conscious thought, she didn't stop. At some point she met the pack members on patrol, acknowledging their presence with a quick nod and a brief wave of one hand.

When she turned the corner to trace the southern border, her mind noted her heavy breathing and the rapid pounding of her heart. And still she kept running, pushing herself. Sweat poured down her face, but she didn't break her concentration long enough to wipe it away.

A dim part of her knew when a wolf started following her, but it didn't speak to her, just ran in her wake, so she ignored it. She slowed somewhat when she could no longer breathe correctly, but kept going, one foot in front of the other. When she stumbled on a root, she lucked out and caught herself before falling.

"Enough," sent the wolf.

"Not yet," she answered. And kept going.

Her lungs screamed from the lack of oxygen, her eyes burned from the sweat streaming into them, and she could no longer feel her legs. She was past pain and moving from sheer force of will. But she wanted to go farther. Her goal was the meeting of the southern and western borders. And past that if she could hold on that long.

She fell again, this time hitting the ground hard enough to scrape the skin off her palms. As she struggled to find the energy to rise, a heavy weight dropped on top of her. *"Enough!"* roared the wolf.

"Just a little more," she pleaded. But the logical part of her brain told her she'd gone as far as her body would take her. It was time to rest.

The walk home took longer as she wobbled at each step. The wolf—she'd finally identified him as Dmitri—stayed alongside her until they reached her parents' house. She barely made it into the bathroom, stripping off her shoes, socks, and jeans before collapsing into the tub already filled with hot water. Dmitri must have alerted her mother before she made it home.

After a few minutes, she noticed the glass of water sitting on the corner of the tub. Lukewarm, not ice-cold, which was good. The first sip revealed it wasn't water at all, but a sports drink. Better, because she needed to replenish the minerals she'd sweated out.

Each time the water in the tub started to cool off, she drained some of it out and refilled it with hot water again. She removed her shirt and underwear without leaving the warmth of the water. Several times, her mother came in to verify she was all right and refill her glass. Thankfully, she didn't push and ask any questions, but Tasha caught her shaking her head each time.

When her body started to return to normal, Tasha pulled herself out of the tub and dried off. Hearing voices in the front room, she wrapped herself in several towels before slipping into her room to get dressed. She wasn't ashamed of her body—living in a shifter village, it was common to see someone nude after a change—but she didn't know who the visitors were. Common rules of politeness decreed she cover herself.

She finally identified the voices—Gavin and Elder Fenner. She stopped to fluff her still-wet hair, aware there was no way to hide her exhaustion from them. With a deep breath, she prepared herself for battle.

"Elder Fairwood, Elder Fenner," she said politely as she walked into the front room. There was no doubt in her mind that this was an official visit. They might yell at her, but at least their presence would stop her mother from fussing over her. Then the look on Gavin's face registered. Having her mother yell at her might have been a better choice.

"What the hell, Tasha?" The anger in his voice nearly broke through her calm facade. But it would take more than an angry alpha to break her.

NINETEEN

Tasha assumed the parade rest position. "Training," she explained. "Not every evade capture scenario allows time for a shift. Sometimes there is a need to get away as quickly as possible to reach a safe place to change."

"Don't preach to me, girl. I've seen combat, remember? Whatever game you're playing can't match the real thing." Gavin stood and thrust his finger into Tasha's chest.

She didn't move an inch. "I don't consider guarding your mate a game, Elder. It is a privilege. One I take seriously. And if that means I have to resort to extreme measures to make sure I'm up to the task, so be it. Besides, what I did today is minor compared to some of the training I received from the Radferds."

Elder Fenner drew in a sharp breath. "I didn't expect them to give you the full course when I sent you there."

"They wanted to go easy on me. I asked them not to. I found the physical demands the training put on me helped me overcome the psychological issues left by my abduction." The pain of the physical wounds she suffered had given her something to focus on besides her memories.

This time the intake of breath came from her mother. "I thought it was to give you time to recover from the silver poisoning."

"That's what I wanted you all to think. The scars went a lot deeper than that. For the first time in my life, I realized I was vulnerable. I'm a wolf, you're not supposed to be able to tie me to a chair and shoot me full of chemicals." Tasha shrugged. "I know better now."

"You should have been a teacher or something!" her mother burst out.

"Sorry Mom, that's not the way this works. I chose this line of work, and now I'm one of the best. You should be proud of me." No matter how many times she and her mother had discussed it, Tasha had never been able to convince her mother that her interest in security was more than a passing fancy. Or perhaps her mother just refused to accept the truth.

To Tasha's surprise, Elder Fenner chuckled. "I told you she was good, Elder Fairwood. There she is, solid as a rock, standing up to you, me, *and* her mother. I don't doubt she's every bit as good as she thinks she is, if not better."

Gavin lowered his finger and took two steps away. She'd have a bruise in the morning, but the praise from Fenner made it worthwhile.

"It is my responsibility to look after the good of the pack and its members," Gavin said slowly. "In the future, if you're going to put yourself through such strenuous training, alert someone first, and take a companion."

"That was the point. Once I go back on duty at

Lapahie, I won't be able to continue training. It would be hazardous for me allow myself to be that vulnerable—for both Dot and myself."

"You plan to return tonight?"

"If I'm not needed here. Thank you for allowing Tanya to stick around and help Samantha, but I'm the expert and getting security up to par there is my responsibility."

"You won't be riding your motorcycle, will you?" her mother asked.

"That's the plan. I want to get back before the bad weather moves in."

"The newest prediction is for the storm to hit tomorrow." Her mother had studied meteorology and acted as the unofficial weather forecaster for the pack.

"Then I'd better take off now." Although Tasha said it nonchalantly, she wasn't sure she was up to manhandling her bike all the way to Lapahie after pushing her body to its limits earlier.

"Or we can issue you a company car. I should have thought of it earlier. It's about time for you to put the bike away for winter anyway," Gavin said.

Tasha hated the idea of swapping her motorcycle for one of the boring generic vehicles the pack maintained, but there would be no winning that argument. She'd won enough battles for one afternoon.

The trip to Lapahie seemed to take twice as long as normal. Between the late start, the unfamiliar vehicle, her weariness, and the different route she'd opted to take, Tasha regretted the decision to not wait until the morning. It was a good thing she'd taken the company car. Her body wouldn't have handled the trip on her motorcycle.

The guards at the northern gate had apparently been warned to expect her because she'd barely pulled up to the gate before it opened for her. Another time, she might have scolded the young men for not verifying her identity first, but she decided she didn't have the energy for it. She didn't even bother getting their names.

The storm clouds rolling in from the west made the night seem even darker than normal, bearing the promise of an early snow. Tasha had her window down, hoping the cold air would help her stay awake. When she caught the first trace of smoke, she assumed that someone had been smoking in the car, never wondering why she hadn't caught the scent sooner. When the odor got stronger, she pulled over to the side of the road, thinking the car had developed a problem.

But when she got out to pop open the hood and take a look at the engine, she realized it wasn't a mechanical issue at all. No, that was wood smoke. Pine, most likely.

Tasha tried to remember if she'd driven past a mile marker on this lonely stretch of road—something to use as a landmark to direct work crews to if this was a forest fire. Even with the recent rain, with all the dead leaves and branches on the ground, it was possible that one had started from a discarded cigarette. Few shifters smoked, but there were always the exceptions.

She locked the car and using her nose as a guide, went to explore. If it was something small, she'd put it out before it grew. With her body still not recovered from the afternoon's exertions, she took her time navigating the unfamiliar terrain.

The glow surprised her. It looked like light gleaming through a glass window. No one had ever mentioned a home this far removed from the rest of the village, so Tasha immediately went into alert status. Crouching, moving from one tree trunk to another, she crept closer.

Although the structure was crumbling, the rough cabin still had most of its four walls and a roof. Smoke rose from its stone chimney and the light in the window appeared to come from a lantern. A figure moved around inside, and Tasha crept closer to see if she recognized him. At least, she assumed it was a him based on his size.

Before getting too close, she opened her mind to try and catch any stray thoughts. She was met with silence. Whoever was inside, they were either not a shifter or had a strong ability to hide their thoughts.

Tasha maneuvered herself into a position where she could see most of the interior of the cabin without being seen herself. The man seemed to have settled into one spot, but it was a corner hidden from her vantage point. Cautiously, she slunk to another tree closer to the cabin.

The man was lying on a cot, his hands tucked behind his head, staring at the roof. Or maybe there was a hole over him and he was star watching. Not that there were any stars to be seen through the thick cloud cover. With the light between her and him, she still couldn't get enough of a look to identify him.

She wanted to take a picture of him and send it to Samantha and Dot to see if either of them knew the man. He might be a member of the Free Wolves seeking some quiet time for self-reflection. If so, she'd sneak away and not bother him. The camera on her cell phone, although not the best, would serve the purpose.

Used to waiting for the right moment, Tasha climbed a nearby oak tree and stretched out along a branch. The added height gave her a different perspective of the interior, but still didn't give her a good view of its occupant. She wondered if there was a way to lure him to the doorway without giving away her presence.

The wind shifted, blowing smoke from the fireplace directly into her face. She fought the urge to cough, not wanting to give her hiding place up. At least the smoke would cover her own scent should the air currents change direction again. She swallowed several times, trying to calm the burning of her nose and throat, wishing she had a mint to suck on.

Her muscles, strained to their maximum earlier in the day, soon protested the forced stillness. When they started to cramp, Tasha tried to work out the knots by tightening and loosening each muscle in turn with only the slightest of movements. The ploy relieved the spasms, but soon she'd need to give up her post.

Finally, however, he got up, glanced at his watch, and stretched. He threw several pieces of firewood on the fire, and Tasha wondered if he thought he'd be able to stay warm in the drafty structure. He walked to the door, paused and looked around, and strode into the woods. The sound of liquid hitting a rock told Tasha what he was doing. She worked her phone out of her jacket pocket and set the volume to silent.

As he returned to the cabin, she got a clear view of

his face. At least, clear to her *other* vision. She took several pictures, but assumed they'd be too dark to see his features well. He stopped by the door to pick up several more pieces of firewood, and when he straightened, his face was fully illuminated for a second.

And that was all Tasha needed. He strode back to the doorway and glanced at his watch again, then returned to the cot. After waiting for him to settle back onto the thin mattress, she dropped to the ground. With a grace that belied her aching legs, she melted back into the woods.

She didn't go very far, just far enough to get a signal for her phone. She tapped the buttons to forward the last picture to Samantha, with the simple message—"Do you know this man?"

While she waited for an answer she stretched, first reaching for a branch above, then dropping her arms to touch the ground beside her toes. She'd only completed two toe touches before her phone vibrated with the response. "No, why?"

"He's holed up in a shack somewhere between the north entrance and the village. Hang tight, I'll get back to you," Tasha texted.

The next message went to Dot and, for backup, Gavin. But if one of them was out of range this time of night, they probably both were. She did some more stretches while she waited to keep her overworked muscles limber. She longed to sneak back to keep an eye on the cabin, but she couldn't do that and get an answer. So she waited impatiently as the seconds and then minutes ticked by.

But eventually an answer came from Gavin. He typed it in all capitols, as if to emphasize its importance. "ARNOLD CHOATE. DO NOT APPROACH! REPEAT! DO NOT APPROACH! WE ARE ON THE WAY!" Then a second text came in "What is your location?"

Wasn't that the name of the old pack member who'd escaped from police custody? The one who had been involved in Dot's kidnapping? Tasha was in Maine when that happened, and she remembered the guilt she'd felt knowing that she hadn't been there to protect her friend. What was he doing on Lapahie holdings? "Old cabin between the north entrance and the village," she responded. "The car is parked on the road nearby." She fought back the urge to run back and challenge Arnold to combat.

The answer came back immediately. "I know the spot. Hang tight."

It would take far too long for Gavin and whatever army he assembled to get to her location. Her reinforcements were only a text away.

The message went to both Samantha and Tanya. "Target identified. Arnold Choate. Bring guns. Don't tell anyone."

"We're on our way."

Tasha figured it would take a minimum of fifteen minutes for them to arrive. That gave her time to sneak back to the cabin and renew her surveillance. If Choate was waiting for someone, she wanted to catch his accomplice in the act.

There wasn't time to climb another tree and get settled in, so Tasha settled for picking a spot that gave her a view of the door. She wasn't concerned with tracking Arnold's movements any longer. Her priority was waiting for his anticipated guest. And hoping that Tanya and Samantha didn't scare his guest away.

TWENTY

Armed with her favorite rifle, tactical knife and the pistol now tucked into a shoulder harness, Tasha sat silent under the protective shelter of a pine. Its branches caught most of the light snow falling, and she stayed relatively dry. The temperature was dropping, and she tucked her hands into her pockets to keep them warm.

She, Tanya and Samantha formed a triangle around the cabin. Samantha was up a tree, a spot Tasha helped her choose. Tanya, having trained with Elder Fenner, found her own hiding hole. As a precaution Tasha insisted on no communication by either cell phone or thought so she had only her own musings to keep her company.

It was nearly midnight, and Arnold was still awake. He occasionally threw another log or two on the fire, then check his watch, reinforcing her belief he was waiting for someone. Every now and then, he'd open the door and stare outside, as if that would make his guest show up. Each time, she shrunk a little further into the tree's shadow so he'd have no chance to catch a glimpse of her.

She sensed their approach first and sent a quick tendril of thought to Tanya and Samantha. "Reinforcements have arrived. Stay tight. I'll meet them."

Gavin, Dmitri and Elder Fenner she'd expected. Jaime she hadn't. Dot she'd expected, but she wasn't there. Tasha raised a questioning eyebrow Gavin's direction.

"We were at The Pub. He was too. He's law enforcement so I invited him along." Gavin responded. *"Dot is on her way to Lapahie Headquarters with a full contingent of guards."*

Tasha nodded. In a whisper, so Jaime was included, she explained the situation.

"So what's the plan?" Elder Fenner asked softly. He and the others were all fully armed. "This is your operation."

"I want to intercept his contact—or contacts—if possible. After that we'll deal with Choate. Dmitri, you backup Tanya. If you circle to the right, she's at a point near the southwest corner of the cabin. Elder Fenner, if you'll back up Samantha please? She's city-bred and out of her comfort zone. She's up a tree at the southeast corner." Tasha pointed to Gavin and Jaime. "You two will be with me." Her hiding spot would be crowded with the addition of two large men, but it had the best position to spot potential trouble first.

At least the additions made her wait warmer because she ended up squeezed between them. Something about Jaime unsettled her. She tried to convince herself that it was because she didn't know his skill level and how he'd react in a crisis. Now was not the time to be thinking of anything but the safety of those she was responsible for.

"By the way, we moved your car." Gavin sent. *"Dmitri brought a spare set of keys for it."*

"Thanks. I was worried about it giving our presence away, but I didn't want to take the time to go back and hide it." Tasha answered. She felt bad about keeping Jaime out of the conversation, but unless it was an emergency, verbal communication was a risk. She glanced his direction to see how he was doing. He looked as if he'd settled in for a long wait, and she guessed he'd done this before.

Tasha had to give credit where credit was due. Gavin heard it first. He bumped Tasha's shoulder with his and lifted his chin in the direction he wanted her to look. Tasha craned her neck to see around him and made out a figure stumbling towards the cabin. She, in turn, touched Jaime on the knee to get his attention.

"What's the plan?" he whispered.

"I want to see how this plays out," she answered quietly. "Gavin, will you please update the others?"

Gavin nodded his agreement, and his face went blank for a moment.

"What was that?" Jaime asked.

"I'll explain later." Tasha put her finger to her lips indicating the need for silence as the figure, another man, got closer. An overstuffed pack on his back seemed to be responsible for his poor posture and footwork. He was leaning forward under its weight, and Tasha wasn't able to get a look at his face. She couldn't put her finger on why he seemed familiar.

The man reached the door of the cabin and knocked. When Arnold answered it, he held a revolver in his hand. That answered a nagging question. "He's armed," she whispered, and her companions nodded. Gavin's face momentarily went blank as he passed the information along.

The new man bowed slightly and Arnold slipped the gun into his waistband and held out his hand. The man bent more and kissed it. Tasha drew in her breath at seeing the long-discarded, human show of respect for one's pack leader. Gavin started to get up, and Tasha put her hand on his shoulder to restrain him. *"Not now. Your time will come,"* she sent.

With the door closed behind them, even with her *other* hearing, Tasha had a hard time listening to the conversation inside the cabin. "I'm getting in closer. You wait here," she murmured before moving into a crouch. Once out from under the branches of the pine, she moved in a ragged zig-zag fashion from tree to tree until she was within hearing distance of the conversation.

"With the coyote gone, your job should be easier," Arnold said.

"Now I have two nosy women in my way," the man replied. "One of them's a pushover, but the other has me worried."

"What kind of wolf are you that a woman can intimidate you?" Arnold sneered.

"She's not a normal female, she's a freak of nature or a government experiment or something, Elder Choate," the man replied. "Hell, she has more muscles then most of the weaklings they call men. Not more than me or you, of course," he added hastily. "And those blue eyes of her—no proper wolf has blue eyes."

Tasha recognized the voice. It was Roy, the young

man she'd confronted on her first full day at Lapahie. She wondered how long he'd been working with Arnold. Was he also a Choate?

"If you can't handle her, I can choose another second."

Tasha almost laughed out loud. If Roy was Arnold's second, he was scrapping the bottom of the barrel already.

"Have you made any progress on getting any closer to the bitch?" Arnold asked.

"Every time she's here, she's surrounded by her admiring fans," Roy said with disgust. "I tried to get put on duty with her the night she made a big show of running patrol, but it didn't work out."

The sound of a fist meeting flesh followed by a grunt made Tasha wince. She wondered if Roy was still standing.

"She ran patrol, and you didn't tell me? Are you stupid? That was the perfect opportunity to snatch her!"

"I'm sorry, Elder, I couldn't get away," Roy whimpered. "The whole place was on alert after I destroyed the classroom like you ordered. It was bad timing."

Tasha couldn't decide if the next blow was a kick or another punch. "Don't think you have any chance of claiming her," Arnold roared. "She is mine by right of challenge. And once I have mated with her, whether she wants it or not, I will run the business as well. If she lives, she will learn to obey me. And all those bitches who think they are free will learn otherwise."

"You promised me first choice of those you don't want," Roy whined.

"The deal still stands, although you are pushing

your boundaries. Don't fail me on this. Bring me the Lapahie bitch and I will honor my word."

She'd heard enough. Or maybe too much. The "her" Arnold kept referring to was Dot. Tasha had no idea how she was going to contain Gavin when she shared the conversation.

She crawled back into the cover of the pine and sat facing the two men, wondering how many guns Gavin carried. He'd use whatever was handy to kill Arnold and Roy and protect his mate. Jaime, as an officer of the law, would be obliged to arrest Gavin for murder. Not a good situation.

"Well?" Gavin asked.

Tasha took a deep breath. "The second man is no threat," she said. "I can handle him with one hand tied behind my back in either human or wolf form."

"And Arnold?"

This is where it got tough. "You must promise me that after I tell you, you will sit here and not move. I know you're my pack leader, but this is my mission and you answer to me."

"That bad?" Jaime asked quietly.

Tasha nodded.

"What did he say?" Gavin demanded.

"It appears his plan is to restore the glory of the Choate pack, as if it ever existed," Tasha said dryly. "And take over Lapahie Enterprises."

"He can't do that."

"Unless he forces Dot to marry him. And he doesn't care how he does it or if she survives."

Jaime moved faster than Tasha imagined possible for a non-shifter, and clasped his arms around Gavin's chest. Gavin struggled to throw him off, and Tasha took the opportunity to snatch the pistol from his hand. *"Quiet! Do you want to give our position away?"*

"I let him live once. Now he's a dead man."

"I agree. But let's figure out how to do it without you ending up in prison for murder."

They left Tanya and Dmitri to monitor the cabin while they gathered on the road to develop a plan. Gavin paced, with Elder Fenner alongside him, away from the others. Tasha suspected a string of non-verbal communication between the two of them. Hopefully her mentor could calm down their pack leader.

"I want to capture Roy," Tasha said. "Drill him for information. Find out who else he's working with and if he's responsible for the missing money."

"Missing money?" Samantha asked.

Tasha nodded. "Someone's been stealing from Lapahie Enterprises and the school. I doubt that Roy has the know-how to do it, but I don't like making assumptions."

"Can't we capture this Arnold fellow and turn him over to the local sheriff?" Jaime asked.

"Yes, but if he escapes again, we'll be right back where we started with Dot's life in danger. Gavin's not going to let that happen. I can take him out with one shot. Better for me to go to prison than Gavin."

"There's got to be a different way," Jaime said.

"There is, but you aren't going to like it. It's the old-fashioned way, at least to us wolves. Gavin calls Arnold out in a challenge, and they fight wolf to wolf.

Gavin has already beat Arnold once, and he can do it again." The story of Gavin's rescue of Dot after Arnold and his cohorts abducted her had spread even to the packs in Maine.

"As game warden, I know better than to interfere in a battle between two wolves. Especially as I'm not equipped with any tranquilizing darts."

Tasha nodded. "If one wolf dies, that's just the way it is. Law enforcement certainly won't waste any time investigating a fight between two wolves. If you don't want to be involved, we'll arrange transportation for you to go home."

Jaime glanced down the road where Gavin and Elder Fenner still walked side by side. "Will he agree?"

"I'm willing to bet he's already reached the same conclusion. And is ready to make it happen."

TWENTY-ONE

Roy's capture was almost a letdown. Against Tasha's better judgment, she let Gavin have a hand in it as a way to release his pent-up frustration. She wanted him to have a cool head for the eventual battle with Arnold.

The setup was simple enough. The path that Roy used to get to the cabin was marked by deep slashes in the tree trunks. Tasha and Gavin picked out hiding spots close to where it met the road. She hoped Roy was drunk enough not to spot her among the sparse foliage.

Dmitri and Tanya confirmed that Arnold and Roy had been drinking. There'd been more than one six pack among the supplies Roy brought. While Arnold had encouraged Roy's drinking, he'd only had two beers, not enough to make a difference in the coming battle.

Tasha didn't need Gavin's mental warning. She heard Roy stumbling his way down the path long before she could see him. At least he wasn't singing, like the drunkards in old movies.

When he was almost even with her hiding place,

she stepped out in front of him. "Boo," she said quietly. Then Gavin had one hand over Roy's mouth and an arm around his chest. "Surprise," Gavin whispered.

Roy put up token resistance, but there wasn't much he could do with one arm pinned to his side and his feet dangling in mid-air. Tasha stood in front of him, her arms crossed and shaking her head. "Roy," she said, "I'm disappointed in you. For being so smart, you really can be dumb. You think Arnold Choate can be trusted? He eats little boys like you for dessert." She nodded, and Gavin dumped the young man on the ground and sat on him. But not before some well-placed kicks showed Gavin meant business.

With rope Elder Fenner had tossed in the back of Gavin's jeep, they tied up their prisoner. Tasha took too much pleasure in sliding the point of her knife down Roy's face and stomach before cutting a strip off his expensive dress shirt to use as a gag. Once he was trussed up, Gavin picked him up and carried him up to the road, dumping him alongside one of the vehicles.

"Where are you taking him?" Jaime asked.

"To Lapahie Headquarters. Dot and her Board of Directors can figure out what to do with him. If they were a typical pack, he'd be forced out. Whatever they decide to do with him will have to wait until I'm done with him." Tasha bent over and drew her knife blade across Roy's throat, leaving no more than a scratch. His eyes widened, and she added, "I'm going to make him talk first."

She straightened, deliberately turned her back on the captive, and winked at Jaime. His expression changed from a look of tension to one of amusement. He winked back. "Don't go too easy on the rat."

Tasha bit her lip to keep from laughing. "Oh, he'll be begging for mercy soon enough."

"Cut the crap," Gavin sent. *"There's serious business to take care of."*

Spoil sport, Tasha thought, but she understood what was going through Gavin's mind. They still had to take care of Arnold.

"Let me sneak in and slit his throat and be done with it," Tasha suggested for Gavin's hearing only. They'd left Jaime and Samantha guarding Roy and the rest huddled near the cabin where Arnold now appeared to be sleeping.

"No. This is my fight."

"How do you want to do this?" Fenner asked quietly.

"Me and Dmitri go in first, with guns. You and Tanya go next. Once Arnold is disarmed and restrained, Gavin can come in and challenge him. He'll know he's a dead man either way, so he'll try to escape. If he runs as a man, a well-placed shot will take him down. If he runs as a wolf," Tasha shrugged her shoulders, "it's anybody's game."

"No, it's not. Sorry, Tasha, you are no longer in charge. I'm taking over. This is my battle, not yours," Gavin said firmly.

"Is this wise?" Tasha sent to Fenner.

"No, but we won't be able to change his mind."

"Whatever you say, Elder Fairwood. I'm yours to command. What's your plan?"

Gavin's lips narrowed to a tight line. "I want to lure him out here. A couple of howling wolves should do the trick."

"I don't know how he'd react," Dmitri said. "He tried to cheat during his fight with you. If he's that much of a coward, he might just crawl under the cot and hide."

Tasha hadn't heard that piece of gossip. How low could a man be? Maybe slitting Arnold's throat was going too easy on him.

A whisper of movement had her reaching for her gun. The other members of the group, except for Gavin, copied her action. His face went blank, and Tasha wondered who he was communicating with. "Damn that woman," he muttered, but he had a trace of a smile on his face. "Put away your weapons. We're getting company."

The five figures glided silently through the pre-dawn mist, flitting among the trees. Tasha picked up on the leader's scent before identifying the face.

"You didn't think you were going to keep me out of the action, did you?" Dot asked.

The lonesome howl of a wolf sent birds flying into the sunrise. It was answered by a short bark and then another wail. Tasha saw the man in the cabin stir uneasily, but not wake.

Then the three wolves howled as one, and he threw his blanket onto the floor, reached for the gun under his pillow, and rose. With his back pressed against the wall, he slid his way to the door. He kicked the door open and peered into the forest.

"Who's there?" he called into the pale light.

A sudden blow from an unseen fist knocked the gun from his outstretched hands, and he was pulled outside. A circle of wolves interspersed with armed humans surrounded him. One man, arms crossed, shared the circle with him.

"You might remember me," Gavin said. "I'm the big, bad wolf."

"I'm flattered," Arnold sneered as he looked around, "that you think it will take all of you to haul me back to the authorities. Who gets to collect the reward?"

"You misunderstand our intentions," Dot said sweetly. "But then your ego was always bigger than your brain. We have no intention of turning you over to the police."

Arnold paled. "Oh, so you're here to sign over Choate enterprises to me and become my mate?" he blustered. "What makes you think I'd have you, bitch?"

Gavin didn't move, but Tasha noted the tendons in his neck tightened. "I can't say I care much for his attitude, Elder Fairwood. He's as bad as the stories make him out to be. Are you sure you want to waste your time with him? I'd be glad to take care of him for you." Tasha drew her knife from its sheath and ran her finger along its edge. "Yup, still sharp. I bet it would take his over-inflated head off that scrawny little neck in one stroke."

"Careful, Tasha," Fenner sent.

"Don't worry. I know what I'm doing."

"And that is?"

"Distracting him, getting him angry. If he's not thinking rationally, he'll be more likely to make a mistake. And it'll give Gavin time to cool down."

"Look at the itsy bitsy girl playing at being a

soldier. Where'd you get your gun, honey, out of a cereal box?" Arnold leered at her. "You should come play in my bed."

Calmly, Tasha looked him up and down. "Nope. I don't need another set of balls to add to my trophy case. Yours don't look big enough to bother with anyway."

"You wouldn't know what to do with a real man."

Tasha yawned and put her knife away. "Whatever. Besides, there won't be enough of you left to mess with once Elder Fairwood gets done with you."

"I should be scared of a man who has a girl fight his battles?"

"Enough talk," Gavin said. "Arnold Choate, I'm calling you out on the charges of abduction, torture, vandalism, theft, and impersonating a pack leader. The challenge is wolf to wolf. The time and place is here and now. If you choose not to accept, I'll leave you to the tender mercies of my second."

The challenge was made in the traditional terms. Tasha waited to see if Arnold would accept in the standard fashion or attempt to run.

"It's customary that my second be present," Arnold said. "So we'll have to put this off until later."

"I don't think so. In fact, the one you named your second last night should arrive in a minute or two." Gavin interlocked his fingers and brought his hands to his chin. "We can wait."

As quickly as Samantha and Jaime arrived, they must have already been on their way. Roy was on his feet, but unsteady, and Jaime was supporting him and pushing him along at the same time.

"You've brought a human to a wolf fight?" Arnold asked.

"An impartial observer. And one that can arrest you if necessary," Gavin answered. "Now are you ready? Or are you going to try to weasel out of the fight?"

"Which one of these losers is your second? I need to know who to drag your body to after I kill you," Arnold taunted.

Tasha glanced at Dmitri. As Gavin's best friend, surely Gavin would have bestowed that honor on him. But Dmitri wasn't a Fairwood by blood, having come from a different pack. That could cause problems.

"I have neglected that duty," Gavin said. "I need to remedy the situation. Dmitri, Tasha, I'm aware neither of you cares for the politics of the pack. Will you share the duty and support each other in supporting me? At least until Dot and I have a child?"

A hiss of surprise rose from the others in the circle. While the idea of two seconds wasn't unknown, it was rare. And it was unheard of for a female to be in the position. A pack leader's second was considered to be his heir. It was impossible for her to question Gavin's motives in the situation without causing him to lose face. No matter what she'd told Gavin before, a part of her was thrilled.

"Of course, Elder Fairwood," she said quietly. "It would be my pleasure."

"Naturally, Elder," Dmitri agreed.

Tasha avoided looking at Dmitri. They'd need to have a discussion later.

"Isn't that touching? It takes two puny Fairwoods to be the equal of my second," Arnold laughed.

Arnold's comments were starting to annoy Tasha, but she shoved her feelings aside. Trash talk was part of the challenge. She couldn't take it seriously.

Gavin must have been tired of it as well. He took off his coat and tossed it aside. "Let's do this."

The field of battle was marked using sticks and rocks from the ground. No rule decreed that the combatants stay within the confines of the boundaries and Tasha anticipated they'd be erased quickly. The longer the battle raged the more likely it was that it would cover a large territory.

Two naked men faced each other. Despite the falling snow, neither shivered. Tasha and Dmitri stood on either side of Roy so he'd be unable to interfere with the battle. She doubted that he had any desire to but she wasn't taking any chances. Everyone waited for one thing—the sun to rise over the horizon.

TWENTY~TWO

Arnold shifted first—and he shifted too soon, based on Tasha's viewpoint. But by the time he leaped and lunged towards Gavin's throat, Gavin had already moved. All Arnold got was a mouthful of air. Then, faster than Tasha had ever seen it done, Gavin made his shift. One moment he was a magnificent man, the next a marvelous wolf. Tasha had seen him in his wolf form many times before, but she didn't remember him being this large or this dangerous.

Arnold landed roughly but spun around and attacked again. Gavin met him head-on, and they bit and snapped at each other before separating, growling as they backed off. Gavin appeared to be unhurt except for a scratch or two, but Arnold's nose was bleeding.

They took spots at opposite ends of the battle zone. Arnold paced back and forth, keeping his eye on his opponent, while Gavin picked up his right paw and licked it, seemingly unconcerned. "I don't remember him being this big," Jaime whispered in her ear. Tasha had been so focused on the fight she hadn't noticed him standing beside her. "But then, I was freaked out at the moment, so I could be wrong."

"No, you're right. I've heard stories about it happening when a male defends his mate. I figured they were just the result of someone's imagination working overtime."

In a sudden burst of flying fur, Arnold dashed at Gavin. Gavin continued licking his paw, and Tasha worried that Arnold had caught him off guard. At the last possible moment, Gavin whirled on three paws and bit into Arnold's flank.

But that gave Arnold an opening to bite into Gavin's hind leg—or try anyway. Gavin must have anticipated the move because he released Arnold's flank, bounded away, and spit out a clump of fur. He'd bit, not deep enough to cause a major injury, but enough to tell Arnold who was in charge.

Only Arnold wasn't getting the message. He attacked again, this time trying to bite into Gavin's shoulder. Gavin stuck out one of his massive paws before Arnold reached him, and the smaller wolf tripped over it. With Arnold on the ground, Gavin chose to walk back to his end of the arena. In the process, he stepped right on his opponent, one paw landing squarely at the spot where Arnold had been bit.

"Gavin's playing with him," Jaime said, drawing in a deep breath.

Tasha agreed. She didn't know what Gavin was trying to accomplish. Normally during a fight, the combatants taunted each other and sometimes the audience. If any of that was happening, it was strictly between Gavin and Arnold. No stray thoughts leaked out to the observers.

The group of spectators was getting larger. It appeared word about the fight had leaked out to the

Lapahie village, and people were coming in three's and four's to watch, making Tasha nervous. Pink stripes on the cheek might only be camouflage instead of a declaration of one's loyalties.

Her instinct was to circulate among the crowd hoping to pick up bits of conversation or body language that would point to potential suspects. But as one of Gavin's seconds, she couldn't leave her position. Elder Fenner stood near Dot, and his all-too-casual posture told Tasha he was in heightened guard status. She caught his eye and sent him a message. *"The crowd is making me nervous. Do you have anyone to monitor it?"*

"Working on it," he replied.

With that off her mind, she returned her attention to the fight. It was at a standstill as Arnold returned to pacing out of Gavin's easy reach. She wondered how long Gavin's patience would hold out. Or was the humiliation of Arnold part of his plan?

Gavin made the next move. He marched along the edge of the circle, stopping to nuzzle Dot before continuing his trek. With every few steps he took, Arnold moved a few steps the opposite direction, maintaining a steady distance between them.

Without warning, Gavin tore across the middle of the battlefield, aiming his body at his opponent. Arnold swung around on two paws and threw himself towards his enemy. But Gavin paused short of the expected meeting point and stepped aside. Arnold, unable to stop his forward momentum, skidded to a halt a few feet past Gavin.

A chant started in the crowd, "Lapahie, Lapahie," but then changed to "Fairwood, Lapahie, Fairwood, Lapahie."

The chorus angered Arnold. He snapped and growled at a little girl at the front mimicking the crowd. Her mother snatched her up and several men moved in front of them.

That was the breaking point for Gavin. He raised his head and howled. The sound sent shivers down Tasha's spine. Other howls joined his, and Tasha had to fight the urge to shift and add her voice to the others.

Arnold studied the crowd as if looking for a friend or a path to escape. All around the edges, the strongest men moved to the front, standing shoulder to shoulder. The moment of distraction gave Gavin an opening.

Since she was keeping an eye on Arnold, Tasha missed Gavin's move. She caught the blur of a massive black form hurtling through the short space and landing firmly on top of Arnold, smashing him to the ground. Gavin bit at his ears, and Arnold yipped with pain as he struggled to get up. But Gavin was far heavier, and Arnold's efforts were futile

The biting moved to the upper neck. Like a mother wolf getting ready to carry her cub to a new den, Gavin grabbed loose skin and pulled. Arnold's head jerked and he whined. A few members of the audience laughed uncomfortably.

Gavin shook his head a few times, pulling Arnold's forequarters around. When he grew tired of the game, he simply walked away. He turned to face Arnold and sat, daring Arnold to charge.

Arnold took the bait. He attacked Gavin with open mouth, trying to reach anything he might be able to bite, dashing in out of Gavin's reach, twisting and turning, desperately searching for a vulnerability.

Gavin matched his movements, writhing as quickly as a snake. For every bite Arnold landed, Gavin returned two.

The battle moved to the edge of the impromptu arena and the crowd backed away and fell silent. All that was heard was the growls and yips of the two enemies. Tasha wondered why Gavin didn't put an end to it—he was capable of it. Was he putting on a show or did drawing out the battle serve another purpose?

The wolves broke apart, panting heavily. Arnold staggered and withdrew as far from Gavin as he could get. There was no doubt who'd been on the losing side of the exchange—Arnold's ears and sides were tattered and bleeding in too many spots for Tasha to count. Gavin had fewer scrapes, but several were deep enough to leave scars.

Arnold licked his wounds while again studying the gathered group. When his eyes strayed to Dot and settled there for a second too long, Tasha's instinct screamed a warning. *"Watch Roy,"* she sent to Dmitri. She backed up, pushing her way into the bystanders gathered behind her. She moved cautiously, trying to stay unnoticed, squirming her way towards the spot where Dot and Fenner watched the fight.

A hiss rose from those around her so Tasha knew the action had picked up again, but she had a mission. Part of the responsibility of a second was guarding the leader's mate. Her gut told her that her services would soon be needed.

Fenner acknowledged her with a nod when she pushed her way to stand on the other side of Dot. Gavin sprawled on top of Arnold again, only this time Arnold lay on his back and Gavin's mouth gripped the soft underside of his neck. All Gavin needed to do was bite a little harder and Arnold's throat would be ripped out, resulting in his rapid death.

"Mercy!" Arnold screamed so everyone could hear.

Tasha caught her breath. Tradition demanded that Gavin release his enemy and turn him over to the Council for punishment. But she was sure that her leader was battling with his animal longings to put an end to his enemy once and for all.

The chant of "Lapahie! Fairwood!" picked up again, but it was interspersed with the cries of "Kill him!" Gavin's whole body shuddered, and his mouth tightened its grip.

Arnold screamed again, but his mental voice sounded weak. *"Mercy! I demand Council judgment!"*

He'd taken the coward's way out. If Arnold survived his injuries, no pack in the country would ever let him join. He'd signed his own death sentence because young wolves would seek him out as fair game to fight to prove themselves. Eventually, one would end his life.

As the crowd booed, Gavin reluctantly loosened his grip and backed away. *"Who will deliver him to the Council?"* he asked. He scanned the crowd as did Tasha, but no one volunteered for the responsibility. No one wanted to protect the loser.

Arnold had other plans. He pulled himself off the ground, blood spilling from the wounds covering his body. He gathered himself on unsteady legs and stared defiantly at the crowd. Something about his stance made Tasha uncomfortable, and she instinctively reached for the knife that hung at her side.

Still, it came as a surprise when he launched himself into the air. *"The bitch is mine!"* She will die with me!"

His wounds slowed him down, and Tasha moved faster. Instead of finding Dot's throat, Arnold found a knife in his stomach. Even as his claws tore through Tasha's shirt, her weapon cut a path upwards to his heart. When he fell back to the ground, he writhed once and then stopped moving, his eyes open and staring blankly at the now-bright sky.

"Well, that's the end of that," Tasha said with a calmness she didn't feel into the stunned silence surrounding her. She started to swipe the blade of her knife on the leg of her pants to clean it and realized she was covered in blood. Reluctantly, she slid the weapon back into its sheath. She'd clean it later.

Only vaguely aware of the many voices that screamed for her attention, she turned to Dot. "Are you all right, Miss Lapahie?" she asked politely.

"I need to be asking you that question," Dot said quietly.

"I'll take care of her," Fenner said, shoving Dot aside. "You go see to your mate." He grabbed Tasha by the arm and pushed her to the ground. She didn't resist. The adrenalin rush was wearing off and the pain from the multiple wounds on her chest was making itself known.

"Can I get a clean cloth and water?" he called out. "Where did he get you?" he added.

"It's just a couple of scratches. Nothing major. I suspect most of the blood is his." Tasha twisted to see Arnold's body, but it had already been dragged away.

"There's an old sand pit nearby they'll to use to dispose of the remains. I heard a discussion during the fight." Fenner splashed water in her face and rubbed it with someone's scarf. She felt like a cub being washed by its mother, he was so gentle.

She didn't protest when he sliced her shirt open and pulled it off her chest. But she couldn't stop a moan from escaping when he poured water on her wounds. She closed her eyes so he wouldn't see the pain reflected in them.

"That's no scratch," he said. "We need to get that looked at. How many others are there?"

"How many claws does a wolf have?"

"If that's your idea of a joke, you'd better not give up your day job." Tasha opened her eyes to see a fully-dressed Gavin hovering over her. "Dr. Tracy is on standby. Is she in good enough condition to take home?"

"I think so," Elder Fenner said.

"Of course I am." Tasha put her hands on the ground and gave herself a push with every intention of standing. Instead, she found herself being lifted by two strong arms. She struggled to free herself, not wanting to display any weakness.

"Hey, take it easy," Fenner said. "I'm your taxi."

Tasha gazed up into his worried eyes. She knew how to pick her battles, and she wouldn't win this one. "I don't seem to have any money on me. Do I need to worry about how I'm going to pay the fare?" She wanted to see him smile.

"We'll worry about that later." His expression didn't change, and as he carried her up the hill towards the vehicles, she concentrated on not allowing him to see the pain shooting through her with every jarring step.

TWENTY-THREE

The forced time off was anything but relaxing. Tasha wasn't used to having people fussing over her and didn't like it. Between her mother and Dr. Tracy, Tasha didn't have much time to be alone. Not with the constant stream of well-wishers who dropped by to gush over her. After getting released from the pack's medical clinic, she'd been confined to her mother's house. She wasn't allowed to get out and run in either wolf or human form, and the inactivity made her antsy.

Dot and Gavin were daily visitors. So far, they hadn't discussed the fight, but she was just waiting for Gavin to tell her that naming her as his second was part of the show. Sure, he'd find another way to reward her for her performance, but it was insane to believe that he'd consider a female for his personal bodyguard. That would create such a huge turmoil among the pack he'd never be able to lead properly again.

She talked to Samantha and Tanya every day. Once the initial excitement over the fight died down, the school and business settled into a routine. With Roy's confession to being responsible for the vandalism, they discussed calling off the extra patrols, but so far they were still running.

Jaime stopped by one evening after he got off work. They sat around the fire pit in the backyard and talked about his day. But he seemed uncomfortable, and the visit didn't last long. She'd seen the reaction before—strong women intimidated some men. She hadn't pegged Jaime as that sort of man, but he wouldn't be the first man she'd misjudged. Either that, or the idea that she'd killed someone created a moral conflict for him.

But this afternoon Dr. Tracy, the Fairwood pack's resident medical expert, was making encouraging noises as she examined the wounds on Tasha's chest. Tasha hoped it meant she'd be freed from her confinement. A week as a patient was more of a test than the physical trials during her training in Maine.

"We may not be immortal," Dr. Tracy said, re-wrapping Tasha's chest with fresh cotton bandages, "but I'm glad to see you inherited the rapid healing gene. Those were nasty cuts. There's no sign of infection and the healing is coming along well. They'll make quite an addition to your collection of scars."

Tasha grinned. "Yeah, the Radferds play rough. But they never hurt me on purpose. Sometimes they forgot I wasn't as tough as they are. I took it as a compliment."

"You have a funny definition of a compliment," Dr. Tracy said with a crooked smile. "Continue using the salve I gave you on those wounds, and I'll see you in a week. Limit your physical activity, use your pain medication as directed, and no shifting yet. It might tear the gashes open."

Tasha moved carefully as she put her shirt back on. She didn't want to show any sign of discomfort while Dr. Tracy watched her. And she didn't want to admit to the doctor that she refused to take the pain pills, fearing they'd interfere with her ability to react to an emergency. She was fastening the buttons when Dr. Tracy surprised her with another question.

"Are you on birth control? I haven't received your medical records from the pack in Maine."

"No. I don't need it. Why?"

"The antibiotics you are on can interfere with some forms of birth control. And if you're considering sex with that good looking game warden, you should use protection."

Why was everyone so interested in her love life? "He's not interested in me that way." Tasha shrugged her shoulders. "I guess I scared him with my Amazon warrior act."

"So why did he come to visit you?"

"I don't know. Maybe I'm a novelty, like a pet rock or whatever the fad is these days. He'll tire of me eventually."

"You don't give yourself enough credit. I've seen how he looks at you. The night Elder Fenner carried you in here, that wasn't just concern for a friend on his face."

Tasha slid off the examination table. She hadn't known it was Elder Fenner who had brought her to the clinic. Of course, she'd been unconscious at that point, not willingly, too weak to protest when someone gave her a shot to put her out. "You're imagining things. I'm not a beauty queen, and I've seen how women react to him. I can't imagine why he'd want to be anything but a friend. I've accepted that I'll be stuck in that role the rest of my life." She'd never admit to anyone that she'd hoped for more from the warden.

"Just because one man hurt you doesn't mean every man will break your heart. You need to take a chance on him, Tasha."

She'd deal with one man breaking her heart at a time, Tasha decided as she sat in Gavin's office. She, Gavin and Dmitri were waiting for Dot to get done with an on-line meeting and join them. Tasha anticipated the meeting was to announce Dmitri would be Gavin's sole second and let her know she'd go back to working at Lapahie Enterprises.

Her suspicions strengthened when Elder Fenner arrived with Dot. Well, perhaps she'd be assigned to work with him full-time. That wouldn't be so bad. She hoped she'd be allowed to finish her contract with Lapahie. They still hadn't figured out who was stealing the money. Until that piece of the puzzle was put in place, she wouldn't be confident Dot was safe.

While Fenner took a seat next to Dmitri, Dot walked around the desk and ran her hand across the top of Gavin's head before sitting next to him. Tasha noticed they were more outwardly affectionate since the fight and the look Gavin gave his mate made it blindingly obvious how much he loved her. Tasha fought back a momentary rush of jealousy. No man would ever look at her like that.

Gavin reached out and took Dot's hand before turning to face Tasha and the other two men. "The incident of last week," he said with no introduction, "has brought to my attention several matters of concern that I should have taken care of long ago but chose to put off. One is a private matter, the other concerns the three of you. We'll start with personal business."

He gave Dot's hand a squeeze. "I have no excuse for neglecting it, other than I was scared. But I conquered my fears, and, after strenuous negotiation, managed to reach an agreement." He coughed and winked at Dot. She blushed. "Dot has agreed to formally and legally bind the Lapahie name with the Fairwood pack and marry me."

Dmitri jumped out of his chair and howled. "It's about time! When's the big day?"

"We haven't set a date yet. That's still under negotiation. But we're going ring-shopping tomorrow."

"We're also hashing out how big the wedding will be. I want it to be limited to close friends, but Gavin says we need to accommodate the entire Fairwood pack." She sighed. "Plus the Lapahie School, plus whatever Council members wish to attend."

Fenner grinned. "Don't forget you'll need to invite the pack leaders from every pack in the country. If you don't, it will cause hard feelings."

"I told you we should elope," Dot groaned.

"That's the price you pay for being so popular." Tasha couldn't keep the smile from her face. "I tried to warn you."

"What did you warn them about?" Dmitri asked.

"I told them they were shifter royalty. Not king and queen, but way up on the food chain."

Dot laughed. "I guess that makes you our white knight."

"Yeah, right. More like the dark avenger who storms in, takes care of business, and leaves."

"Which brings us to the second issue," Gavin said. "The matter of my second."

Here it comes, thought Tasha. I wonder how he'll break the news.

"The elders have been pushing me to name my second for months. I've ignored their suggestion, not wanting to face the fact that, despite the legends, I'm not immortal. When I named the two of you as my seconds, it was a gut reaction."

Gavin leaned back in his chair. "Dmitri, although you're my best friend and I trust you implicitly, you're not a Fairwood. That could cause resentment among the pack.

"And Tasha—well, you know the problem. You're female, and that goes against every tradition for a second."

"I understand, Elder," Tasha said formally.

"I'm not done. On the other hand, Dmitri, you and I have backed each other up many times. I can count on you to support me, no matter what."

Dmitri shrugged. "That's what friends do."

"And you, Tasha, you risked your own life to save my mate. You saw the potential for danger and stopped the enemy I couldn't. I'll never be able to thank you enough."

"It was my honor." Tasha said. "Besides, Dot is my friend, and just like Dmitri has your back, I have hers."

"I know. So I've made my decision. I'm listening to my gut and want the two of you as my seconds. Neither of you likes to deal with the politics of the pack, so I'm hoping that by working together it will be easier on both of you." His smile spread across his face. "Close your mouth, Tasha."

She did, but then opened it again. "How will the Elders react?" The thrill of being officially asked to take the position couldn't override her need to protect her pack leader.

Gavin's face darkened. "If they object, I'll make it clear they are free to resign their positions. I've kept all of my father's appointees to ease the transition to my leadership, but the time has come to bring in fresh blood."

"Besides," said Fenner, "both of you are rather popular right now. I can't imagine anyone will complain too loudly."

"Do you approve?" Tasha asked bluntly.

"Absolutely. I can't think of two finer people for the job."

"Well," said Gavin, "do you accept?"

"Dmitri, you're being awfully quiet," Tasha said. He'd been sitting with his head down as if the pattern in the carpet fascinated him. "Do you have a problem with the arrangement?" She'd never pegged him as a chauvinist, but maybe he figured the position should be solely his.

"I do." Dmitri raised his head. "I refuse to let anyone call me 'Elder.' It's just not right. But if we can work around that, I'll agree to the arrangement."

"One down. How about you, Tasha?" Gavin asked.

"I'm considering it, but I have a couple of conditions. One, I agree with Dmitri. I won't answer to 'Elder.' Two, I need to finish up my commitment to Lapahie before I take on any duties here. Three, I need to make sure that Dmitri's girlfriend has no objections. I imagine he and I will spend a lot of time together."

Dmitri grinned. "Crystal? She's a Free Wolf and in favor of women not following traditional roles."

"When are you two going to officially mate?" Dot asked.

His grin got bigger. "She's playing hard to get. And as long as we're both still having fun pretending we haven't caught each other already, I don't mind playing along."

There was one more hurdle to get past. Tasha examined herself critically in the mirror. There wasn't much she could do about the bruises on her face or the overly-loose shirt and baggy pants. She couldn't risk re-injuring any of her wounds wearing something more professional for the hastily-called elders' meeting.

One of the traditional roles of the pack leader's second was to maintain order at these meetings. She and Dmitri had discussed it with Gavin, and they'd decided to come prepared. After adjusting the shoulder harness that held the Sig Sauer, she double-checked the blade on her knife to make sure that Arnold's body hadn't dulled it. She'd cleaned the knife several times, and it gleamed in the light before she slid it back into its sheath.

She decided to forgo her rifle. The strap across her chest would be an irritation she didn't need, and she couldn't imagine there'd be any use for it. Besides, the meeting room was too small for it to be effective.

They met up at Gavin's office. He'd changed into a deep blue dress shirt and gray pinstriped suit. "Looking good," Tasha said.

Dot reached up and straightened his tie. "Got to remind them who's in charge once in a while," she said. "Would you disagree with this man?"

Not if you knew what was good for you, Tasha thought. Gavin looked as if he'd be as dangerous in a board room as he was on the field of battle as a wolf.

TWENTY-FOUR

The murmurs started as soon as Dmitri and Tasha walked into the meeting. Dmitri, equipped similar to Tasha, entered first followed by Gavin, then Dot, and finally Tasha. Gavin made room for Dot to sit by him at the end of the table, and Tasha and Dmitri stood behind them, arms crossed, their eyes roving around the table. It was meant to be intimidating, and although Tasha didn't crack a smile, inwardly it amused her to see how well it worked.

She'd taken the spot behind Gavin while Dmitri stood behind Dot. They'd worked out the ploy beforehand, just another way to manipulate any of the elders who might object to their appointment.

"Since when have weapons been allowed in our meetings?" demanded Elder Talbot, a wizened old man. Tasha recalled that not only had he served Gavin's father, he'd been one of the elders during Gavin's grandfather's time.

When Gavin smiled, it held a threat. "Have you forgotten? The moment I shift I'm a weapon, Elder Talbot, as I recently proved to an old enemy. And it's traditional for the pack leader's second to carry weapons."

"Dmitri I understand, but her?" Talbot snarled.

"Perhaps you should wait to voice your objections until the meeting starts so they are on the record." Gavin looked around the table, then at his watch. "It's early, but everyone is here. Shall we begin?"

Tasha noted the various reactions of the Elders. They apparently were not used to Gavin being so authoritative. As old as most of them were, they probably still thought of him as a youngster.

"I have two announcements to make that could not wait until our normal meeting," Gavin said. "I didn't want the news to reach you as rumors. As the pack elders, you deserve to know first." He held up one hand. "And before I begin, I warn you. I've made these decisions as is my right as pack leader, and although I will listen to your concerns, neither one is up for a vote.

"The first," he continued, reaching out and taking Dot's hand, "is that Dot and I decided to confirm our status as mates in a legal sense. The details will take time to work out, but as soon as we can, we're getting married."

"Does that mean we're finally acquiring Choate Enterprises?" someone asked.

Gavin glared at the speaker. "Choate Enterprises no longer exists. Lapahie Enterprises is and will remain a stand-alone company that we are pleased and honored to partner with. Are there any other questions?"

"When is the customary challenge going to be?" Elder Talbot asked.

Gavin raised both eyebrows. "Where did you get

the idea there would be a challenge? Dot is my mate, she will be my wife, she is and will continue to be the alpha female for the Fairwood pack. There will be no challenge. And clearly, Elder Talbot, you haven't been doing your job of listening to the members of the pack, otherwise you would know that she is well-liked and admired."

Elder Blackhaw rose unsteadily to her feet. She was the pack's historian and the oldest person of the pack. She was old enough that she claimed she'd forgotten how old she really was. Tasha assumed the information was hidden in her massive stacks of records somewhere, deliberately buried until she died and the person who followed her into the position resurrected it. Elder Fenner rushed to help her, inquiring politely if her arthritis was acting up. She brushed him away but leaned on the table as she spoke.

"Since none of these yahoos have done it yet, let me be the first to congratulate you on your upcoming wedding." She paused while others around the table voiced their agreement. She cleared her throat and continued. "It's about time. And as far as the challenge goes? As the oldest female in the pack, let me tell you something. It's a stupid tradition, and I'm glad you're not following it. Dot makes you happy, and that's what counts. I can't imagine being hitched to a mate just because she outfought your pick. Bad enough for a woman, let alone the pack leader."

Tasha worked to keep her face expressionless. Elder Blackhaw had never been shy voicing her opinion. Sometimes it upset people but she didn't care.

"Thank you, Elder. I appreciate your support. Now to the second item of business." Gavin paused just long enough to make the silence uncomfortable. "Some of you have been urging me to name my second. I have done so."

"So why isn't he here instead of these two?" Elder Talbot asked.

"Isn't it obvious?"

"Shoot, I figured it out the minute they walked into the room," Elder Blackhaw said. "Good idea."

"You're not naming this outsider as your second, are you?" Talbot spluttered.

"No." Gavin grinned with satisfaction. Elder Talbot relaxed. "No. I'm naming Dmitri and Tasha as my co-seconds."

There were several times during the ensuing argument that Tasha thought she might need to use her new authority to restore order. Each time, just before things reached a physical confrontation, Gavin stepped in and reminded the room who was in charge. When the shouting was over, Talbot had agreed to take a long vacation to visit his daughter in Seattle at Gavin's expense.

The rest of the elders agreed to support Gavin's decision, some wholeheartedly, others reluctantly. Tasha tracked the body language during the meeting and noted whose words matched their feelings. She'd share the info with Gavin after the meeting.

Protocol dictated that Gavin leave the room before the elders, so the four of them filed out in the same order in which they entered. They headed straight to Gavin's office. "Wasn't that fun?" he asked sarcastically shutting the door behind them. "But at least it's over and done with."

There was a knock on the door, and Tasha answered it. "May I join you?" Elder Fenner asked.

"Come on in, Mark," Gavin said. "You're always welcome."

"Well, that was interesting. I expected Talbot to object to Tasha's appointment, but I never expected him to be so adamantly opposed to Dmitri."

"I suspected he might be." Gavin sat on the edge of his desk. "I remember when Dad first suggested allowing women to serve as elders. You would have thought he was recommending we dissolve the entire pack structure."

Fenner grimaced. "I'd forgotten that. You were still a young cub then. I'm surprised you remember."

Gavin chuckled. "You're not that much older than me. That was one of the first times I realized how important Dad was. I didn't quite understand it, but it impressed me anyway. Which reminds me, I'd better call him and tell him about the wedding before someone else does."

"That's our clue to head out," Tasha said to Dmitri.

"Yes, but will you two join Dot and I for supper tonight? You too, Mark. We have unfinished business to discuss. I'll provide the steaks. I assume everyone likes them rare?"

If Gavin ever wanted to switch jobs, he'd make an excellent chef. Tasha couldn't figure out what seasoning he'd used, but she ate more steak than she'd ever done before, at least in human form. A long run would help work off the calories. But that wasn't going to happen, not only because of doctor's orders, but they hadn't even settled down to talking business yet.

"Anyone want another beer?" Gavin asked as he carried several plates into the kitchen. "Dmitri, I see you're ready. Tasha, are you sure I can't talk you into having one?"

"Not unless you want to explain to Dr. Tracy why I'm mixing alcohol with my medicine."

"Heaven forbid! She still hasn't forgiven me for not telling her about the scratches I got in the fight."

Tasha picked up her glass of soda and carried it into the front room where Elder Fenner was relaxing in an easy chair. She sat on the end of the sofa close to him, and Dmitri took the other end. Gavin and Dot settled into the loveseat, and Gavin threw his arm around her shoulders, drawing her close.

"How does it feel to be making history?" he asked no one in particular.

"You're the one who should answer that question." Fenner leaned forward. "Have you informed the Council about your decision yet?"

"Which one? I left a message for Counselor Carlson, didn't give him any details. It could prove an interesting conversation when he calls back." He ruffled Dot's hair. "Maybe I should get Dot to tell him. He has a crush on her."

Dot swatted him playfully on his thigh. "Yeah, right."

Tasha grinned at the exchange. She suspected it might be true.

"Let's work out more of the details before I talk to him. I don't expect either of you will want an office, right?" Gavin asked.

"I expecting to keep my old job at the motor pool," Dmitri said. "You don't need us hanging out with you twenty four-seven."

"And I hate being stuck behind a desk," Tasha said. "Besides, I need to finish up the job at Lapahie first."

"Is that all I am to you, Tasha? A job?" Dot's words didn't match the huge grin on her face.

"Yup. And one of these days I expect to see the big paycheck I was promised."

Gavin snorted and almost spit out a mouthful of beer. He swallowed wrong and coughed. Dot pounded him on his back until he caught his breath. "Actually, there is something I want to give you," he said. "There's no way I can ever thank you enough for what you did, so I tried to come up with something tangible as a reward. Be right back."

He patted Dot on the knee before getting up and disappearing down the hallway. When he came back he was carrying what looked like a magazine and an envelope. "Dmitri mentioned your bike is getting worn out. He's maintained it as much as possible but replacement parts are hard to come by. So, here." He handed her what he was holding.

It wasn't a magazine, but a catalog for motorcycles. Ones she'd never be able to afford. She looked at Gavin quizzically. "Open the envelope," he said.

From the grins on the faces of everyone else in the room, they already knew what the envelope held. She carefully tore it open. "What..." she said as she pulled out a slip of paper and rapidly read it. When she looked up, she was fighting back tears.

"You probably won't want to go shopping until next spring," Dot said. "But don't worry, it'll still be good then."

"This is crazy," Tasha said. "You're buying me a brand new motorcycle?" She held a gift certificate for a nearby dealership.

"Well, it comes with a few strings," Dot said.

Of course it did. "Like what?"

Dot winked at her mate. "Well, you know how Gavin is about me going for rides by myself, even on that fancy new bike he bought me. So now you'll have a bike that can keep up with mine, and we can ride together. Deal?"

Tasha was already plotting how she could rig the motorcycle of her choice to carry her weapons. "Deal," she said.

Tasha didn't think anything about it when Elder Fenner said his good nights at the same time she did or when he started walking beside her. After all, his house was a few doors down from her parents' home. It wasn't the first time their paths took them the same direction.

"There's one thing we haven't discussed yet," he said a short distance down the street.

"What's that?" she asked.

"What your duties will be when you are back here permanently."

"I had a few ideas, but now I'm not sure they'll work."

"I'd like to hear them."

Tasha hesitated. "Don't laugh, but I thought I could contract out to other packs to help them improve their security. Especially packs that might have businesses like we do. I figured it would improve our pack's reputation."

"Good idea. But you're right, that may not be possible now that you're Gavin's second." They were approached by a wolf, and Tasha listened in as he gave his report to Elder Fenner, *"All clear,"* before running off again.

"Any other ideas?"

"I considered the possibility of working with you, Elder."

He stopped walking, and Tasha backed up a couple of steps. "Let's get something straight," he said. "Now that you're the pack leader's second, we're equal in rank. In fact, you might rank a little higher than me in traditional pack hierarchy. So just like you call Elder Fairwood 'Gavin' in informal circumstances, I'd like you to call me 'Mark.' If you don't, I might start calling you 'Elder' as well."

Tasha grinned. "That's going to be hard. I mean, you were an elder even when I had a teenage crush on you."

"You had a crush on *me*?"

"Yeah. While the other girls were crushing on Gavin, I fixated on you. That's why I got interested in security. I wanted you to notice me. And I dragged Tanya along so I wouldn't look foolish."

They started walking again. "I had no idea."

"You didn't hear us giggling all the time?"

"If I did, I assumed it was directed at someone else. Why would you be interested in me?"

"Because you were handsome, and I wanted to heal your broken heart."

His lips twitched. "You were going to rescue me? At least I now know when your knight in shining armor complex started."

"I've always been a sucker for the underdog."

"I don't see Jaime as an underdog."

Tasha sighed loudly. "Why is everyone so intent on pushing Jaime at me? He's seems to be a nice guy, but we haven't even gone on a date."

"Could it be that he's the first guy in a long time you've shown any interest in and they want you to be happy?"

"Could be. But the harder everyone pushes, the more I want to push back."

"Always the rebel."

They reached her parents' house, and Tasha hesitated. She wasn't ready to go in yet. It was nice not to be fussed over all the time.

"Are you headed back to Lapahie tomorrow?" Mark asked.

"Yes. Even though the weather is supposed to be good, I'll be taking one of the company cars. It was part of the bargain with Dr. Tracy. She doesn't want me riding yet. In fact, she told Gavin to make sure to give me an automatic to make it even more boring."

He grinned. "Will you stop by in the morning and see me before you leave? I'd like to discuss this idea of yours."

"Which one?"

"Working with me. You didn't think I shipped you off to the Radferds and don't expect to get something out of it, did you?"

Elder Fenner—no, Mark had a pot of coffee brewing and a box of bagels on his desk when Tasha arrived. "Help yourself. There's cream cheese in the fridge."

"No donuts?"

"I'm pretending to eat healthier." He grinned. "Dr. Tracy is after me to add more fruits and vegetables to my diet."

"She tells everyone that. Not many people listen." Tasha bent carefully to retrieve the cream cheese from the small unit on the floor.

"Too bad. She's a smart lady, and we're lucky to have her."

Tasha poured herself some coffee and settled into a chair across the desk from her long-time mentor. The mounds of paper in front of him made her wonder if he needed a secretary. She hoped that he didn't have her in mind for the task because she'd turn him down. "I assume you have a plan for me. What is it?"

"I've been debating how to use your talents for some time, even before you went to Maine. And although you weren't ready then, you certainly are now."

"Ready for what?" Tasha spread a generous helping of cream cheese on her blueberry bagel and bit into it, the flavors melding together perfectly.

"I've talked to Gavin about it before, and he said it was my decision. Then he went ahead and named you as his second, stealing my thunder."

Usually Fenner—Mark—wasn't this evasive. "What *are* you talking about?"

"I've been getting along with various interns and temporary assistants for years."

"Yes." Tasha was starting to get an inkling of where he was heading.

"It's time I named a permanent second."

Her gut was right. "It won't work."

Mark shook his head. "No. Not now. Can you imagine the hell the other elders would raise if I named you my second now? So we need to come up with a different title for you. Got any ideas?"

TWENTY-FIVE

It was a good thing nobody expected her to climb the ladder and install the security cameras because Tasha wasn't sure she could. After Samantha and Tanya got done hugging her on her return, she was sore in spots she'd thought were healed. But Ella, the school's resident hardware expert, was having fun crawling up and down the ladder and aiming the cameras just the way Tasha wanted them. Besides, from what Ella told Tasha, it gave her a break from the task of setting up the dozen or so computers an anonymous donor had gifted the school.

They saved Mr. Dillman's office for last. Tasha's theory was that he'd be less likely to be involved in a major project at the end of the day. Ella just seemed happy not dealing with him.

"Is he really that bad?" Tasha asked as they gathered the needed supplies from the storeroom.

Ella, a slim brown-haired lady, sighed. "When I first got here, I heard other people running him down, but I tried to ignore it. I know what it feels like to have everybody hate you because you're different. My pack wouldn't accept that I wanted to be a computer technician because I'm a female. So I gave Mr. Dillman a chance. Said hi when I walked by, tried to talk to him, but it didn't work. He seemed determined not to like me, so I gave up."

"Maybe he's shy?"

"He didn't come off that way. I had the impression he figured he was better than me and I was a lowly peon because I don't program." Ella grimaced as she handed Tasha a bundle of blue cable. "It's not uncommon."

"That's too bad. Do you get the same attitude from other people here?"

Ella shrugged. "It's there, but Dillman is the worst. It upsets him that I'm more knowledgeable than he is in repairing computers. I've had to work on his several times, but he refuses to let me replace it."

"I thought you computer folks were always looking for the newest and most up-to-date gadgets."

"That's what makes it so weird." Ella added pliers and other tools to Tasha's load. "He's had the same setup for so long he's worn the letters off some of the keys on his keyboard. He won't let me give him a new one."

"I wonder if he's got pictures of his late wife stored on his computer and is afraid he'll lose them," Tasha suggested as they headed upstairs.

"I don't think he's ever been married," Ella said.

"That's not what he told me."

"That's strange. I overheard him tell someone on the phone he never had a wife. That was a few years ago, but I'm pretty sure that's what he said."

Tasha added another task to her checklist—check out Dillman's personnel file.

"I didn't think you were ever going to show up," Mr. Dillman grumbled when he opened his office door.

"Sorry," Tasha said. "I was in an accident and have been out of commission for a while. Plus, the supplier had the camera on back order. But now we're here, so is this a good time for us to install it?" She'd decided the grouchier he got, the more cheerful she'd pretend to be.

"Sure, go ahead."

His office was small and crowded, and made even more crowded by the two extra bodies and a step ladder. Tasha could see Dillman's frustration growing and decided to get him out of the way so Ella could work without his supervision.

"I feel like I'm slowing down the process," she announced. "I'm going to get coffee. You want to come along, Mr. Dillman? My treat."

She'd never known a computer guy to turn down coffee. Mr. Dillman hesitated but picked up his stained mug and said, "I guess that would be all right."

This late in the afternoon, the break room was empty and the coffee looked old and stale. Tasha emptied the remnants of the last batch and washed the carafe before starting a new pot. "Have you had any problems recently?" she asked while they waited for the coffee to brew.

"No."

He wasn't much on conversation. Tasha tried again. "Got any plans for the night? Any good shows on?" She had him pegged as the kind of guy who went home, grabbed a drink, and planted himself in front of a TV.

He sighed heavily, and Tasha caught the slightest

trace of alcohol on his breath. "Not tonight. No games either."

That gave her a lead. "Who's your favorite team?"

"Steelers."

Well, that hadn't worked. The coffee was done, and she grabbed herself a foam cup from the nearby stack. "How's their season looking?"

"They need a new coach. Or a better quarterback. Or both."

She filled her cup and then his. "I heard they've got a shot at making it to the division rounds."

"Hopefully."

Tasha was ready to give up. She hoped she'd given Ella enough time to complete the job. When she and Samantha had talked to him before, he hadn't been this withdrawn. Was he just having a bad day? Or this was his normal personality and their first meeting had been an exception.

She took a gulp of her coffee so it wouldn't slosh when she walked. "Should we head back and check if it's ready yet?" she asked. "I'm anxious to see how this setup works."

Ella glanced down from her perch on the ladder when they returned. "Almost got it," she said. "Just trying to get both the door and your desk in the view. Take a look and tell me what you think."

"Isn't getting the door good enough?" Dillman asked as he sat.

"Not with these guys. I want to record your screen too in case someone accesses your computer remotely and messes with your stuff."

"More to the right," he said. "There, that's good."

After tightening several screws, Ella got off the

ladder. "I've got this set so you can turn it on when you leave for the day by clicking this button. Standard set up—if the light is red it's off, green means on. If you want to view the recording, you go to the shortcut called Camera. I'll check in with you in a couple of days to make sure it's working correctly."

Tasha stepped into the hallway so Ella had room to gather up her tools and maneuver the stepladder out of the way. "Have any questions?" Ella asked. "I don't want to bore you with too many details. You're smart enough to figure out how the camera works without reading the manual, but I left it for you anyway."

Dillman just brushed her off. "Close the door on your way out," he said gruffly.

They hadn't gotten very far before Ella swore softly. "Damnit! I was nice as pie and didn't even get a 'thank you.' Lousy old man."

"Don't worry about it. I appreciate what you've done, and I have an in to the woman at the top of the food chain. I'll let her know, and I'm sure she'll thank you. Besides, people like Dillman aren't worth wasting your energy on."

"You're right. It's just so frustrating." They'd reached Ella's workroom and Tasha helped her put her tools away. "Thanks," Ella said as together they boosted the ladder onto its storage hooks. "And thanks for getting Dillman out of there. I hate having people breathing down my neck while I work. Besides, it gave me the chance to install another program that I've needed to add and could never get him to let me do it."

"Nothing bad, I hope."

Ella grinned. "As tempting as that is, I'm a professional. No, now I can back up his files to a safe place so if his computer crashes, the company won't lose anything he's stored. And he's been here so long, who knows what he's got?"

"I'd like a chance to look at those files. I probably won't understand what most of them are, but I'd like to browse through them anyway."

"I don't mean to offend you, but I can't do that. You may know about physical security, but I'm the expert on our system security. If you want to see those files, you'll need the okay from someone higher up than me."

Tasha grinned. "Good for you. That was the perfect answer. What if I get it in writing from Miss Lapahie? Would that be good enough?"

Ella relaxed. "That would work. When I have it in my hand, I'll let you see Dillman's files."

The day took more of a toll on Tasha than she realized. Extreme tiredness didn't hit her until she sat down for supper. The simple act of warming up the leftovers her mother had sent along took more energy than she had left. Dr. Tracy had warned her that between the antibiotics and the healing process she might tire rapidly, but she hadn't expected it to be that bad.

Thankfully the house was quiet. She assumed Samantha and Tanya were out working with the patrols somewhere, and the others were with friends. She forced herself to eat before heading to the bathroom to clean up. A quick shower was all she was allowed, and it did little to revitalize her.

Before re-wrapping her chest in fresh bandages, she lay on her bed to rest for a few minutes. It wouldn't hurt to give the scabs a chance to dry completely before covering them. She closed her eyes to ease the glare of the bare bulbs in the overhead light fixture.

The room was dark when she opened her eyes again, and she was covered by the sheet. She tossed it aside and stretched, slowly waking up. When she swung her legs over the edge of the bed, she realized her chest was still bare and cursed. She hadn't meant for anyone to see her condition.

"I'm your sister. You should have told me, goddammit," Tanya said from the other bed.

Tasha's training paid off, and she didn't even flinch. "I've told no one. I suspect Dr. Tracy and Gavin are the only people who know the extent of my injuries. Even Mom and Dad weren't told."

"If it looks like this now, how bad was it originally?" Tanya asked. "They threw a blanket over you the night of the fight, and I didn't see."

"The bruising makes it look worse than it actually is." Tasha reached for a fresh roll of gauze. "But now that you've seen me at my worst, do you want to help me put fresh dressings on?"

Tanya grabbed the roll of cotton gauze from Tasha's hand. "Put your arms up and I'll get this done in no time flat. And tell me if I'm too rough. You don't have to play hero for me."

"I don't try to be a hero." Tasha took a deep breath as Tanya hit a sensitive spot. "I just happened to be in the right place at the right time."

"Yeppers. You seem to make a habit of that. And this time your habit almost got the better of you. You could have died."

"I'm a warrior, Tanya. Once I understood that, a lot of pieces fell into place. This is what I'm meant to do with my life. And yes, that means that one day I may run into a bigger, better opponent. I know the risks, and I accept them." Tasha smiled, hiding the sadness her words conveyed. "Not all of us are cut out to be programmers."

She pulled her twin into a hug, and the tears that flowed from two sets of eyes said more than words ever could.

Twenty-Six

Dot was due to arrive soon, and Tasha wondered if Gavin was coming with her. It was only natural that the CEO would want to be there when the auditors arrived. Tasha hesitated before choosing her outfit. She could wear most of her clothes without a problem now as her wounds were almost healed. But finding clothes that looked business professional and still gave her the ability to move freely in a battle wasn't easy. Her standard black dress slacks and blazer would have to do.

She chose to wear a colored shirt. The bright red one projected power and made her stand out. She didn't want to blend into the background on this occasion; she wanted to advertise her presence to discourage any potential troublemakers.

The custom-made blazer had an interior pocket that allowed her to carry a handgun without wearing a shoulder harness. Another pocket was perfect for stashing several clips.

The pants held their own secrets. The strip of elastic in the crotch made it easier to kick or run without popping a seam. And the legs were loose enough that she could strap a knife to her leg and have it remain undetected. The outfit had been part of her gear for several missions she'd run with the Radferds.

At the last minute she pulled on black gloves and added a pair of dark sunglasses. Not that the sun was bright enough to need them, but it was another intimidation factor. If her eyes couldn't be seen, no one would know what she was looking at.

Tasha hoped she'd have at least a few minutes alone with Dot. She reminded herself to call her Miss Lapahie. It would be a breach of protocol to call her anything else.

She met Samantha and Tanya coming in the front door as she prepared to leave. The job of organizing security patrols was still theirs while she concentrated on getting her strength back. At least that's what everyone thought. In reality, she'd spent a lot of time reviewing the recordings from the security cameras. She wasn't convinced the Choates might not have another plant among the students.

"Wow," said Samantha, cocking her head. "You look like the big bad wolf."

"Either that or she's trying to *attract* the big bad wolf," Tanya teased. "There are more than a few males who'd find this getup sexy."

"Those are the guys I don't want to attract," Tasha tapped the side of her jacket and smirked. "Once they find out my gun is bigger than theirs, they lose interest."

Samantha giggled and Tanya grinned. "Glad to see you're getting your sense of humor back," Tanya said.

"You're always the one cracking jokes," Tasha said. "I'm the straight guy."

"That's because your jokes aren't funny."

"Are you going to let her get away with that?" Samantha laughed.

Tasha smiled. "Unfortunately, she's right. My jokes go right over most people's heads. They aren't smart enough to catch the meanings. Tanya, on the other hand, knows how to dumb her jokes down for the audience."

"You're bad. Are you implying that you're smarter than everyone else?"

"Not everyone. But even if I'm a little smarter than average, it's safe to say I'm more intelligent than fifty percent of the people around me." Tasha raised an eyebrow and shifted her eyes back and forth between her sister and her friend. "So who wants to own up to being in the lower fifty percent?"

"Ouch. You'd better let Tanya make the jokes. Yours hit too close to home."

Tasha sighed. "I can't win, can I? Okay, I get the hint. Tanya, I'll go back to being your fall guy."

"Good call."

Tasha raised a hand, interrupting the easy conversation. "Hear that? It's Elder Fairwood's Jeep."

"How can you tell? Sounds like any old car to me," Samantha said.

"It's got a slight rumble that stands out if you listen hard enough. Front and center ladies, it's time to go to work."

They got to the parking lot as the Jeep and a rental sedan pulled in. *"Open the doors for Dot and Gavin,"* Tasha sent. *"Let's give our leaders the full treatment in front of company."* She didn't allow the smile in her voice to reach her face which remained solemn.

Gavin seemed surprised when Tanya opened his door. Samantha mimicked the movement on the passenger's side, but extended her hand to assist Dot with hopping down.

"Good morning, Elder Fairwood, Miss Lapahie," Tasha said impassively.

"Two can play this game," Gavin sent. "Good morning, Elder Roeper, ladies," he said.

Startled, Tasha almost broke her deadpan expression. *"Was that wise?"* she asked as she watched three people, two men and a woman, exit the second vehicle.

Gavin turned, angling his body so the visitors couldn't see his face and winked at Tasha. *"The council has been informed, so it's time the news becomes public. Besides, based upon how hard of a time your sister is having keeping a straight face, I'd say somebody already knows."*

She sent the mental equivalent of a sigh. *"Point conceded. I might have informed one or two people. As always, you win."*

Tasha led the way to the conference room set aside for the auditors contracted from an allied pack. Rosa, looking somewhat flustered, was waiting for them. Dot had given her the assignment of running errands for the trio, keeping them supplied with drinks, snacks, and whatever materials they needed. Dot's hope was that the job would help boost Rosa's self-confidence which was severely lacking.

The initial meeting was to be between Dot and the auditors so Tasha felt safe heading downstairs and trying to find Ella. Samantha and Tanya would be returning to the security office. Tasha had Dot's written permission to look at Dillman's computer files in her hand, and she hoped Ella would have time to review the files with her. There hadn't been a peep out of Dillman since the camera's installation.

She found Ella in her workroom, the guts of a computer spread out on the table in front of her. Tasha knocked softly on the door, not wanting to startle Ella too much.

"Come on in," Ella said, without looking up. "I'll be with you in a sec."

Tasha waited while Ella snapped one piece into place and screwed down another one. She set down her screwdriver and stretched. "What can I do for you?" Ella asked, turning around. "Oh! It's you. Sorry to make you wait, but I didn't want to lose track of what I was doing. How can I help you?"

"I'm hoping you've gotten a copy of Dillman's files and have time to help me understand what they are. I've got Miss Lapahie's permission." Tasha handed Ella the paper.

"The files copied and I'd love to help you but I'm kinda busy right now."

"Anything I can help you with?" Tasha asked, more out of politeness than any real expectation of getting a positive answer.

"Unless you're any good at diagnosing a RAM error, no."

Tasha grinned. "I think I know what that means, but no, I can't help. When should I come back?"

Ella glanced up at the clock on the wall. "Half an hour or so? And that's if no emergencies happen."

"I'll be back."

Tasha didn't want to wander off too far in case Dot or Gavin needed her services for something. And she didn't want to appear as if she had nothing to do, so she needed to create a quick project for herself. She decided to check out the company's personnel files, a chore she'd put off for too long.

Despite Lapahie Enterprises being a software company, most of their hiring and payroll files were stored on paper. The clerk in charge of the files wasn't at her desk, and the file room was open. Tasha grimaced. She'd have to bring the lapse in security to Dot's attention and let her figure out a resolution.

Luckily for her quest, the files were clearly marked and it didn't take Tasha long to find what she needed. She wanted to start with Dillman's file. As the most senior employee of the company, she expected his file to be the thickest. Once it was out of the way, the others would be easy.

There was a small table and one hard chair in the room, and Tasha set the several folders marked with Dillman's name there. She removed the sunglasses and tucked them in the pocket of her jacket. The overhead florescent fixture provided lighting that was hard on the eyes, but Tasha didn't want to overlook any faded bit of writing.

She skimmed the earliest paperwork because she suspected the information if provided would be no longer accurate. Surely in that amount of time he'd moved, changed positions, gotten married or had children.

Remembering his fixation on money, she decided to peruse the folder holding his payroll records. It seemed normal enough. Small raises each year, likely cost of living and a little more. An occasional larger bump matching a promotion here and there. Nothing out of the ordinary.

Then the bonuses started. Every six months or so,

he'd receive a significant amount of money for unknown reasons. The records showed no justification for why he got the money. She did discover one slip of paperwork from about five years earlier ordering a payment and signed by Damyon Choate.

The bonuses stopped a couple of years after they started. When Tasha reflected on the timing, she realized it was just after Dot took over the company. She'd have to compare that pattern against other employees who'd been around before the takeover.

Information about his family was non-existent. She couldn't even find anything about next-of-kin. Maybe the paperwork had been pulled after his wife's death and never updated. It was the only theory Tasha could come up with.

The next file she pulled was Chief's, more out of curiosity than anything else. Much smaller that Dillman's, it contained nothing Gavin's contacts hadn't uncovered.

She decided she'd done enough for one sitting and after putting away the files, exited the small room. The clerk had returned to her desk and gave a little scream when Tasha appeared. "Where did you come from? No one's allowed in there."

"The door was open," Tasha said dryly. "I'll come back another day to give you my recommendations for security. In the meantime, lock it up every time you leave."

She ignored the clerk's mumbled "Pain in the..." and headed to Ella's office. She'd lost track of time and hoped Ella would still be there and not immersed in another project.

Ella had her back to the door again, but this time she was staring at a computer screen. "Take a look at this," she said before Tasha even knocked. "You'll find it interesting."

"Heard me coming?" Tasha asked, surprised. "I'm a quiet walker."

"I caught a whiff of medicine and remembered it from earlier. Sore muscles?"

"Something like that." If Ella hadn't attended the fight, Tasha wouldn't share the gory details. "What did you find?"

Ella grinned. "Computer forensics is a hobby of mine. This gave me the opportunity to practice what I've learned. On the surface, Dillman's computer is clean. Almost too clean. That's what got me interested.

"Normal people have garbage on their system. If you surf at all, you're going to have traces of your activity. Dillman didn't have any cookies or temp files. Even the log file of me installing the security camera was gone."

"And that means?" Tasha asked.

"Either he's phobic about keeping his files clean or he's hiding something. So I dug into a few places that people don't think about. That's where I found some weird shit."

"Like what?"

"Unless he has job responsibilities I'm unaware of, there's no reason for Dillman to have a photo manipulation program on his work PC. Or a couple of other programs he installed. Or scanned copies of bills."

TWENTY~SEVEN

"Are you sure? Because if so, you found the answer we're looking for." Tasha hated to believe it—Dillman hadn't seemed like the kind of guy to steal from his employer—but she also didn't think Ella had manufactured the evidence. No one at Lapahie knew the reason for the investigation. "Whatever you had planned for the rest of the day, scrap it. There are people upstairs who will want to talk to you."

She sent a careful tendril of thread to Dot. *"Ella discovered important information the auditors need to be made aware of. Can we interrupt?"*

"Ella?"

"One of the company's computer techs." One that deserved a raise in Tasha's humble opinion.

"Let me check."

They'd reached the top of the stairs before Dot got back to her. *"I'll meet you at the conference room."*

Happily, their path didn't take them anywhere near the programmers' work area. Tasha didn't want rumors spreading, and Ella might be tempted to say something to her friends. She picked up a definite vibe of happiness from the computer technician. Was Ella happy that she'd found evidence against Dillman, or that she'd finally put her skills to work? Although Tasha's curiosity was aroused, she didn't want to ask the question.

As promised, Dot waited for them at the conference room door. Ella seemed startled to see her, and a little nervous. *"Does she know why you brought her here? What information does she have?"* Dot sent.

"The auditors need to verify, but she's pointed us in the right direction to figuring out who's been stealing the money."

"Are you going to tell me who?" Dot asked as she opened the door for them.

"I'll let Ella take the glory. She deserves it."

The three auditors barely looked up from their computer screens when Tasha and Ella walked in. "I hope this is important," the woman said, sounding bored. "Our time is expensive."

Ella hesitated. "Tasha says so. This was her idea."

"Go ahead."

"I was working on a programmer's machine. He's got financial information stored, and I can't figure out why."

Tasha inwardly grinned at the way the auditors' heads popped up. "I need to see that computer immediately," one of the men said.

With him and Ella gone, Dot asked the question on everyone's mind. "Whose computer?"

"Dillman. One of the original employees from the Choate days."

"No!" Dot exclaimed. "Not Norm!"

"You know him?" Gavin asked.

"I've met all the employees," Dot put her hand on

his arm. "He seemed like a sweet old man. I can't imagine he'd steal from the company."

Tasha decided not to tell her what the other employees thought about him. "Ella is only looking at a copy of his computer. We should get him out of his office and away from the actual machine."

"How do we do that?" Dot asked.

"I'll use the excuse of checking if his camera is working out, then see if I can get him to go get coffee with me. Or offer to buy him lunch. Or you can stop by and check on him, Miss Lapahie, and tell him to take the rest of the day off with pay. Tell him he's been working too hard and deserves a break. He's sweet on you, so maybe he'll fall for it."

"If that doesn't work?"

"Have a fire drill. Once he's out of the office, we swoop in and grab his computer."

"You seem convinced that he's involved," Gavin said.

"Let's say I have reasonable suspicions." Tasha frowned. "And I don't want to give him a chance to destroy potential evidence."

Dot made a leisurely trip through the cubicle farm, stopping to chat with everyone along the way. Most of the programmers were male, and Tasha watched in amusement as they fawned over their employer. It was a good thing that Gavin had stayed in the conference room.

Dot spent over half an hour making her way to Dillman's office. Although the main room had gotten noisy during her tour, he hadn't peeked out of his door even once. Tasha maintained her distance when Dot disappeared through his door. If needed, she was only a mental shout away.

Five minutes later they came out together, with Dillman smiling and putting on his coat. *"Let me walk him out,"* Dot sent to Tasha. *"I'll tell you when he's left the parking lot."*

It seemed like a good plan, and Tasha responded with a mental nod of agreement. It was better, and less noticeable than keeping an eye on him through the windows.

"He's gone," Dot sent in a few minutes. *"Do we have to do it this way?"*

"Sorry, but yes. We don't want to give him the chance to hide any of the evidence." Or give anyone else time to get into his office and plant any either. Although Tasha believed Dillman to be guilty, she'd protect his right to be shown innocent.

Several minutes passed before Ella and the auditor showed up. More than a few heads popped up over the cubicles to watch when they exited Dillman's office with Ella carrying his computer under her arm. It was her turn next.

Tasha sauntered over to the office, listening to the buzz that followed her. The security camera blinked red in the corner as she took a seat at the desk. She wasn't sure where to start, but the papers piled on the top of the desk were as good a place as any. It was the least likely place to find any evidence based on Dillman's previous behavior, but she didn't want to risk overlooking anything.

Everything was work related, although some so outdated Tasha wondered if Dillman had hoarding tendencies. She couldn't think of a valid reason to keep a printed out copy of an email from five years earlier concerning an upcoming holiday. She was tempted to ball it up and throw it away, but didn't. Instead, she returned it to the stack in case Dillman returned and needed it.

The desk drawers were next, but a quick tug proved them to be locked. That wouldn't be a problem with the right tools, but Tasha didn't own a set of lock-picks. Did he take the key home each day or was it stashed somewhere in the office? Tasha looked in a couple of the normal places—taped under the desk, hidden under the keyboard, beneath the coaster for his coffee cup—and came up empty.

She twirled around in the chair looking for other hiding spots. There were too many to make a search easy or efficient. Ella might have a small enough screwdriver in her workroom to spring the lock.

But as Tasha stood, she noticed the plaque on the wall given to Dillman by Elder Choate was crooked. Very crooked, as a matter of fact. She carefully took it off the single screw that served as a holder and turned it over and spotted not one, but two keys attached to the back.

The smaller one looked like a typical desk key and she carefully pulled it from its place, stuck it into the desk lock, and turned it. She heard the satisfying click as the mechanism released. This time the drawer opened easily.

One glance at the mass of papers inside made Tasha wish for a handy pot of coffee. The task of going through them individually could take longer than she had. And a two-drawer file cabinet had to be inspected.

"Finding anything?" Dot sent.

"A fire hazard. Dillman must not throw away anything."

"That's good for us, right?"

"Only if we have a week to sift through the garbage. Besides if he's smart, he shreds anything incriminating. He's got a shredder beside his desk. Either that or it's electronic. That's up to Ella and the auditors to find."

"So where do we go from here?"

"Give me a few minutes to come up with a plan."

The way Tasha saw it, she had two riddles to solve. One was obvious—where would Dillman hide something he used on a semi-regular basis but didn't want anyone else to find? The answer to that was dependent on the second question—what was she looking for in the first place?

Idly, she ran her fingers over the keyboard as she thought. It didn't matter what keys she hit because it wasn't connected to anything. Remembering the stories of people hiding their passwords under their keyboard, she flipped it over, laughing at herself. Surely a computer professional wouldn't do such a thing.

Of course, he hadn't. But if Dillman only accessed financial systems once in a while, would he have those passwords stored in his head or write them down somewhere? If written down, where in the myriad of sheets of paper would they be?

Tasha frowned. Where would she put something like that? It had to be somewhere within easy reach, but where no one else would see it.

She ran her hands around the monitor and come up with nothing but dust. She wiped her hands on her pants before squirting a dollop of the hand sanitizer on the desk into her palms and rubbing them together. It was almost empty, and she felt guilty using up any of the little he had left.

Whatever brand it was it had a good smell. The label was facing the wall, so Tasha picked it up and turned the bottle around. One corner of the label was peeling off, and she started smoothing it back into place when she noticed the outline of something under it.

The small, folded up piece of paper was stuck to itself and Tasha gingerly worked a fingernail between the layers to separate it. Unfolding it without ripping the paper was a challenge to her patience, but she didn't want to destroy the information it might contain. Opened, it was about an inch tall by two inches wide and held several lines of seemingly random letters and numbers.

"I've got it!" she sent in a mental shout.

"I hoped you wouldn't find anything," Dot said. "But between these passwords and the information Ella got from his computer, it's clear Norm is guilty." They'd returned to the conference room where their discussion couldn't be overheard.

"If you need more proof, we can have a handwriting expert compare this writing to a sample of his from something else he wrote," Tasha suggested.

"No, that won't be necessary." Dot released a deep sigh. "I have enough evidence to fire him."

"Can I get a cardboard box or two for his personal items? I want to examine them before we arrange to get them to him."

"That's so impersonal. I want to meet with him

face-to-face when I let him go. I can give him the boxes then."

"You're not going to prosecute him?" Gavin asked.

"I could. But what I want to do is make a deal with him—if he can explain to me why he did it, I'll let him retire. No one besides us will know the reason behind it."

"You're more forgiving than I am," Tasha said. "I'd like to see him spend time in jail."

"That would draw unwanted publicity to the company. I'll include a gag order in the agreement. I don't want rumors getting out to our customers that would make us seem untrustworthy."

It made sense. "I don't want you meeting him by yourself," Tasha said. "I'll be in the office but I won't say a word."

Gavin nodded. "I want to be there too."

Dot smiled tenderly at her mate. "You'll scare him so badly he won't be able to talk. Tasha will have to do."

Tasha was already plotting how both she and Samantha could hide in Dot's office. Two bodyguards were better than one for the occasion.

TWENTY-EIGHT

Stretching was getting easier but Tasha didn't want to overdo it. Still, there wasn't much else for her to do as she haunted the company parking lot waiting for Dillman to show up. She'd been waiting for over an hour, but his assigned space remained empty.

Her mission was to intercept him upon his arrival and take him to Dot's office. Samantha would be alerted as they made the short walk through the hallways so she could take a position in the corner of the room. Then Dot would confront him with the evidence and try to extract his confession to the thefts.

But if he didn't show up soon, their planning would be for nothing. And they hadn't come up with a Plan B, not imagining a need for it. Tasha hoped Dillman hadn't gotten wind of their arrangement ahead of time.

"Has he called in sick?" she asked Dot.

"I checked with his supervisor a few minutes ago, and no, he hasn't."

"I'm ready to give up. I don't think he's coming."

"You might as well. We'll get the guards at the

gates to watch for him. Come in and let's figure out where we go from here."

"Do you have Dillman's home address handy?" Tasha asked as she strolled into Dot's office. Samantha had gotten there first.

"I can get it in a sec." Dot picked up the handset from the phone on her desk. "Are you thinking of checking on him?"

"Maybe driving by his place and seeing if his car is there, making sure he hasn't split. I don't plan to confront him."

"I'm going too," Samantha said.

"Why don't you stay here in case he shows up? The situation is making me nervous. For a man who took pride in his attendance record, this is out of character."

Samantha looked as if she wanted to argue, but Tasha stopped her with an unspoken plea. *"Please, Samantha? I can't imagine anyone attacking Ms. Lapahie here, but I don't want to take any chances."*

"You should stay, and I should go check on Dillman."

"If you two are arguing over me, you can stop." Dot twirled a knife she'd pulled out of nowhere in the air. "It'll take more than an old man to get to me."

"It's not worth facing the wrath of your mate for leaving you unguarded." Tasha grimaced. "I'm surprised he's not hanging around here, keeping his eye on you."

"He had a big meeting today. After being here yesterday, he couldn't justify skipping it. If it makes you feel any better, he asked Mark to come with me. He didn't want me driving alone."

There was a knock on the door. "Can I interrupt?" Ariana asked timidly.

"Of course. What's up?" Dot asked with a warm smile.

"Two of the boys are missing this morning. Their roommates say they're taking part in the traditional coming of age hijinks."

"Which two?"

"Lars and Stavros."

"Isn't Lars too young for it?" Samantha asked.

"What are you talking about?" Tasha questioned. She'd developed a fondness for Lars and had taken him out for field training exercises several times.

"There's a tradition for students to skip school and hang out in one of the nearby towns for a day or two when it gets too boring here," Samantha explained. "When they come back, everyone pretends nothing happened. The teachers don't encourage it, but they don't discourage it either. Usually it's just the older teenagers who can look after themselves that go."

"I don't like it," Dot said, "but it helps keep motivation up. I worry someone will get hurt, but so far nothing has happened."

Or they aren't telling you when it does, Tasha thought. Still she could imagine the admiration the feat would earn a young shifter, slipping past the security patrols. Or were the patrols in on the plans, and allowed it to happen?

"Please let the guards know to watch out for them," Dot continued. "And let me know if they aren't back for supper tonight."

When Ariana left, Tasha said "I'm surprised you're being this calm."

Dot shook her head. "The first few times it

happened I was a nervous wreck. I've gotten used to it now so I can pretend I'm alright with it, even though it bothers me."

"So where is Mark? I want to say hi."

"He said something about checking out the armory. He wanted to be useful." Dot waved a hand in the air as if brushing Tasha away. "Why don't you go find him? And take Samantha with you. I've got work to do, and you two are a distraction."

"Yeah, whatever. Call if you need us."

When they were out of Dot's hearing, Samantha said, "I'm not comfortable with this."

"Me neither. I keep expecting Dillman to show up with a gun and start blasting away."

"One of us could hang out in her outer office."

"Which seems a waste of our time."

"Too bad there aren't two of you," Samantha said with a grin.

"Tanya!" Tasha stopped in her tracks. "She's working on a project for her boss back at Fairwood anyway. No reason she can't haul her laptop over here instead of sitting at the house."

A quick phone call resolved that issue. Next stop was the clerk that maintained the personnel records. The woman plastered a fake smile on her face when Tasha walked in.

"It's locked," she said.

"Good. Can you please give me Norm Dillman's home address? It's for Miss Lapahie."

"How do I know that?"

Now you're going to be strict in your duties, Tasha thought. She stared down at the woman. "Should I

241

have her have call you? Although I hate to bother her for such a minor thing. What's your extension?"

Like a light bulb turning off, the lady's attitude changed. "Well, if it's for Miss Lapahie." She typed something on her keyboard and then scribbled on a notepad. "Here you go," she said. "Please give Miss Lapahie my regards."

Samantha stayed quiet until they exited the building. As they headed for the armory, she broke the silence. "Wow," she said. "You have a touch of alpha, don't you?"

Tasha shook her head. "Unlike a real alpha, that's a technique that can be taught. A combination of facial expressions and body language, it works best if you're in a position of authority."

"I'd like to learn how to do it."

"I'll teach you before I leave."

"I wish you didn't have to."

"Have to what?"

"Leave. I enjoy hanging out with you. You've taught me a lot. I was hoping you'd stick around."

Tasha's face broke into a slow smile. "And here I've been worried that I short-changed you. All the time I've had to spend away from here had me feeling guilty."

"It's not like you could do anything about it."

"I'll make you a deal. When this is over, I'll come back to visit as much as I can."

"Sounds great." Samantha held out her hand. "Shake on it?"

Shaking hands seemed far too cold to Tasha. Instead, she pulled Samantha into a tight squeeze to seal the agreement.

There was a cough from somewhere nearby, and they broke apart. "Pardon the intrusion," Mark said.

"But I heard you ladies were looking for me. I hope you don't mind I came and found you instead."

Tasha hastily wiped the moisture from her eyes. "Did you find the armory satisfactory?"

"A little short on supplies but in perfect order. I recognized your touch, Tasha. Your hard work shows."

Tasha nodded her thanks, but coming from him, the kind words carried extra meaning.

He turned to Samantha. "Good to see you again. I enjoyed working with you the night of the battle. You have real potential."

Samantha smiled. "Thanks, but go easy on the praise. I don't want to make Tasha jealous. She's half in love with you."

Tasha reddened. *Thanks a lot, Samantha.*

To her relief, Mark grinned but otherwise ignored the remark. "So what are you plotting?"

"The guy who is causing all the fuss, including you being dragged over here today, didn't show," Tasha explained. "I want to go by his house and check it out. Unless Miss Lapahie let something slip, or someone here clued him in to what happened, there's no reason we can come up with for him not to report to work today."

"You've got someone assigned to Dot—Miss Lapahie?"

"Tanya. She's working in an office down the hall so it's not too obvious."

His lips twitched, but he didn't respond to Tasha's comment. "Who's driving?" he asked instead.

The house, about half an hour's drive from Lapahie headquarters, wasn't what Tasha expected. She figured Dillman for a small but neat ranch-style home, with a yard that had its share of weeds and bare spots. Not this unkempt old farmhouse with no nearby neighbors.

"Are you sure this is the right place?" Samantha asked, leaning forward from the back seat.

"It is, according to the mailbox," Mark said, studying the paper from the human resources clerk.

"Maybe it was his wife's dream home and he's let it rot since her death," Samantha suggested.

"You know, I didn't see anything about a wife or family when I looked in his file yesterday. I don't know if he lied to me or not." Tasha parked the car at the end of the long driveway, wishing she'd brought her binoculars with her. She leaned against the steering wheel to get a different view. "Anyone spot his car?"

"No, but it might be in the garage," Mark said.

Tasha wouldn't have risked putting a car in the structure he indicated, as it looked ready to tumble into a pile of scrap at a moment's notice.

"Should we drive up and knock on his door? Use the excuse we were worried about him and wanted to make sure he was all right?" Samantha suggested.

"Not unless you want to risk being mauled by his watchdog," Tasha said, pointing to the "guard dog on duty" signs attached to the falling-down wooden fence.

"You suppose he really has a dog?" Mark looked doubtful.

"Easy enough to find out." Tasha turned off the engine and climbed out of the car. They'd brought the company car because it was nondescript enough it would be hard to remember. She stood by the gate and waited for ferocious barking. When nothing happened, she sniffed the air.

"I don't smell dog," she reported, climbing back into the driver's seat. "I do however smell shifter—wolf, to be exact."

"Oh?" The lack of inflection in Mark's voice hinted at a deeper meaning.

"That's not all." Tasha restarted the motor. "I also spotted what appears to be a sophisticated and expensive intrusion alert system."

TWENTY~NINE

"You think there's something shifty going on?"
Samantha asked.

They parked a mile away in the driveway of an
abandoned house. Far enough away and behind
enough trees that a ground-based camera couldn't
spot them from any vantage point at Dillman's place.

"Definitely shifty," Tasha said, with a half-smile.
"Which is interesting because he's a non-shifter. I
suppose he might have made friends with someone
from work but if so, he never mentioned it. And why
would a place that run-down have a huge security
system? Dillman struck me as odd, but not paranoid."

"Why do we care?" Mark asked.

"Good question. Easy answer is we don't. Better
answer is—this is the guy who's been stealing money
from Lapahie Enterprises. What else does he have
going that we don't know about? And is it a threat to
Dot? But you knew that."

He nodded. "I just wanted to make sure you did.
How do you want to proceed?"

Tasha leaned casually against the car. "Without
equipment we don't have access to, we'll resort to the

old-fashioned method." She grinned and allowed her canines to drop. "I sneak in and pray he doesn't spot me."

Cooler heads prevailed, and she got a lift from Mark to reach the first branch of an old sycamore across the road and up a hill from Dillman's house. She could have done it on her own, but she wasn't above accepting his help. She inched her way as close to the top as was safe. By using her *other* sight, she'd keep an eye on the place until Samantha returned with her long-range scope. Mark maintained a position at the base of the tree, keeping an eye on the limited traffic using the road. Although someone with sharp eyes could spot them from the house, Tasha doubted the surveillance equipment was programmed to look up the hill.

"*The curtains are closed,*" she sent, "*so I can't see inside.*"

"*No surprise there.*"

"*There's at least one car behind the house. Can't tell you make or model. I'm not picking up any sounds, not even a TV.*"

"*The wind has shifted and it's blowing towards the house.*"

It seemed like everything was playing against them. Tasha wiggled along her chosen tree branch, trying to get a different perspective of the house and the other buildings nearby. Besides the garage, there was an old storage shed and a pump house, both in bad shape.

"*You think he spotted us when we came by earlier?*" Mark asked.

"*There's not much traffic that comes by here. I'm*

hoping that we drove off quickly enough to make it less suspicious."

There was a long stretch when neither of them said anything as they concentrated on their surveillance. *"What's your theory on his motivation?"* he sent eventually.

"Easy answer would be drugs. But it doesn't fit unless he's good at hiding the signals."

"What else could it be?"

Tasha didn't answer right away. A curtain had fluttered, and she wondered if someone was peeking outside. But even her enhanced vision wasn't good enough to see any more than that. *"I haven't got a clue. It seems to be about money. Maybe he gambles and owes the wrong people? I don't have enough information to come up with a plausible theory."*

"How long do you want to keep this up?"

"You bored already? If I was doing this for a paying client, the correct answer would be as long as it takes. But I have a feeling we don't have that long, so we need to make something happen. Once Samantha gets back, we'll develop a plan."

Samantha didn't only bring back the scope and other equipment Tasha had requested, she also brought food and water. So after one more glance at the house to reassure herself that nothing had changed, Tasha climbed out of the tree and joined Mark and Samantha at its base. The water sliding down her throat eased the tickle building at its base.

"What's happening back at the ranch?" Tasha asked as she bit into a sandwich.

"Miss Lapahie wants us to keep an eye out for the

two missing boys," Samantha answered.

"Unlikely we'll see them out here. Anything else?"

"Tanya asked me to pass along that two other guys didn't show up for work today. And here's the interesting thing—I did some checking. They were both young men of the Choate pack that Miss Lapahie allowed to stay after the pack dissolved."

That got Tasha's attention. *"Do they live on the grounds or have they moved and commute to work?"*

"They share a house with other men. No one knows where they went. One of them has a car and it's gone too."

"That doesn't seem like a coincidence," Mark sent.

"No, it doesn't." Tasha shoved the last bit of her sandwich into her mouth and grabbed the scope.

It was more difficult climbing with the device because Tasha didn't want to bump it around or risk dropping it. She chose a different branch to crawl out on but hesitated when it gave more than made her happy. After deciding it was just adjusting to her weight, she shimmied a little farther out and raised the scope to her eye.

Nothing appeared any different and Tasha wondered if the whole thing was a colossal waste of their precious time. *"We should ask the local sheriff for a wellness check,"* she sent. *"Try to stir up some action."*

Mark disagreed. *"And alert anyone inside to the fact that someone is concerned?"*

"I'd like to know what's going on at the back of the house," Samantha said. *"We may be missing something important."*

"Me too. And now you're here, we have enough bodies to do that."

From her perch, Tasha marveled at how seamlessly Mark, in wolf form, disappeared into the uncut meadow grasses. His passage was marked by nothing more than a slight rocking of the tips, as if the grass was stirred by a gentle breeze. She tracked his path until it vanished into the edge of the woods that grew at the back of the property.

With him out of sight, Tasha returned to her vigil of watching the house. Every now and then, she'd catch a shadow moving past an upstairs window, but it always melted away before she identified any features.

She spent part of her time studying the motion of the cameras mounted on each corner of the front porch. They made the same sweep every twenty seconds, and she detected a dead spot between the areas they scanned. A small one, but it gave her something to work with.

The wiring that ran along the top of the fence bothered her more. Either it was electrified or it powered a series of sensors. She'd spotted a series of electrified pads along the base of the fence when they'd parked at the gate earlier. Hopefully, Mark would find a break in the fence at the back of the property.

"See anything?" Samantha asked. She'd taken over Mark's duty of watching the road.

"Nothing new." Tasha moved to relieve the pressure of the branch on her chest. She hated to admit it, but she might have to swap duties with Samantha. Her injuries, still not completely healed, itched.

"How long do you expect Elder Fenner to take?"

"Don't they teach patience in martial arts training?"

"That's one thing I was never any good at." Samantha sounded embarrassed and Tasha grinned. She felt the same way but wouldn't admit it.

"He'll take as long as he needs. If there are any problems I'm sure he'll let us know."

"You think Dillman has an idea he's being watched?"

Tasha considered the question. *"No. And I want to keep it that way."* She was pretty sure they'd been out of range of the cameras, and she doubted Dillman's eyesight was good enough to have identified her.

She tensed as a car came into sight, but it zoomed down the road without breaking its speed. Probably someone taking a shortcut between one point of nowhere to another or a lost tourist. No one of interest to her.

A red-tail hawk settled on the roof over the porch and preened its feathers before turning its head towards Tasha's position. It blinked once and fluttered its wings. Then, with a screech, it launched itself into the air and flew away. That's what they needed—a bird shifter to circle the house and peer in its windows. They existed but Tasha had never met one.

It was time to switch with Samantha—she was getting distracted too easily. But a trace of movement in an upper window captured her attention once again. For less than five seconds, a man was framed in the opening. Tasha had time to determine it wasn't Dillman before he moved away.

"Dillman's not alone in there if he's there at all."

"Who was it?"

"No idea." Tasha sent Samantha a mental snapshot of the man she'd seen. *"Do you know him?"*

"Can't say that I do."

"I'll ask Mark when he gets back." It made Tasha wonder how many other people were in the house. It helped to know the numbers of the enemy before an attack. Her training included preparing for contingencies.

The muscles in her left calf cramped and Tasha jiggled it to work the tension out. *"You want to trade places?"* she asked. *"I need a break."*

"Sure."

Tasha shimmied backwards until her legs bumped against the main trunk. Getting down wasn't much easier than going up, especially as she was tired and sore. She dropped the last ten feet to the ground, landing with a thump and rolling away before standing.

"Show off." Samantha grinned. She took a few running steps that turned into a cartwheel. *"How's that?"* She rubbed the palms of her hands on her jeans, wiping off the dirt and grass that had stuck to them.

"Not bad." Tasha considered what move would outdo Samantha's. She suspected nothing in her bag of tricks matched her partner's best. She was better off conceding before they got so involved in the contest they lost track of what they should be doing—keeping their eye on Dillman's house. *"It should be no problem for you to scramble up the tree and check if anything is happening."*

Samantha grabbed the nearest branch and easily pulled herself up. *"I did gymnastics in high school. You should see me on a balance beam."*

Tasha handed her scope. *"If you can get to a different spot than I did you might get a better view."*

"I'll try."

Tasha leaned backwards to trace Samantha's upward path. After studying the options, Samantha settled on the same branch that Tasha had used.

"They get thin up here," she sent. *"But this one's alright."*

After walking back and forth for a few minutes to get her circulation going, Tasha settled into a spot where she could see anything coming down the road from either direction. It also gave her a view of the house and surrounding property. She wondered how Mark was making out—there'd been no noises to indicate he'd been discovered, so she guessed his mission was going as planned.

He had more experience in reconnaissance than she did, the result of years of pack wars. Still, she couldn't help but worry. They faced a situation with unknown potential for things to go wrong.

"Here he comes." It made sense that Samantha, from her higher vantage point, would spot Mark's return first.

"If nothing is happening at the house, why don't you climb down and listen to his report."

"On my way."

Less than thirty seconds later, Samantha gracefully dropped out of the tree. They turned as one to face the wolf trotting up the small hill. *"I've got good news and bad news,"* he sent.

Tasha waited while he completed the transformation back to his human form and held out his clothes. *"Bad news first."*

"There are at least three men in the house." Mark

reached for his jeans and pulled them on. *"Maybe four. That's including Dillman."*

"I can guess who two of them are," Tasha said as she handed him his shirt.

"So now we can speculate there was a conspiracy to steal the money," Samantha sent. *"Where do we go from here?"*

"Do you want the good news first?" Mark sat on the ground to pull on his socks and shoes. *"I found a way in. Behind the house, the fence runs across a ditch, and there's no security in the gulley. We can crawl in."*

"Remind me again why we need to get in," Samantha said. *"Shouldn't this be left to the police to handle? We don't have any authority here. Especially as we're dealing with a non-shifter."*

It was a needed dose of reality. Tasha shrugged. *"She's right. We've had our fun. It's time to pack up and head out."*

The atmosphere turned gloomy as they gathered their leftovers and garbage. Tasha barely looked up when a car barreled down the road. But its squealing brakes caught her attention. When it stopped at the gate to Dillman's driveway, her curiosity was aroused. She retrieved her scope and studied the occupants, two men seated in the front. Neither was worthy of more than a casual glance. But the bundle in the back seat put her back in battle mode. That was a human wrapped in a heavy blanket, and unless her eyes failed her, rope held the blanket secure. And the rope glittered silver.

THIRTY

"Mark," Tasha hissed, handing him the scope. "Look in the back seat."

"What am I looking at?" he asked as he raised it to his eye.

He only had a few seconds to observe because the gate opened and the car proceeded up the drive. Tasha followed its path until it drove behind the house and out of her view.

"Did you see what I saw?"

"I believe so."

"What?" Samantha demanded.

Rather than trying to explain, Tasha sent her a mental picture.

Samantha set the bag of garbage on the ground and clenched her fists. *"So what are we going to do about it?"*

Tasha quickly calculated the odds. *"You said there were four men in the house already, one of them being Dillman."*

Mark nodded.

"Add in two, take away one because Dillman is no threat, that leaves five."

Both he and Samantha nodded.

"That's five against three. No need to wait for backups, my friends. The odds are in our favor. Let's go rescue us a shifter."

"You can't mean that," Samantha's eyes widened.

"Surprise is our best tool. We hit them in a few minutes while they're still congratulating themselves and their expectations for an attack are low. The longer we wait, the greater the possibility of them getting reinforcements."

"We have no idea how skilled they are as fighters," Mark pointed out.

"True. I'm assuming they are remnants of the Choate pack, and we have experience with their fighting skills. The best of their fighters are either dead or in prison. So these have to be second stringers."

"That's a big assumption." Samantha rubbed her forehead as if she had a sudden headache.

Tasha nodded, her lips a tight line. *"I know. It's a risk I'm willing to take. But I can't do it alone. If you guys want to wait for reinforcements, that's how we'll play it."* She stiffened as a mental scream reverberated in her brain, then cut off.

"That does it." Samantha clenched her fists and bounced up and down on her toes, warming up. *"I'm in. What are we waiting for?"*

They made the barest outline of a plan. They didn't have enough guns for each of them to have one, and they weren't intending to kill anyone anyway. The idea was to incapacitate their enemies long enough to rescue the captive. Tasha had her Sig strapped to her leg and was glad she didn't have to give it up. She gave her tactical knife to Samantha who had training in using one although she'd never fought an opponent in anything but practice matches.

Mark, of course, had his own handgun, the same Smith and Wesson .357 he'd carried as long as Tasha had known him. He could reload it as quickly as most people could swap out the magazines of a semi-automatic.

He ended the call to Gavin and stuffed his cell phone back into his pocket. They had agreed that someone should know what was going on besides them. *"Remember, the goal is to put them out of action, not to kill them,"* he sent gravely. Tasha suspected the reminder was as much for himself as it was for her and Samantha. *"Are we ready then?"*

Samantha took a deep breath as if steadying her nerves. *"Yes."*

Tasha met Mark's eyes and nodded. It seemed natural for him to take the lead.

The path he led them on circled away from the house before sharply turning back. The last five hundred yards followed a dry creek bed. It didn't provide much cover, but they ducked as low as they could without resorting to crawling. That would happen once they reached the fence at the back of the property.

A branch cracked nearby. *"Down!"* Tasha sent and dropped to the ground. Mark and Samantha followed her lead without a question. *"Did you hear that?"*

"What?" Mark asked.

"It sounded like someone walking nearby."

The three of them lay on the rocks that the dried up creek had left behind for a long moment. Overhead, a squirrel chattered. A chipmunk ran a short distance along the bank and disappeared back into the undergrowth. Crows cawed in the treetops, but as hard as Tasha listened, nothing seemed out of place.

"Maybe it was my imagination," she sent. She flipped over to sit up when she caught the sound of a rustling in the dead leaves that still covered the ground, followed by a whiff of damp fur. *"Or not."*

Instinctively she reached for her knife before realizing she didn't have it. Her pistol seemed like overkill until she knew what she was facing, but she drew it anyway. Mark copied her action and rose to a half-kneeling position.

She relaxed when she heard panting, but didn't put away her gun until the head of a muddy cocker spaniel popped into view. He barked once and bounced over to Samantha who was the closest. He put his paws on her chest and nudged her, wanting to be petted.

Samantha obliged, but sent a questioning *"Now what do we do with him?"*

"He's got a collar, so I'm guessing he's lost. He seems to like you. Do you think he'll stay if you tell him to?" Tasha grinned as Samantha received a doggie kiss.

"I doubt it, but let's see what happens." Samantha stood and held out her hand, palm facing outward. "Stay," she said sternly.

The dog licked her outstretched hand. *"That didn't work."*

"We can muzzle him using his collar and tie him to something so he can't bark and can't follow us," Mark sent. *"We'll come back and get him afterward."*

If they were still alive then, Tasha thought. But if

they tied him loose enough, he'd be able to work his way free.

Tasha wished they'd brought along one of the leftover sandwiches. The dog looked as if he hadn't eaten for a few days. He whimpered when they left him, but it was better that way. He'd make little more than a snack for a hungry wolf.

They stopped again when they reached the fence. At this spot, several strands of barbed wire were pulled loosely between two posts. There was, however, a single strand of electric wiring supplying power to the boxes tacked to the supports.

On this side, only one corner of the house had a camera. Tasha timed its slow sweep. *"I don't think we can make it to the house in one dash without getting caught on camera. I wish we had a distraction out front."*

"Can we hide behind that big tree?" Samantha asked.

"One or two of us could, but not all three," Mark responded with a shake of his head.

"How about behind the cars?"

"The camera is trained longer on them then on other parts of the yard," Tasha told her.

"Should we take turns going to the tree then?"

"It would be an even greater risk because of the longer time it would take," Mark explained. *"If it was a shorter distance it might work but not this far."*

"Let me in front." Tasha crawled to a spot even with Mark. *"I'll head for the small pine to the left. It's enough cover for one person. You two can take cover*

behind the big tree. Then all three of us will make the final dash at the same time. Once we're alongside the house, we'll be hidden from the camera."

"It's too risky," Mark objected.

"This is what I've trained for. It's about time I put it to use."

"It's hard for me to stop protecting you." The message was to her alone.

"I know." Their eyes met, and she winked at him. *"Don't go getting all maudlin on me. Let's do this."*

Mark nodded. *"Tasha, you count it down."*

She ticked off the seconds of the camera's swing, took a deep breath and exhaled. *"On three. One,"* she sent, *"two, three."*

She may have jumped the gun slightly, but it was better than cutting herself short. She wasn't safe until she reached the cover of the pine. A well-aimed bullet could end her run. Like a baseball player headed for home and trying to beat the throw, she dove the last five feet. She curled up behind its branches. Finally she twisted to check on her companions.

Neither was in sight. With her *other* hearing, she picked up the faint sound of their breathing. *"When you're ready,"* Mark sent.

She tracked the path of the camera again while she caught her breath. This close, she wouldn't have as much leeway in her timing. She got into a crouching position so her take-off would be faster. *"One, two,"* she sent, *"three."*

Her vision narrowed to a small point near the back door. She faltered when she stepped in an unexpected dip in the ground but steadied herself before she fell. The wounds in her chest burned as she pumped her arms. A few more feet to safety. She dared not look up to see where the camera was aimed. It didn't matter. She had to make it.

And then she was there. Tasha pressed herself against the wall of the house. A heartbeat and a half later, Samantha was beside her on one side and Mark on the other. *"Impressive,"* he sent. His hand reached out and covered hers for a quick squeeze.

Tasha nodded. The gesture surprised her, but she couldn't allow herself to be distracted. Her entire focus had to be the business at hand.

"Let's hope the door is unlocked," she sent.

"That would be a good thing," Samantha agreed.

"It won't be that easy," Mark warned as he drew his gun.

"A girl can dream, can't she?" Tasha followed his lead. The handle of the Sig was cool against the warmth of her palms. The success of the mission depended on what they found inside the door. If they were met by the men inside armed and ready, the three of them were dead. There was no turning back now. They'd come too far.

"Ready?" Mark asked.

"As ready as I'll ever be," Tasha sent.

"Me too," Samantha agreed.

"On the count of three then. One, two, three."

Mark hit the door first. It flew open easily, the frame around the lock splintering from the force of his blow. Tasha pushed by him as he regained his balance. Her gun swung from side to side as she surveyed the room. Mark's reminder that the mission was to incapacitate, not to kill, pounded in her head like her blood pounded in her veins.

THIRTY-ONE

Samantha made her grand entrance with a running cartwheel that turned into a flying kick. The twenty-something-year-old man standing by the refrigerator with his mouth open and a can of beer in his hand staggered backwards from the force of the blow. With an evil grin, she held one finger to her lips. The knife in her other hand pressed against his throat.

"Be a good boy," Tasha whispered. "Lie on the floor and put your hands behind your back." She was doing him a favor. His shaking legs wouldn't hold him upright much longer.

While Mark kept an eye on the doorway into the rest of the house, Tasha and Samantha tied the man up using a handy dish towel. "Sweet dreams," Samantha whispered as she pinched a nerve in his neck and put him to sleep. That accounted for one of the missing programmers from Lapahie Enterprises.

One down, four to go. The odds were getting better. At Mark's nod, Tasha dashed to the other side of the doorway. She wished for a mirror to use and see into the next room without sticking her head into the opening. Instead, she listened intently to figure out where in the next room the two speakers were positioned. Her best guess was that they were on opposite sides of the room, but the blaring game show on the TV made it difficult to tell.

"Why don't Samantha and you take on the ones down here while I cover the stairs?" Mark suggested. It seemed to be the best choice because Samantha didn't have a gun.

She nodded but had the sudden realization he planned to make the charge up the stairs solo. *"Be careful,"* she shot at him, hiding her concern.

He winked at her before holding up one finger. His turn to go first. She waited, watching his hand. Two fingers. He moved in unison with the third finger being raised.

He was halfway up the stairs before Tasha chose her target, a middle aged man relaxing in a recliner. She was surprised at how quickly he started his shift. But even an experienced fighter was at a disadvantage compared to one with a gun ready for action.

"Do you really want to try it?" she asked, allowing her fangs to descend.

He hesitated for a second before he bunched his muscles and prepared to leap. A clean kill would be easy, a bullet between the eyes. Tasha gently squeezed the trigger. A trail of red appeared from his right forequarter and halfway down his side, He yelped and stumbled.

Tasha closed the gap between them. A swift kick sent him tumbling to the floor. He recovered and, in a flash, charged at her.

She sidestepped at the last moment, and his momentum carried him past the spot he'd aimed for. When he twirled back around, she fired another shot.

The bullet struck his left leg, crippling him on both sides.

The rest of the fight felt like cheating to Tasha. There wasn't time to allow pity for her opponent to slow her down. After two aborted runs by the wounded wolf, she picked up a small end table with a marble top. On his next attack, she swung and struck him in the head. A sharp but short bark, and he collapsed.

She took a moment to check on Samantha. The boy—and it was a boy—was no match for her. Tasha even knew his name. She'd met him when they helped Lars with his shifting. It was Stavros, and Samantha was giving him lessons of a different sort. His nose bled profusely and bruises showed on his arms. If he wasn't smart enough to give up, Tasha wouldn't waste her breath suggesting it.

"I'm headed upstairs," she said, her movement matching her words. Samantha nodded without looking her direction.

Tasha took the steps two at a time. Both Mark and his attackers were in wolf form. She couldn't use her Sig without the potential of hitting him.

The risks of her next move were huge. She knew them before she launched into action. But Mark was outmatched in a two-against-one fight. She needed to even the odds.

The smaller of the enemy wolves yipped in surprise and staggered under her weight as she landed on his back. She wrapped one arm around his neck and tightened her grip. Her free hand pulled at the scruff of his neck.

He shook himself and swung around, trying to bite her. She rode him like a rodeo bull, squeezing his sides with her legs and trying to cut off his airway. He fell.

She muscled him onto his back. With a fist, she punched him in the neck with all of her strength. He passed out.

She ripped off her shirt and tore it in half. One half went to tie up his front legs, the other to muzzle him.

As she prepared to stand, she glimpsed a bundle of gray charging towards her. She rolled to the left, but not far enough to avoid the scrape of teeth along her side. She curled into a protective crouch and ignored the wrenching pain. When the wolf came at her sooner than she thought possible, she was ready. The hard soles of her boots were the best weapon at the moment, and she kicked him on his chin.

The move caught him off-guard. He stepped to the side and stared at her. *"You fight like a girl,"* he sneered.

"Thanks. I appreciate the compliment. Ready for more?"

She stood, and he paced back and forth, assessing her. He feinted, and she dodged, wishing for her knife.

"You get those scars playing with your cubs?" he taunted.

"I earned them in my last kill. Do you carry any or do you let others do your fighting for you?"

He snarled at the implied insult and, mouth snapping, tore at her. She twirled and her foot met his side. Not a crippling blow, but the damage would add up. Still, she couldn't win this fight with her feet alone.

The gray wolf was momentarily distracted by a dog barking in the hallway. Tasha seized the chance to shift to wolf form. She reached for the inner sense of *other.* Her canines extended, her face lengthened, fur sprung out on her limbs and body. Her clothes ripped away, and her hands and feet became claws. Her limbs became legs, and she was *other*. The change happened in the blink of an eye. She'd practiced it many times, and few could match her speed.

Although her wolf was smaller than his, his age showed. To the casual eye they might appear to be evenly matched, but she trusted her training gave her an unseen advantage.

"Are the Fairwood men so weak they have to send girls to fight for them?"

Startled, it took Tasha a moment to reply. How had he known she was from the Fairwood pack? She eyed him with suspicion. She couldn't place why he seemed familiar. *"The Fairwood men are so strong they prefer their women to be strong too. They don't need to enslave them like a weak man."*

They circled each other. She was dimly aware of Samantha standing in the door, but her world narrowed to herself and her enemy. Attack and spin. Avoid and retaliate. Snap. Bite. Growl. Crouch. Attack.

"No wonder you fight. You're too ugly to be someone's mate." He resorted to childish insults as they backed away from each other in the confined space of the small, furnitureless bedroom.

"You're showing your age, old man. All you do is talk." Tasha sneered at him. *"And you must be getting senile, because you don't make any sense."*

"I'll teach you respect. Before I kill you I'll show you what a pack leader is entitled to from his females!"

Pack leader? He really was senile. *"You're so old I bet you can't get it up anymore."*

He howled and sprang. Snapping, she grabbed his front leg and clamped down on it. Her teeth penetrated flesh and hit bone. His mouth scraped her rear flank. Instead of moving away from it, she moved into it, throwing him off-balance. She shook her head and tore flesh from his leg.

They were both bloodied. She'd inflicted the most damage. She sprang on top of him and bit his neck. The injury the bite caused was minimal, but its intent was to demoralize her opponent. As she released him, she raked her front claws down his side. He backed away Snarling, she pressed her advantage. Bite. Snap. Bash. She caught an ear and shut her mouth on it. If he bit her, she didn't feel it. Her world narrowed even further. Growl. Bite. Snap. Snarl.

He panted heavily. She sensed him weakening. Time to move in for the kill.

"Incapacitate!" a voice screamed in her skull.

She shook her head. *"Kill!"* she screamed back.

"Lars is safe! No kill!"

Lars? What did Lars have to do with anything? Her world widened and she studied the gray wolf. The kill would be easy.

"We need him alive," the voice insisted. Her world broadened, and the voice became Mark.

She paced. Her enemy tracked her every movement. She stood over him and bit his nose. He whimpered and rolled over, offering her his throat. The temptation to rip it to shreds overwhelmed her. She reached out with one paw and ran her claws down his stomach. He'd have scars to match hers.

She sat back on her haunches. *"He's all yours,"* she sent regretfully.

Tasha-wolf lay stretched out on the couch, her head resting on her now-clean paws. She'd been licking them clean when Samantha rushed over and insisted on washing them with fresh water and a cloth. Tasha-wolf thought it a waste of tasty fresh blood, but let her. She'd also let Samantha sponge off her various cuts and bite marks.

Samantha performed a similar service for Mark, who was in human form. He'd found some clothes and although they were too big for him, they were more serviceable than the blanket he had been wearing. Tasha-wolf thought it was too bad he'd felt the need to shift back to human and cover himself. She'd seen his wolf form many times and fought beside him several times, but there had been something different about this battle.

Or she had changed. She saw herself as his equal, not a little girl who worshiped an imaginary dream. When she looked at him now, she saw him as the man he was, with all his strengths and flaws. And she found him attractive.

She'd heard of this phenomenon before. The reluctance to return to human form, especially after battle, but she'd never experienced it. She'd have to switch eventually, but she was putting it off as long as possible, pleading exhaustion.

While there may have been some truth to it at first, it was now only a handy excuse. She wanted to go for a long solo run, kill and eat a rabbit or two, and rejoice in her wildness.

Mark could go with her to celebrate their victory in a different way. Tasha-wolf shook her head. The old wolf said it correctly. She was too ugly and bore too many scars for any wolf to pick her as a mate.

With a soft whimper, she licked a scratch on her front leg. She'd chosen this life and didn't regret it.

Now she was a hero, and no one would pity her.

The clean-up crew from Lapahie had come and gone, taking the prisoners with them. Tasha-wolf had heard bits and pieces of the story, but she knew the whole story wouldn't come out until they had been grilled for answers by Council representatives. Samantha went with them, taking her new best friend, the dog.

Mark stayed behind, so it was just the two of them. He kept himself busy examining the various security measures around the house and disabling them. But Tasha-wolf sensed his growing impatience with her.

He came out of the kitchen, and she closed her eyes, pretending to be asleep. But she knew her ploy hadn't worked when he stopped by the couch and sighed. *"It's time to get your act together, Tasha. We have work to do."*

Tasha-wolf opened one eye a crack. *"A little while longer?"* she whined.

"No. It's nearly dark and I'm tired too. It's time to go."

She opened both eyes, yawned and stretched. *"If I have to. But I can just run back to Lapahie."*

"What kind of game are you playing?" he asked sharply.

Huh. Maybe he wasn't familiar with this particular after-effect of extended fighting. She'd have to explain it to him. But that required shifting back to human form. And she wasn't sure she wanted him to see her naked, although it had never bothered her before. With her mouth, she reached for the blanket crumpled on the floor beside her, intending to pull it over herself before the shift.

She caught the question in his eyes, but he didn't

say anything as he reached over to help her cover up. Before he straightened, she raised her head and licked his cheek. She could always blame the gesture on her wolf.

The shift back to human took several seconds. Tasha spent more time adjusting to her wounds before standing and wrapping the blanket around her naked body. "I guess I'm as ready as I'll ever be. It'll be a long walk back to the car."

"Samantha parked it out back for us."

"That's not so bad then." Tasha took a step and stumbled. She'd forgotten the bite she'd received to her left foot.

Mark was there in a flash, supporting her. "Do you want me to carry you?"

She flushed. "No, I just need a moment to adjust." In reality, she enjoyed the warmth of his arm around her. "Dr. Tracy will yell at me, won't she?"

"Probably. But not as much as she'll yell at me for letting you do this."

"You couldn't have stopped me."

"*I* know that." He reached out with his free hand and shoved some hair away from her eyes. "Ready to try again?"

She scolded herself for reading anything more into that simple gesture but the caring of a friend. "Ready," she said, faking a smile.

THIRTY~TWO

The Council gathered in Pittsburgh instead of the neutral territory of Atlanta to allow more witnesses to testify. From the back of the room where she stood guard, Tasha studied the proceeding. When questioning revealed the intent of the conspirators had been to return the Choate Pack to its former supposed glory, Gavin called in the Council to handle the matter. And although women were still not a regular part of Council meetings. Counselor Carlson made an exception for Tasha. After all, she was responsible for the capture of the rogue Damyon Choate, the former pack leader of the Choates.

She couldn't wrap her mind around the fact she'd taken down an alpha, even if he was old and well past his prime. That was supposed to be impossible, except by another alpha. Dot had been able to do it because, even though she wouldn't admit to it, she was an alpha too.

Tasha wasn't the only guard. Carlson traveled with a hand-selected group of his own bodyguards, chosen from packs throughout the country and strategically placed around the room. One she recognized as having spent time at the Radferds while she was there. He'd acknowledged her presence with a nod and the barest of smiles.

The discussion of how to punish the conspirators went on for several hours and Tasha desperately wanted to change positions to ease her stiff muscles. But until they declared a break, she was stuck pretending she was a statue. Granted, her eyes constantly roamed the conference hall, but she moved nothing else.

"Miss Roeper," Counselor Carlson called, snapping her out of her semi-trance. "As one of the aggrieved parties, do you think the suggested punishment is fair and equitable?"

They'd been arguing about sending the men to Alaska. All except for Dillman who they held no authority over. But his life was ruined because he'd lost his job and his pension. Dot had also negotiated him passing over ownership of his house to the school in exchange for not being prosecuted in human courts. It turned out he'd married one of Damyon Choate's nieces, and the Choate leader used that relationship to manipulate the man even after her death. He'd also been against the kidnapping of Lars which the group plotted as retaliation for the death of Arnold Choate. Still, Tasha couldn't summon any sympathy for Dillman.

"May I approach the Council?" she asked. It would be easier to talk calmly if she was closer. Besides, she suspected some of the men at the table wanted a better look at what they considered a freak of nature. A few had found an excuse to wander past her during their short breaks.

"Naturally," Carlson agreed.

She ignored the many eyes focused on her as she walked forward. She'd dressed for the occasion in a somber black business outfit, and she looked as if she'd fit in at any company meeting. Except, that was, for the knife strapped to her leg, the pistol evident in her shoulder harness, and the rifle slung across her back. She stood at the end of the table, silent long enough that several of the Counselors appeared irritated. If they expected her to be a sweet, nurturing female all dressed up for Halloween, they were in for a shock.

"In answer to your question, Counselor," she said politely, "my wolf pronounced a death sentence on Elder Choate and stands by it." She grinned to herself as she studied the reaction her statement caused. "As a human, however, I'm willing to accept whatever sentence this group determines, as long as the punishment ensures Miss Lapahie and Lapahie Enterprises will never be threatened by the guilty parties again.

"I would ask for some level of mercy for Stavros, the youngest of the conspirators. The young are easily misled and perhaps he can be rehabilitated."

Murmurs of approval rose from several of the men around the table.

"I suppose you want him to go to the Radferds," one man grumbled.

"He doesn't deserve the honor that implies. I suggest taking him out of his normal surroundings however. Is there a desert pack willing to work with him?"

"Thank you for your recommendations, Miss Roeper. The Council will take them into consideration." Carlson turned so he faced her and winked. "You may return to your post now."

She nodded and, hiding her surprise, took her time getting back to her assigned spot, using every possible moment to stretch her tired muscles. The guard closest to her subtly nodded his approval as she resumed her previous position.

She didn't have to maintain it long. Before the final vote, protocol demanded she and the other observers except for the most senior bodyguard, leave the room. Because they were in a public hotel, they had to leave their weapons in the conference room. Tasha noticed the other guards placing their pistols into their waistbands or hiding them under their suit coats. She removed her shoulder harness and slipped the Sig into the case strapped to her lower leg. The move earned her approving glances from several of the other guards as they exited the room.

The outer room was reserved for all those people who were there either to testify or were affiliated with the men inside. She scanned the room with two motives; first to verify the absence of a threat and second to locate Gavin and Dot. They weren't hard to find although they were surrounded by a crowd of admirers. Mark hovered close by, clearly uncomfortable with his lack of control.

She caught his eye and gestured to the knot of people with her chin. *"I'm still not sure if he understands how he affects people,"* she sent.

Mark chuckled. *"Oh, he does, but he hides it well. It's part of his master plan. I'm not sure that even Dot knows."*

"I wasn't aware he had a master plan."

"He wants to drag the pack structure into the twenty-first century. The more friends and allies he has the easier that will be."

"You mean like opening up leadership to females? If I'm causing resentment towards him from other pack leaders, perhaps I should step down."

"You can't do that. You're part of his master plan."

"Me?"

Mark grinned. *"Yes, you. You're his prime example of what a female can accomplish given the right opportunities. Even more so than Dot. That was sheer luck and totally unplanned. He really does love her and would have mated her no matter what the cost to him personally. You, on the other hand, he picked out from the day you started training under me."*

"I had no idea."

"That's the way he wants it but it's time you know. Standard rules apply here."

"Standard rules?"

"Yes. If you ever tell anyone we had this conversation, I'll deny it."

"May I have a moment of your time, Miss Roeper?"

Tasha looked up from her seat on the conference room floor, cleaning her rifle before packing it up for the trip home. The decision had gone as well as she could have hoped. Stavros was being sent to live with a pack in Arizona and the other conspirators transported to a wolf pack above the Arctic Circle. The only way out was by foot or by plane and neither of those was likely to happen.

"Of course, Counselor." She wiped her hands on a rag and started to push off the floor. He extended his hand to help her, grasping hers when she took it and giving her a firm pull up.

"Let's walk while we talk," he said.

She looked around and raised an eyebrow. "Shouldn't one of your bodyguards accompany us?" He was, after all, the leader of the group that worked to keep the peace among the wolf packs of North America, not an easy task. Having enemies came with the job.

His smile reached both ears. "Normally, yes. But I suspect you've got enough weapons with you to protect the both of us."

Grinning, she raised her pant leg just enough for him to see the holster there. "Where are we going?"

"Around the block once or twice should be sufficient. Far enough we can speak freely without being overheard and yet close enough my guards won't have a heart attack."

He led the way outside, and Tasha blinked when the rays of the setting sun hit her face. It had been a long day, and she was eager to get home. But, as protocol demanded, she waited for him to speak.

"I suppose you're wondering why I asked you to be a guard today," he said when they were halfway down the block. It took her only half the distance to verify they were followed by his senior guard.

"Not really. I figure you saw it as a reward for my part in capturing Elder Choate and his followers or it was a test. More likely, a combination of the two."

Counselor Carlson coughed, and Tasha suspected he was trying to cover a laugh. "I was warned that you speak freely,"

"Then I'm glad I didn't disappoint you. Don't you get tired of people saying what they think you want to hear?"

"I can neither confirm nor deny that." They walked a few more steps, and Tasha waited for him to continue the conversation. "There are a couple of things on my mind," he said. "The first concerns Damyon Choate. He is not expected to live long enough to be sent to Alaska. His wounds aren't healing, and he's given up the will to live. He may linger for a week or two, but my personal physician has examined him and doesn't believe he will last much longer than that. It's the truth this time, not like the bogus paperwork Miss Lapahie received saying he had Alzheimer's." The auditors had figured out that money earmarked for his care went straight into Dillman's personal account, and he passed it on to the Choate conspirators.

Tasha took a moment to process the information. "I suppose I should feel sorry for him, but I don't. It was his poor judgment that led to all of this. If he would have reached out to Miss Lapahie when her mother died, none of this would have happened."

"True. I've heard that he was a good leader until his son's death, but I never knew him then, so I can't be sure." They'd walked around the entire block and Tasha knew they hadn't got down to business yet. So she waited while he greeted several pack leaders waiting for their cars at the entrance to the hotel.

Finally he started walking again. "I have a favor to ask," he said. "But you guessed as much, didn't you?"

She employed his tactic. "I can neither confirm nor deny that."

A real smile lit his face, replacing the artificial one he'd assumed earlier. "No wonder Elder Fairwood talks so highly of you. So here's the question—how do you feel about joining my guard?"

Tasha stopped abruptly. Counselor Carlson kept walking, and she hurried to catch up. "It would be a bold move on your part," she said.

He inclined his head in acknowledgment.

"But you and I both know that the packs are nowhere near ready for it. So although I thank you for the honor, I respectfully decline. Besides, I have a commitment to the Fairwood pack to fulfill before I can think about anything else."

"I figured as much, although I appreciate your reasoning. So I have a second question. There are times when it would be beneficial to have a woman working for me. For example, when I first met Dot. If I'd had a woman available to guard her then, maybe she wouldn't have slipped out of my influence. There are other instances too that I'm not free to share at the moment. Do you think that Elder Fairwood would consent to lending your services to the Council on an as-needed basis?"

"That sounds feasible." And in line with her own original plans for her future. "Of course, Elder Fairwood needs to approve the arrangement. And my commitment to the pack is my priority. There's a rather big event looming in the future."

"You're referring to the wedding?" It was Carlson's turn to stop abruptly. He shivered dramatically. "All I can say is may the gods save us. Welcome to the team, Miss Roeper."

THIRTY~THREE

It took Tasha twice as long as she'd estimated to go through the day's reports because of all the interruptions. But the one person she'd hoped to see had been a no-show. She didn't know if Mark was using the opportunity to relax or if he was avoiding her.

It was her fault, she supposed. He'd been acting this way ever since she'd allowed her wolf hormones free reign after the battle. Except for the day at the hotel, he spoke to her as little as possible, and she was getting tired of it. Even Gavin had mentioned it. Tasha was able to deflect his inquiries, but she needed to do something about it. A week of Mark's shunning was a week too much.

"Have you seen Elder Fenner?' she asked the trio coming in off guard duty.

"He was at the shooting range awhile back," the team leader responded.

"Thanks." Tasha continued looking through the stack of papers in front of her, waiting for the three to leave.

"Do you need him for something?"

She looked up, keeping her face bland. "No, I was just curious and didn't want to interrupt him."

"Okay, see you tomorrow." With cheerful waves, the three headed off, probably to celebrate another successful patrol with drinks at The Pub.

After filing away the paperwork, she stood and stretched, pretending there was no urgency in her movements. Not that anyone was watching, but old habits were hard to put aside. Once outside she hesitated, as much for the show as to reassure herself she really wanted to do this.

She took off at a jog. Nothing unusual about that; everyone was used to seeing her run from place to place instead of walking. When she reached the meadow at the end of the street, she sped up. Each time her feet struck the ground, she imagined herself as nothing more than a whisper of the wind. It was a technique some claimed made a person's presence invisible, even to an alpha. Tasha didn't know if it would work or not, but she'd always meant to try it.

She took an indirect route to the firing range, hoping Mark would still be there by the time she arrived. The sound of rapid gunfire reverberating among the trees revealed his presence before she could see him. She paused to calm her breathing before walking to the wooden stump where spectators routinely sat.

Mark was in the middle of reloading, and she said nothing as he fired off another six shots. As he studied the results, he asked offhandedly "Is there something you needed from me? Or did you come to say goodbye?"

"Goodbye? Am I going somewhere?" she asked, puzzled.

"Rumor has it that Carlson asked you to join his guards." Mark avoided looking at her as he collected his spent shells and tossed them into the metal box nearby. "I can't see you turning down that offer. It's what you've trained for, after all. And it's the most prestigious security job out there for a wolf."

"That's true," Tasha answered quietly. Was he jealous or did he think she should have asked him for his advice? Was that what caused the strain between them? She forged ahead. "The Counselor did ask me, and I turned him down. Mostly."

"Meaning what?"

"That if special occasions arise when a female is a necessity, and if it doesn't interfere with my duties here, I'll help out."

"That was foolish of you."

"What was?"

"Turning down the opportunity."

In the loneliness of the time when he'd been avoiding her, Tasha had thought the same thing. But deep in her gut, she knew better. "My commitment has always been to the Fairwood pack first and foremost."

"Are you telling me you'll be content spending the rest of your life here playing second fiddle to me?" Finally turning to face her, Mark crossed his arms and stared at her.

"I still have lots to learn. Here is as good of a place as any to learn it."

"And you expect me to teach you."

The discussion was going nowhere, or at least not where Tasha wanted it to go. "Would that make you happy? To pigeonhole me back into the student role so you don't have to face the fact that I'm an adult? That I'm no longer off-limits?"

The frontal attack staggered him for a minute. "Are you referring to what happened when your wolf took a liking to me?"

"You mean when my wolf woke me up to what I refused to admit for years? Yes." Tasha stood and took a step towards him. Just one. She didn't want to scare him off by moving too swiftly too soon.

"As if a one-time incident means anything," he scoffed.

She took another small step. "And all the times you found a reason to touch me since I returned? Did they mean nothing?"

"Impaired judgment on my part."

Another step. "Impaired by what?"

He put his revolver back in its holster and turned away from her. "Guilt. I should never have agreed to Gavin's scheme."

"You mean his master plan?"

Mark spat out his answer. "Yes. His master plan. His grandiose idea. Prove to wolves all over the country and the world that women are capable of doing more that raising pups."

A little closer. "He succeeded, didn't he?"

"But look at what it cost. How many times have you come close to dying so he can prove his point?" His body jerked as he gestured wildly.

"And that matters to you?" A few inches, no more.

"Of course it matters! I care about all my students."

"Is that what I am to you? Just a student?" Like a hunter moving in on the prey, she stealthily changed her position, ready to spring.

"What do you want me to say, Tasha?"

"Tell me I mean something to you. That what you feel for me is not what you feel for a student."

He looked at the ground, bent over and picked up an imaginary shell, but didn't answer.

"You can't say it, can you?" She smelled the sweat forming on his forehead. "So tell me the truth. That I'll never be more than then one of your favorites."

"I can't tell you that."

"What can you tell me?" Tasha wanted to howl with frustration.

"When I shipped you off to the Radferds," he said slowly, "I wished you well with every inch of my being. I never expected to see you again. And that would be a good thing because it meant I'd no longer have to worry about you getting caught in Gavin's scheming. I truly believed that you would find your mate there, and I'd be happy for you. I fought Gavin when he suggested that we bring you back, using the excuse that you needed more time, but he won. He always wins."

"What would make you happy, Mark?" Two steps closer. She was close enough to reach out and touch him.

"My chance for happiness died years ago."

Tasha backed away a step. "I thought so too. That we only had one chance for happiness in this life and that I'd missed mine somewhere along the way. I had to find a different path to follow, one that included friends but no mate and no children. But being close to death will change your perspective."

"Do you want children?"

She cocked her head. "I suppose I could change my mind, but no. Tanya better settle down soon and have a handful, because I'd love to be an aunt. I want to be able to borrow someone else's kids and give them back when I'm tired of them. Maybe that's selfish of me, but

I don't think I'd be a very good mother."

She'd let him think he'd distracted her on purpose. Time to move in for the kill. "Do you want children?" she asked innocently.

He snorted. "Me? At my age?"

"Is that the problem? You think you're too old for me?"

"Tasha, I don't know what game you're playing, but it's time to stop."

"This isn't a game, Mark." She moved and stood toe-to-toe with him before he had a chance to back away. "It's a chance for us to find a future. Or fail miserably but knowing at least we tried."

"What do you want?"

"This." She put her arms around his neck. "We try this once, and if you can truthfully say it means nothing, I'll write it off to battle fatigue."

"Tasha..."

She didn't give him a chance to finish. She'd always wondered how his lips would taste, and this was her chance to find out. The first touch was hesitant, barely there, but even that sent a tingle down her spine. She withdrew and tried again, this time with more confidence.

Then his arms clasped around her lower back, pulling her close. His mouth pressed firmly against hers, as if he was imprinting the contact into his memory. Her whole body responded, reveling in the closeness it had been denied for so long, and she pushed herself even tighter against him. Her reward was a small moan and a renewed attack on her lips.

When the kiss finally ended, they remained clinging to each other, each supporting the other's weight. "Tell me," Tasha demanded.

Mark pulled back enough to look her in the eyes. "Tell you what?"

"Tell me you felt what I did."

He groaned. "You know the answer to that."

She captured his eyes with her gaze. "Yeah, but I'm a weak female and I want to hear you say it."

Mark laughed and the sound broke the building tension. "This from the woman who beat a male alpha wolf. And don't tell me it doesn't count because he was old. Yes, I felt it. And now I can't get enough of it."

His admission was rewarded by more kissing, this time less frantic.

"What's the protocol on this, Elder Fenner?" Tasha asked solemnly as they headed back to the village sometime later. She couldn't keep the happiness out of her voice no matter how hard she tried.

Mark replied in the same way. "I believe we are required to inform our pack leader, Elder Roeper, as it involves his second and his security chief. Although I suspect this is the first time in recorded pack history that those two titles have been linked in this way."

"Do you suppose it was part of our esteemed leader's master plan?"

He put his arm around her shoulder, drew her into the shadow cast by an old elm and kissed her on the forehead. The sun had set and the streetlights were on and they weren't ready to make the change in their relationship public yet. "I can't imagine even Gavin could have foreseen this."

"Good. We need to keep him on his toes."

"I agree. He's been too smug for my liking ever since the Council meeting."

"Did all the adoration give him a swelled head?"

He kissed her again before they headed back to the sidewalk. "Don't push him too far," he warned.

"We'll see how it plays out in the morning."

"We should tell him tonight."

"Are you in a hurry?" Tasha assumed his switch in the form of communication meant he wanted to keep the conversation private.

"I hoped you'd spend the night with me. Or am I moving too fast?"

"By human standards, yes. By wolf standards, no."

Mark growled, a deep rumbling sound. Not many of the pack could reproduce the sound so well while in human form. *"I'm feeling a bit wolfish."* He grinned and extended his canines. *"Besides, I want to keep you to myself for now. If Gavin doesn't like it—too bad."*

They'd reached the sidewalk in front of his house. *"You know how to turn a girl on, don't you, Elder Fenner?"* Tasha started to reach out to touch his cheek but quickly stuck her hand back in her pocket when she noticed shadows moving among the trees in the empty lot next door. *"I see the patrols are on duty."*

"As is proper. And they report all is well. We need to make sure they start including you in their reports."

The last of her concerns fled. *"Then I guess it won't matter if we distract each other for a little while."*

"A little while? I intend to take all night."

It was not unusual to hear a wolf howl in the Fairwood village, especially at night. So when a deep, mellow howl rose as the moon reached its crest, Tasha didn't stir. With Mark's shoulder serving as a pillow, and his arm draped across her chest, she had no desire to move.

But when a second wolf added its voice, the urge to join was irresistible. Wolf voices rose from throughout the cluster of neat little houses and she was tempted to shift and add her own howl to the song.

Mark ran his fingers down her arm. Her skin tingled along their path. "They're singing for us."

She untangled herself from his body and pushed herself up on her elbows. "Want to join them?"

"Not tonight." He gently tugged until she collapsed on top of him, kissed the tip of her nose and wrapped his arms around her once again. "Tonight it's just me and you."

EPILOGUE

Gavin Fairwood, CEO of Fairwood Enterprises and leader of the Fairwood pack, was unsure what to make of two of his most trusted advisers standing stiffly in his office, waiting for his permission to speak. Clearly this was official business as they were both dressed in dark business suits. Each carried guns as was proper for their position. They had shown up without appointment—not that it was necessary—but he didn't have any idea why they were there. Especially this early in the morning.

"Elder Fenner, Elder Roeper," he said. If they wanted to be formal he would accommodate them.

"Good morning, Elder," Fenner said, a little too cheerfully for this early. Gavin hadn't even started on his first cup of coffee. "Elder Roeper and I are here to inform you of a change that may impact our working relationship."

"I wondered when the two of you would settle whatever you were arguing about." He'd expressed his concerns to Tasha—Elder Roeper—a couple of days earlier, so perhaps that had been the impetus for this meeting. "Or do you need me to mediate your discussion?"

They both stared out of the window behind him, their eyes never straying elsewhere. But if he was correct, both of their lips twitched at his question. It appeared they were hiding something, but what?

"No arbitration is necessary, thank you, Elder," Roeper said. She cleared her throat. "We thoroughly negotiated the arrangement and are here to, as tradition requires, notify you of the agreement."

Sometimes tradition was a major pain in his side. He picked up his coffee and took a swallow. He wanted caffeine in his system to help himself brace for whatever was coming. "Notify away. I have work to do."

They changed their stance to stand at attention. He found it odd how they moved in unison. Roeper spoke first. "It is my duty and honor to notify you that I have possibly found my mate. It is still early in the relationship, but I have every belief it will be a long and successful pairing."

Gavin smiled. "I didn't know you and Jaime were still seeing each other. I'm happy for you. He seems like a good man. I must say I'm surprised you broke your rule about non-shifters."

The barest hint of a smile crossed her face. "I don't believe I mentioned the warden. Perhaps you should allow Elder Fenner to say what he needs to before jumping to a conclusion."

One of these days, he'd get tired of her attitude, but that day was a long way off. "All right then. Mark?"

"Elder, it is my duty and honor to notify you that I have possibly found my mate. It is still early in the relationship, but I am confident it will be a long and successful pairing."

The implication took a minute to sink in. He hastily took another drink of coffee and leaned back in his chair. "You and you?" He pointed to each in turn. "Together?"

"That would be correct, Elder." Mark reached out and tenderly took Tasha's hand. "We've discovered we're compatible in many ways."

Gavin set his cup on his desk, interlocked his fingers and rested his chin on his hands, studying the pair. A trace of red rose in Tasha's cheeks, and he wondered which of them had made the first move.

There was only one correct way for him to react. He vaulted over his desk, scattering paperwork everywhere, and grabbed both of them, pulling them into a three-way hug. "Congratulations! That's wonderful! I'm thrilled for the two of you!" He pulled away. "Now *that's* going to take some getting used to."

The sound that came from Tasha sounded suspiciously like a giggle. He shook his head. He hadn't heard her giggle since her return from Maine. "Supper. Tonight. My place. We'll celebrate then. Now, unless there's something else, I have work to do and I know you do too."

After escorting the two out of his office, Gavin stood staring out the window, hands clasped behind his back. How had he missed the signs? He sighed. There went one of his long range plans. For a moment he wondered how it would be to rule like his great-grandfather, deciding everyone's fate to please himself. He thought about his own mate, soon to be his wife. She hadn't been part of his plan either. No, it was better when life was filled with surprises.

THE END

OTHER BOOKS BY P.J. MACLAYNE

Wolves' Pawn
Book 1 of the Free Wolves

Dot McKenzie is a lone wolf-shifter on the run, using everything available to her to stay one step ahead of her pursuers. When she is offered a chance for friendship and safety with the Fairwood pack, she accepts.

Gavin Fairwood, reluctant heir to the Fairwood pack leadership, is content to let life happen while he waits. But old longings surface when he appoints himself Dot's protector...and becomes more than a friend.

But her presence puts the pack and her new friends at risk, and Dot must go into hiding again. When old enemies threaten the destruction of the Fairwood pack, it will take the combined efforts of Dot and Gavin to save it.

Can anything save their love and Dot's life when she becomes a pawn in a pack leader's deadly game?

The Marquesa's Necklace
Oak Grove Mysteries Book 1

Harmony Duprie enjoyed her well-ordered life in the quiet little town of Oak Grove—until her arrest for drug trafficking. Cleared of all charges, she wants nothing more than to return to the uneventful lifestyle of a historical researcher she once savored.

But when her beloved old car "George" is stolen and explodes into a ball of flames, it sets off a series of events that throws her plans into turmoil. Toss in a police detective that may or may not be interested in her, an attractive but mysterious stranger on her trail, and an ex-boyfriend doing time, and Harmony's life freefalls into a downward spiral of chaos.

Now she has to use her research skills to figure out who is behind the sinister incidents plaguing her, and why. And she better take it seriously, like her life depends upon finding the right answers.

Because it might.

Her Ladyship's Ring
Oak Grove Mysteries Book 2

Harmony Duprie is back, and so is trouble in Oak Grove.

When a man is murdered in the back yard of the old Victorian house she is remodeling, Harmony is determined to help locate his next-of-kin so he can be put to rest properly. But with her ex-boyfriend Jake out of prison, back in town and one of the suspects in the murder, she takes on the challenge of solving the crime.

With Eli, her current love interest, in Florida and Jake close by, old emotions come back to haunt her. Can Harmony clear Jake's name and solve the mystery of her own heart?

Coming Soon:
The Baron's Cufflinks